Proper Secrets

Rachel Francis

Rachel Francis

ISBN 978-0-9858346-5-4

Cover art: Design by Rachel Francis with stock photos provided by Big Stock contributors Hanna Hrakovich, Bragin Alexey, and Tamara Kushniruk.

Font: Copyright (c) 2010, 2011 Georg Duffner (http://www.georgduffner.at)

If there is anything I know, it's that historical fiction readers do not like having the facts tampered with. This is the chief reason why I decided not to write a historically accurate Regency romance. The book you are reading now is set in an alternate Europe, and none of it is to be taken as more than fiction. I love history--it was my major in college, and when I see it misrepresented, I cringe and fume for days. It would break my heart for such an error to spring out of my book.

On that note, I did write this with modern readers in mind. Language has changed, and I am hard-wired to write a certain way, being both of the late 1900's and American. I cannot replicate Jane Austen or the Brontë sisters, and hope that my personal style can be enjoyed for what it is, as character-driven fiction.

In the appendix, I've included some helpful information about the world I've created. Endland is the country in which the story takes place, and I didn't plan on it sounding quite so much like England, but it stuck. It is the country at the "end" of the continent, and shares a land border with Sypass. These two countries have been engaged in a border war for decades. If you read no more of the background I've provided, this information will get you through the novel. If, however, you wish to know more about the history and customs of Endland before joining Miss Worthing on her quest for truth, a map and other reference can be found in the aforementioned appendix.

Happy Reading,
Rachel

What is feeling if it is all for naught?

1. When First We Met

To keep a secret is to sacrifice another's journey for truth, a horrific offense against the chief occupation of any sensible person. It is foolhardy to assume that obstructing the natural instinct to acquire information by actively concealing details bearing consequences, makes one caring or helpful.

To be clear, some things should not be known, just as some actions should not be taken. This is the line between curiosity and insanity, or moral weakness.

The Worthings were a family of knowledge-seekers. No tome passed through the bookseller's without ending up in their library, no craft too lowly for them to master. Their relative state of wealth may have been their only defense against the snickering hyenas of high society that would not bend to light their own candle. Mr. Worthing would not be convinced that his children should cloister themselves instead of contributing to the household. It flew in the face of what was proper, and yet, not a word could be said against the manners of the Worthing siblings, as well bred and clever as they were. With Mrs. Worthing's repeated episodes of enduring illness, even more fell on the shoulders of the eldest daughter, Emily. Whilst the firstborn son Peter could assist his father with business, she took to running the house in her mother's stead.

"Bridget, I'll tie my bonnet up in knots the first time you are not the last to be ready for an outing," said Emily. A peek into her sister's room found her dressed, but with hair still flowing down her back. Bridget wrinkled her nose and swept the locks up into a flawless bun, complete with dangling ringlets.

"Your patience for me is endless, I know," said Bridget, pinning her work in place.

"If it were, we might never leave Charlton for the world beyond," laughed Emily. She continued on down the hall, knocking at her mother's door.

"Come in," called Mrs. Worthing.

"Mama, do you need anything from town?" Propped up in her bed clothes, Elizabeth Worthing, matron of Charlton, tilted her head to think.

"Some pretty ribbon that matches my blue gown, for the ball."

"Wide, lace? Or thin and straight?"

"Thin and lacy, if you please. Oh, and remind your father to have the stand cleared for the musicians before Saturday," said Mrs. Worthing. Emily nodded her understanding and sought Mr. Worthing in his study off the massive Charlton Library. His study smelled of books and fresh air, owing to his habit of propping the window open at the slightest hint of a breeze.

After reminding him as her mother asked, Emily said, "Bridget and I are going to town. Is there anything you require from the shops?"

"After the frills that might attract a suitor, are you? I require nothing, thank you, save a small present for your mother. A necklace or whatnot to accompany her dress. Worries of appearing ill have wrecked her nerves, and no energy need be spent on that rather than meeting with friends," said Mr. Worthing. He teased her with twinkling eyes, a feature he'd given all his children.

"In the same breath you dote on my mother to distract me from your assumptions. Very well, sir, I shall find Mama a special trinket, and forgive you for guessing wrongly at my intentions," said Emily with a smile.

"Hide it all you like, my dear. I will not be fooled!" Mr. Worthing called after her as he went back to his writing.

"Bridget, can we go at last?" Emily inquired from the top

of the stair. Swirling her skirts, Bridget posed.

"I am ready," she said, sighing like a maid in love.

"Oh, saucy girl! How will I ever be at ease with you in polite society?" They grinned at each other.

"You shall suffer it, as I suffer your badgering," said Bridget. Emily descended the stairs, unaffected by criticism.

"You will understand one day, when you are responsible for more than yourself." Their good-natured banter kept them company all the way to Tripton, the bustling country community to which Charlton lay closest. It was a town built around the harvest of the neighboring estates, owing much of its prosperity to the good fortune of Mr. Worthing. The music of the morning played at once, transforming natural birdsong into rattling carriage wheels and good-natured shouts of greeting.

"Muster your strength, Bridget, we have not the time to visit the bookseller today," said Emily. Spotting them through the window, the bookseller himself rushed outside.

"Miss Worthing, Miss Bridget, any suggestions for a good book? Several customers have been asking your opinion on the latest volumes," said Mr. Brandichant.

"Through the Towering Forest was quite good, don't you agree, Bridget?" said Emily.

"Yes, yes, eerily fantastic. The Dark One, too."

"Thank you Misses!" he said. They nodded and bravely walked on, away from the literature shop.

"How much pocket money do you think we've given Mr. Brandichant over the years?" inquired Bridget. Fresh dye and fabric dust blew past them into the street from the clothing store, their first stop. Emily ran her hand over the bolts of soft wool and cotton on her path to the ribbons. A gown in progress lay over a form in the corner, half the trim hanging under the bust, yet to be affixed to the empire waist.

"Our pocket money is nothing to Papa's monthly requisitions. He could keep several wordsmiths fed and clothed with his appetite. Mama requested thin lace, matching her blue gown, help me," said Emily. They picked through the finery until Mrs. Johnston, the proprietor, sidled over to gossip.

"Good day to you Miss Worthing, have you heard that someone has taken up residence at Reddester?" Emily dropped the spool she admired, hastily stooping to retrieve it.

"I had not, Mrs. Johnston. Is it true?"

"I have seen the lady of the house myself. Very fine, Miss Wingrave," said Mrs. Johnston.

"Miss? She is not married?" asked Bridget.

"No, ma'am. She will keep house for her brother, Mr. Wingrave. Have you not visited them?" said Mrs. Johnston.

"No, we have not. I wonder if Papa knows of them? We have been extraordinarily busy planning the ball," said Emily. Mrs. Johnston leaned in close.

"I feel you will be very pleased with the showing at your

ball. I've been selling the finest of my wares in preparation, ma'am," she whispered. Miss Worthing smiled at the genuine enjoyment Mrs. Johnston had from her occupation. Her passion created some of the most elegant dresses Emily had seen anywhere, awash in the social escapades of her customers.

"Thank you, Mrs. Johnston," said Emily. With a grin, the woman scuttled away to greet newly-arrived ladies.

"That is news, indeed. How out of sorts our information gathering is," said Bridget, "Ah! Here, this will do nicely." She held up a length of ribbon, perfectly suited to the task.

"Excellent choice. I agree, we have not been as social in the last fortnight as is expected. Of course, in the several fortnights preceding this one nothing of import occurred," said Emily. Bridget chuckled under her breath. The sisters completed their errands with enthusiasm, happy to be out of doors after a bout of bad weather. When Emily stopped to look for a present for Mrs. Worthing, Bridget admired the jewelry, but peered at her sister.

"You hardly ever shop here," she said.

"Papa wants a necklace for Mama," said Emily. He had given her the money for nearly any piece Mrs. Worthing could desire, so she applied it with good taste.

"I wish I had someone to dote upon me," said Bridget.

"You do. Papa gave you a handsome pony for your

birthday," said Emily, pressing the package into Bridget's hands.

"It's not gifts I want, it's to be valued by one I love," said Bridget.

"We all love and value you." They strolled down the road out of Tripton, content with the day's work so far.

"You know it is not equivalent to one's spouse. If I could have someone look at me the way Papa sees our mother, I should be very happy."

"Have you been reading an abundance of romances again? You know what Mama said--"

A passing carriage wheel flung a rain of slick mud high in the air, which landed in the only proper place—Emily's dress. She froze in horror as it absorbed a brown most unbecoming to females of elegance. Shielded from the onslaught, Bridget gaped at the sludge dripping off her sister's clothing. Were she not born into a respectable family, Emily may have let slip a word worse than the color now soaking through her undergarments. As it was, she couldn't speak without fear of humiliating herself further.

The carriage came to a sloshy halt when the occupant became aware of the condition inflicted on her. A man alighted from the vehicle, pleasing in stature, with a charming face and manners. He addressed them straight away, after dodging over several more puddles in the street.

"My most severe apologies, Miss. I will have another

dress made for you in recompense, or this one professionally laundered should it be a favorite," he said. Jaw wide open, Emily made no reply.

"Excuse my sister, she must still be in shock," said Bridget, nudging Emily out of her embarrassment. Looking between her sister, the gentleman, and the ground, Emily worked to gather her wits.

"Yes, excuse me, I must get home before I catch cold. Please do not trouble yourself," she said, giving a short curtsy. Nothing would have assisted her more than for the gentleman to ignore what had happened.

"May I have your name so that I might endeavor to please you, when you are in better spirits?"

"Miss Worthing, and this is my sister, Miss Bridget Worthing." The man colored at hearing their names.

"I am Mr. Wingrave, and I insist upon your joining me in the carriage. I will usher you home."

"No, please, I can still walk," said Emily. A faint shiver betrayed her play at bravery.

"No, Miss Worthing, I will have this courtesy. I shall think you very ill-mannered if you do not accept." His gallant smile and attempt at humor lengthened Emily's temper.

"Come sister, we would not want to fall in the opinion of an acquaintance just made," said Bridget. Finally, Miss Worthing accepted and even allowed Mr. Wingrave to assist her over puddles to the carriage door. They settled into an awkward acceptance of their situation.

"So, Miss Worthing, where shall I direct the driver?"

"To Charlton, please," said Emily. Mr. Wingrave gave the direction, and the driver coaxed the horses into a gentle start. Bridget politely conversed with him when Emily could think of nothing to say.

"You are passing through the neighborhood?" she inquired.

"No, I've taken a house, Reddester Hall, a few miles out on the other side of Tripton."

"We've all expressed our sadness at its being empty so long. I'm glad someone has taken it."

"It's a fine house. Mr. Roland Worthing is your father, I presume?" said Mr. Wingrave.

"Yes, you know of him?" said Emily. Mr. Wingrave's easy manners and shelter from the cold wind softened her reserve.

"It's difficult to pass through this county without hearing of him."

"Papa is a good man," said Bridget.

"I'm pleased to hear it," said Mr. Wingrave. He sat back in thought. Bridget kept up friendly chatter about the weather until the carriage stopped in front of Charlton House.

"Miss Worthing, I hope you can forgive the unhappy

circumstance of our meeting, and remember only that we met as friends today," said Mr. Wingrave once he had handed them down.

"Thank you, Mr. Wingrave, I shall try," she said. The great door of the house opened to Mr. Worthing's joyous welcome.

"Girls! Girls! Are you back with Mrs. Worthing's present? Why, Emily, what happened to you?"

"I stood too close to the road, Papa," said Emily, blushing again at her dress.

"Is that you, Mr. Wingrave? What brings you to Charlton?" Emily and Bridget lifted their heads at their father's familiar greeting. The two men conversed as respected equals, unexpected for one of Mr. Wingrave's age.

"I apologize, Mr. Worthing, for calling unannounced, but I am the one who ruined Miss Worthing's dress."

"Oh. Well, Mrs. Worthing will be happy to hear she was ferried quickly home. You are still attending our ball Saturday eve?" Emily squinted at her father's casual dismissal of her plight.

"I was delighted to receive an invitation so soon after arriving, and will be even more so Saturday night, if I may engage Miss Worthing for the first dance," said Mr. Wingrave.

Forced to be courteous in front of her father, who looked on her in anticipation, Emily said, "You may, thank you."

"Excellent, I shall see you all then. Farewell," he said, bowing and returning to his carriage.

"You should have been more accommodating, Emily," said Bridget, "A handsome man offers you any redress and you could not find your tongue? And one of good fortune, too."

"Because he is handsome and rich I should be grateful my clothes are ruined?"

"Of course not, but you must admit he could not control the state of the roads. Besides, anyone who would still ask for a dance when you appear so disheveled must be charitable." Vexed and truly cold, Emily did not reply.

"Papa, why did you not tell us you had invited our new neighbors to the ball?" said Bridget.

"I thought it would be a fine surprise, knowing myself how amiable and handsome Mr. Wingrave is, to give everyone a good hour of gossip after their arrival," said Mr. Worthing, "Emily, for goodness sake, has the mud affected your nerves? Get inside and change clothes before you are too sick to dance. Your mother wants you, when you are presentable." Mr. Worthing left them for his study.

"I am still shocked at your taciturn treatment of Mr. Wingrave, considering all that he did to make amends," said Bridget. The girls trudged up the stairs to their room.

"The horses did the most work," replied Emily.

"Without man the horses would run free."

"Bridget, if I need a lecture after I wash, I will call on you."

"Fine, fine. Hurry to see Mama. I won't show her the ribbons until you come," said Bridget. Emily nodded and closed the door behind her.

Nursing her wounded vanity and pride, Emily took in her image reflected by the mirror on her wall. Logic told her that Mr. Wingrave would not think less of her for muddy clothes he caused, but the memory of his concerned expression caused a flash of heated embarrassment that overrode her logical assumptions. She huffed and found clean things in her closet.

"Mama, you should have seen it! Emily could barely speak," said Bridget. Emily favored her with a scathing look as she plumped Mrs. Worthing's pillow.

"Just remember how loud you crow, Bridget, is often how loud you will be crowed at," said Mrs. Worthing. She sat up and stretched while Emily adjusted the bedclothes.

"Do you want to walk today, Mama?" said Emily.

"No, my dear. Saving up my strength for tomorrow. If I sit and talk, I'll be able to stay downstairs longer."

"The doctor said you were getting better, earlier today. Is that true?" said Bridget.

"So far. He has changed my diet and it seems to be

improving my health, but we will have to wait to be sure. I do
not want to raise hope yet," said Mrs. Worthing. She laid back
on her pillows and sighed.

"I understand that young man has asked you to dance,
despite seeing you covered in mud. That's quite a compliment,"
Mrs. Worthing continued.

"It is likely he didn't want to make me feel as foolish as I
looked," said Emily, sitting on the edge of her mother's bed.

"You think he was humoring you?" laughed Bridget.

"You do not think as highly of yourself as you should,"
said Mrs. Worthing. Emily focused on an imagined flaw in her
skirt. She gritted her teeth in annoyance. Had he been
motivated by beauty?

"I'd have my entire face covered with mud if it would
keep him from approaching me for my physical charms," she
said. Mrs. Worthing and Bridget laughed at her assertion.

"The mud monster of Charlton. Papa would have to beg
men to dance with you," said Bridget.

"Really, Emily. Your beauty shines from the inside. Do
not be so concerned if at first men are attracted to your face
instead of your mind, for that will drive away all but the most
serious of lovers," Mrs. Worthing said.

"Mama!" cried Emily. Bridget broke into giggles.

"Emily, is that you?" came a sweet voice from the hall.
The Worthing's youngest child Genevieve rested her head against

the door, dark curls framing her genuine expressions.

"Yes, dear. Are you finished with lessons today?" said Emily.

"Not yet. Ms. Pierce allowed me respite to come see Mama while she prepares the sheet music," said Genevieve, "Why were you laughing Bridget?" Emily cast a warning glance at her sister.

"Nothing of import, love. Mama told us a fine joke," Bridget said.

"Are you pleasing Ms. Pierce with your progress today?" inquired Mrs. Worthing, gesturing for her youngest to come sit at her bedside.

"I think I am. She calls me bright."

"Indeed you are. We are all very proud of your accomplishments," said Emily.

Genevieve smiled and replied, "You would be proud if I barely managed a song, just for the effort."

"Such is love, clever girl."

"Aren't we all grateful she has given us something to dote upon other than a few ill notes?" said Bridget.

"Exceptionally grateful," said Mrs. Worthing, "In fact, I told your father to put an instrument in my sitting room for tomorrow, so that my daughters could play for me during the ball."

"I hope you mean Em and Gen. Bridget might end the

ball early."

"Peter!" cried Bridget as the ladies turned to the door, "You abuse me!" The eldest Worthing sibling stood handsome in a fresh coat. He grinned like their father, and smiled like their mother, never too far from making them all laugh.

"If I encouraged you to do what you ought not to, it would be a disservice to a fair lady," said Peter, as he stepped in to lean against the bedpost.

"I hope I taught my son better than to charm women by openly announcing their faults," said Mrs. Worthing.

"Is it a fault to lack aptitude in a particular skill? I cannot play and I doubt anyone would fault me for it."

"Perhaps then, brother, we should entertain with a duet. Peter and Bridget Worthing, a shameful, musical legend."

"I, for one, would like to keep all my acquaintances," said Emily.

"Oh yes, if Mr. Wingrave knows what you looked like draped in mud and does not mind, that you have two siblings of no musical talent will definitely do in his regard," said Bridget. Emily blushed at the presumption that she would care what Mr. Wingrave thought.

"Have you found a beau to your liking at last? That will be news for three counties," said Peter.

"Hold your tongue, Bridget, for the glory of your sense. I claim no one, we only met Mr. Wingrave today. Bridget fancies romance everywhere," said Emily.

"I fancy nothing! Mr. Wingrave is the brave soul who asked you to dance. I merely surmise his intention is to discover how a pleasant face may match its innards."

"All this talk of innards and romance makes me quite anxious. If you must fuss at each other, leave me in peace," said Mrs. Worthing, shooing them out, "Emily, darling, bring me a good book from the library, will you?"

"Yes, Mama," said Emily. They rose and left their mother to rest. "Genevieve, Ms. Pierce waits for you. We'll see you at dinner."

The youngest of them at thirteen-going-on-fourteen years of age, Genevieve sighed and meandered back to her schoolroom.

"Well sisters, are you prepared for the ball?" said Peter as the three of them stopped on the downstairs landing to part ways.

"I was prepared. Now I wonder if my brother and sister will embarrass me by spreading false rumors," said Emily.

"You worry about us more than is required. As soon as you stand up with him the rumors will spread without our help," said Peter.

"Do not underestimate the importance of origin. If they start here then it can be supposed our family was seriously talking of a romantic attachment between Mr. Wingrave and myself. If they start in public because of one dance, then the rumors are easily shrugged off as fantasy."

"Must they be shrugged off? What if Mr. Wingrave finds your prickly disposition towards strangers appealing?" Bridget said. Emily gave a cross sigh.

"Then he will be extremely disappointed," she said.

"All right, Emily. I shall trouble you no further," laughed Bridget.

Emily shook her head and walked toward the library, away from the good humor of Peter and Bridget. As devourers of learning, the library held the consequences of the Worthings dedication. Shelf after shelf of books overwhelmed Emily when they normally calmed or intrigued her. A chair sat close, so she made use of it to steady her nerves. Admitting that it was not the books, but her own thoughts that unsettled the quiet of her mind gave no relief. Bridget could not have known that her teasing would affect Emily so greatly.

Emily plotted to wait out the storm of gossip that would inevitably follow the ball. Mr. Wingrave deserved her courtesy despite being the fuel for several kinds of speculation. With her course set, Emily picked an old favorite and a new volume for her mother's pleasure and delivered them post haste.

"Mr. Wingrave! Good to see you again," said Mr. Worthing.

People lined up to the doors of Charlton, greeting their host and admiring the grand party arranged for their amusement.

"Mr. Worthing, you met my sister, Miss Mary Wingrave. Let me introduce you to my brother, Mr. Jonah Wingrave, my cousin, Mr. Sheridan, and a friend of Mary's Miss Olive Morley."

"You are all a welcome addition to Charlton tonight! Mrs. Worthing has a small sitting room to the right if you would not mind calling on her sometime this evening, she is quite excited to meet you. Illness will keep her from joining us in the ball room, I'm afraid," said Mr. Worthing. Mr. Wingrave took his leave, moving on to greet Peter, Emily, and Bridget. He introduced them also to his party of friends and relations.

"Do you not have a younger sister?" inquired Mary Wingrave.

"Yes we do, Miss Wingrave. Genevieve is having a fine time, entertaining our mother in the sitting room. May I escort you there?" said Peter.

"Yes please, I have already heard reports of her talent, if you do not mind," said Mary. The two departed the greeting line, leaving Emily to be reminded of her obligation.

"Miss Worthing, you have not forgotten our engagement I trust?" said Mr. Wingrave.

"No, sir. The first dance is reserved."

"This is the lady you afflicted? What good aim you have

cousin!" said Mr. Sheridan.

"'Twas not my aim. I would not wish the cold misery she
endured on a lady just so that I may become acquainted with
her."

"Then I praise the good aim of the carriage wheel for a
chance to meet such a lovely creature." Mr. Sheridan clasped her
hand with vigor.

"Thank you, Mr. Sheridan, for putting my beauty above
any inconvenience," said Emily. Her tone was lost on the
intended receiver, but brought color to Mr. Wingrave.

"You are very welcome!" said Mr. Sheridan.

"Let us find the refreshments, Sheridan, and allow these
ladies to welcome the rest of their guests," said Mr. Wingrave.
He and his party moved on as Bridget hid a chuckle at the
awkward meeting.

"What an admirer Mr. Sheridan is. At least Mr.
Wingrave's brother appeared pleasant, though shy in his youth,"
she said.

"I am surprised you recognize bashfulness, Bridget,
being so unfamiliar to it yourself," said Emily, laughing at her
sister's witless surprise. "You see, Mama was right. A loud
rooster makes a large target."

"Loud rooster, indeed. If you did not have someone
around you to pull out a laugh now and then, you would die of
gravity," Bridget replied. When the rush of incoming party-

goers subsided, Emily and Bridget visited their mother's room. Genevieve played softly for a small crowd. Peter and Mary stood to one side, conversing, yet Mary would not look directly at him, instead focusing on Genevieve's music. Emily chanced to stand where she could hear.

"She is lovely," said Mary. Peter reassessed petite Genevieve, noting with some astonishment that she would be a woman soon.

"It is good then that she has an older brother to chase away young men. I've had great success on that front with Emily and Bridget," he jested. Mary nodded as if it were the most natural thing for him to do.

"What lucky girls that you were born first," said Mary. Mrs. Worthing congratulated Genevieve as she completed the piece.

"You are an angel, darling, but you need not stay in here all evening. Go find your friends and enjoy the ball," said Mrs. Worthing. Genevieve gave her a kiss and disappeared into the crowd. With no one at the piano Mary answered Peter with more animation. Emily smiled at her brother's playful manner, putting Miss Wingrave at ease.

"How are you, Mama?" she asked Mrs. Worthing, slipping away to stand by her seat.

"Delighted. I have missed seeing everyone and having chats in a lively atmosphere. Everyone who visits me in bed comes under the weight of my sickness. Here, spirits are lifted, including mine," said Mrs. Worthing. Emily did see the notable happiness in her mother's countenance, but also the weariness. The dancing had not yet started and already Mrs. Worthing tired of the excitement. It was an improvement over staying in her room, as she did during their last party, so Emily took it as a sign of increased health.

Mr. Wingrave approached Mrs. Worthing.

"Mama, allow me to introduce Mr. Wingrave, our new neighbor at Reddester," said Emily.

"I am honored to make your acquaintance, madame," said Mr. Wingrave.

"The pleasure is all mine after hearing so much about you," said Mrs. Worthing. Emily dared not look at him smiling for fear of reddening.

"I'm sorry that it was not all good, and further apologize for Miss Worthing's dress," he said.

"Who said it was not all good?" laughed Mrs. Worthing, "I think it marvelous that fate brought our families together, even if Emily was made uncomfortable for a short time." Emily frowned in betrayal, but had no time to defend her right to bodily peace before Mrs. Barham ambushed them.

"Elizabeth, are you keeping Mr. Wingrave hidden away back here?" she said.

"On my honor, I am not. We've just been introduced,"

said Mrs. Worthing.

"How do you do, Mrs. Barham?" asked Mr. Wingrave.

"Much better now that I see your party here. I am hoping to learn more of you, neighbor, and introduce you to my daughter Anne." Unlike many ladies of station, Mrs. Barham did not flutter about. She reminded Emily of an arrow, always bent to a single-minded purpose.

"I would be delighted to meet her, but first I hear the musicians warming their instruments. Miss Worthing?" said Mr. Wingrave. He smiled upon taking Emily's hand, and led her into the ballroom, leaving a disgruntled Mrs. Barham to plot her next ambush.

To distract herself from the man at her right, Emily took in the room as a whole. The guests and trappings made up an all-too-familiar scene, and yet the undefinable quality that accompanied a ball lit a spark of impulsivity in the hearts of everyone present. Mrs. Worthing, though unable to spend any time in the larger ballroom, still had a presence in her tastes--soft and elegant, as if the whole manor were an expertly-made gown.

"You are radiant tonight, Miss Worthing," he said. Emily blushed.

"Better than yesterday, I hope." A cheery tune sounded from the fiddle and the other instruments joined in a light number meant to warm up the dancers. Mr. Wingrave thought about her response.

"Yesterday was the everyday Miss Worthing. Today is a Miss Worthing accentuated by finery. Both have their charms."

"I am not bathed in mud every day, Mr. Wingrave," said Emily, resenting the implication.

"No, but if one cannot see past the occasional bout of bad luck then they are doomed to miss out on an impeccable dance partner here and there," said Mr. Wingrave.

"You flatter me, sir, but I must inform you that amends are made. I already forgave you for your accidental transgression."

"Do you suppose I compliment you falsely?" A turn of the dance interrupted their conversation and sent them in different directions. Emily did not mind her alternate partner, earning her a scowl or two as she thought of an answer. When the two rejoined company, no conclusion had been reached as to the propriety of giving him an affirmative.

"I cannot merit all the compliments you have given me, and knowing well how I appear to strangers, you would be quite gallant to continue your attentions," said Emily. Surprised by her deprecating self-assessment, Mr. Wingrave fell silent. The dance came to an end and Emily feared he had taken offense. He did not leave her side though, instead taking her on his arm and strolling toward the drinks.

"Do you make many friends this way, Miss Worthing?" he inquired.

"Only the ones I think are worth keeping. I honestly present myself; no one is surprised that way, either the acquaintance by my frankness, or myself when those who would hide in subterfuge dismiss my company."

"That is quite a principle to stand on. I guarantee you that I shall speak just as honestly. My previous compliments pass this test, so I offer them to you again, free of any perceived obligation on my part." Intrigue forged an infuriatingly endearing smile on his lips.

"Then I thank you for them," said Emily when no other argument could be grasped. Mr. Wingrave took leave to speak with his brother. She had never felt so alone in her home. Surrounded by people, Emily poured a cup of wine with her shaky hand.

"Careful with that, Emily. Two days of clothing disaster would be unsupportable," said a woman near her ear. Emily turned to see Anne Barham of the neighboring Barham Park.

"Dear Anne," said Emily, grinning.

"How are you today, Miss Worthing?" said Anne.

"Out of sorts, I'm afraid. Bridget and Peter think themselves jesters since yesterday."

"I see you had a dance with Mr. Wingrave, the mysterious gentleman. Mama has been ferreting out whatever information she can. Apparently he's rich, though no one knows how rich."

"That is all we know, hm? Perhaps it is for the best. I see several ladies already setting their cap at him," said Emily.

"None of them have had the pleasure of a dance." Anne gave Emily a weighted look.

"Do not be ridiculous. As my closest friend, I forbid you from speculation."

"Ah, here he comes now. Couldn't stay away long, could he?" Mr. Wingrave did approach, followed by his sister and her friend.

"Miss Worthing, my sister Mary was just asking where Genevieve learned to play so beautifully," said Mr. Wingrave.

"Genevieve's education is handled by our governess, Ms. Pierce, though I also give her music lessons," Emily replied.

"She is a well-behaved young woman?" Mary inquired.

"Oh yes, of a very sweet temper. We all look after her, since she is the youngest. Bridget teaches her to paint, Peter demands she play chess and I sing with her. And we all press her to read," said Emily.

"A full schedule for one entering womanhood. She'll have no trouble finding a husband with a list of accomplishments like that," said Miss Morley.

"If a husband were a woman's sole aim," said Anne.

"That is how a female gains security, is it not?" Emily felt the heat of offense rolling off Anne.

"Assuming the right man may be chosen. Security is not

better than love, is it Olive?" said Mary.

"I suppose for certain families it is of no consequence if their daughters marry. Excuse me, I've promised the next dance," said Miss Morley. Anne and Emily reeled from the impolitic manner of the girl.

"Forgive me," said Mary, coloring from chin to hairline and exiting the circle.

"Well, Mr. Wingrave, what brings you to Tripton?" inquired Anne to break the tension.

"I needed someplace quiet to settle. Reddester Hall pleases me more as the days pass," he answered.

"It's been vacant so long, we were afraid it would fall into disrepair," said Anne.

"I saw that the garden was already overgrown from the road, a great shame. I've always wanted to take a turn through there," said Emily. Mr. Wingrave smiled.

"The gardener has been at them for several days now. Hopefully the gardens will be fit for a walk from Miss Worthing soon," he said.

Anne was taken aback by Mr. Wingrave's obvious preference for her friend and gave Emily an expressive look to the meaning of, "The rumors are true." Emily did not acknowledge Miss Barham's warning. She found it easier to laugh around Mr. Wingrave when another person was present. The three of them chatted on about the area for a bit, then the various residents.

"Miss Barham, have you any other siblings? I believe you have a younger sister?" asked Mr. Wingrave.

"Aye, and two older brothers. George and William left for the border as Swordtenants just a few months ago."

"Two brothers gone at once? That must be difficult."

"'Tis. Mama has turned her focus to my sister and me. She plans marriage, and will not be denied," said Anne.

"You certainly do go about denying her anyway," said Emily.

"Of course, I would not break our pact."

"You have a pact? Of what sort?" asked Mr. Wingrave, mystified by the inner workings of the feminine sex. Emily bit her lip at how their independence would come across in conversation.

"A pact against marriage, good sir. We shall not be traded about like possessions," said Anne.

"And what if one of you were to enter an equal partnership?"

"Equal? How is it possible for us to be equal under the standards of society?" Anne inquired.

"How indeed, when women do not wage war or own land?" said Emily.

"I do not think war should be waged by either sex. But of land, I see the difference. Would either of you choose a man that might leave you without the means to support yourself?"

"It matters not, for we will not choose men, is that not so Emily?" At this, Emily could only nod her adherence. She quickly changed the subject to the upcoming feast Mr. Worthing had planned for the evening.

"What can he mean by it, Mama?" said Emily. The last dance went on in the ball room as Emily visited with her mother. Mrs. Worthing held up tolerably well, but would take dinner in her room instead of with the party.

"I cannot say, love." Mr. Wingrave had engaged Emily for two more dances in between standing up with his sister and her friend. When they were not dancing, he kept close to her conversations, even if he did not join them.

"He displays a familiarity we do not possess. I fear the censure this will induce."

"Indeed I have not heard one word of censure. You may be more sensitive to it than the rest of us," said Mrs. Worthing, "Besides, what if he prefers your company? Do you not like him?"

"Talking with him is not unenjoyable."

"But...?"

"But two unmarried people are always assumed to be developing a romance," said Emily. She looked down at her hands, imagining Mr. Wingrave's fingers wrapped around her own. He had promised to be honest when he spoke with her, but she had discerned that he was not as he seemed. His hands were not the hands of a young gentleman. They were rougher, stronger, as if he had labored for years.

"Oh Emily, you are silly. If it is love, it is love. If it is friendship, it is friendship. You have the free will to shape your situation. Now stop this melancholy worrying and play me a song before I go upstairs." Emily obeyed, picking one of her mother's favorite songs. Though the room had emptied in preparation for dinner, guests came in to hear as Emily tapped the first few notes.

"On the hills and the glen,
I cannot remember when,
Last I saw my darling love,
From the sky and above,
Stars they fall in a line,
Signaling it is our time,
Leave me now and love me then,
I cannot remember when,
Last I saw my darling love."

The music brought Emily alive, eyes sparkling and cheeks rosy. She prepared to sing the second verse, meant for a man's voice, when Mr. Wingrave sat beside her and played the complementary piece. His voice made her heart flutter and pound simultaneously, his clear tone obviously a result of practice.

"On the road I travel now,

Though I cannot tell you how,

Fate took me from truest love,

From the sky and above,

Stars they fall in a line,

Signaling it is our time,

Wait for me and love me now,

Though I cannot tell you how,

Fate took me from truest love." With a hope that her blushing could be passed off as exertion, Emily continued into the third and final verse, which they sang together.

"'Cross the room I see you here,

For us, my love, I shed a tear,

We were only kept apart,

By a lie, a friendless art,

Stars they fall in a line,

Signaling it is our time,

Love me once and for all,

Answer my love's call,

And forever be mine." A large audience had gathered for the exhibition, and when the last merry note hung in the air, they applauded with enthusiasm.

"I did not know you were musical, Mr. Wingrave," said Emily.

"There are many things you do not know about me, Miss Worthing." He excused himself and left the room after accepting congratulations on the fine performance, leaving Emily to escort her mother to bed.

"The nurse can do this, Emily," said Mrs. Worthing.

"I do not mind, I need space clear of people," said Emily. She took her mother's arm and they made a slow progression up the stairs.

"You look and sing well together," said Mrs. Worthing.

"He sings well." Gritting her teeth would give Emily a headache if she were not more careful.

"His regard for you blossoms. You should have seen how he watched you before joining in."

"Mama, please. We've known each other for exactly two days. He will recover from his fancy in due time when I become no friendlier than I was at the first." Mrs. Worthing's room was prepared for the night, so Emily bid her a good sleep and went to the dining room. Most everyone enjoyed the meal. Pleased to see she and her sisters were set close to each other, and that Mr. Wingrave's party had their own table, Emily took her place.

"Is mother settled in?" Bridget asked.

"Yes, ready for food and sleep. She did wonderfully tonight, don't you think?" said Emily.

"I visited her many times and she was always alert and attentive. I hope she is better for good," said Genevieve.

"Don't we all. I may have been too busy watching Emily dance to note anything else. I think this is the most you've danced in months," said Bridget. When Emily made no reply, Bridget went on, "Peter seems quite enamored of the Wingraves as well, one of them, at least." Ignoring the planted barb, Emily sought her brother sitting at the right hand of Mary Wingrave. He perked up whenever she addressed him. Emily insisted on no more talk of the Wingraves so that she could eat her dinner in peace, much to the upset of her two sisters who desperately wanted to know what Mr. Wingrave had said and how he said it.

After dinner when the guests fell to talking, Mr. Sheridan proved he had imbibed too much drink by stumbling toward groups of women. He spotted Emily and lumbered over to her, missing his mark entirely. When Mr. Sheridan attempted to recover and halt his progress, he lost the contents of his cup-- maroon liquid splashed up and out. Emily's luck held as it narrowly flew past her and soiled Miss Morley's gown instead.

"Mr. Sheridan, you drunken dolt! How dare you ruin my gown?" Miss Morley rebuked him far more than was necessary for the droplets that colored her skirt. He straightened up, ashamed.

"Take it in grace, Miss Morley. Mr. Sheridan did not mean to offend you," said Bridget. Miss Morley stormed off to seek a wet cloth.

"That's quite right, Miss Bridget, no offense meant!" he

said.

"I learned from my sister. Even doused in stormwater she would not behave so," said Bridget. Emily gave her a warm smile.

"Stormwater nor Hell's beasts could make Miss Worthing so... disagreeable, that's the word. Wingrave chose the right lady," said Mr. Sheridan. Not a soul in the room of over a hundred people missed the remark, so loudly given, though he certainly meant "right lady to splash."

"Come Sheridan, your tongue ails you. Lie down on a sofa until the party is over," said Mr. Wingrave.

"Wingrave, there you are! I was just telling these ladies..." Mr. Sheridan said as he was led away. The gathered crowd may as well have shouted their speculation at Emily, so crudely did they whisper their suspicions.

"How unfair! She doesn't even want to be married."

"I say by this time next year. What a match!" The endless variations burned the pit of Emily's stomach into an ashy hole. How could she have let this happen?

Until the last carriage was sent off, Emily avoided being alone with Mr. Wingrave, disappointing many gossip mongers in the crowd who had watched them after their song together. She wondered what made everyone lose their heads when even the illusion of romance presented it self.

"Good night, Miss Worthing," said Mr. Wingrave with a

bow.

"Good night, Mr. Wingrave," she replied.

"I daresay I hope to see you again soon, miss," said Mr. Sheridan, still drunk and unstable.

"Yes, soon," said Emily. As their carriage faded into the darkness, Bridget gave Emily a wry smile.

"Not a word more," Emily warned her.

2. Dinner at Reddester

Three days after the ball, and Emily had not heard the end of it. Peter, at least, was away on business. Genevieve and Mrs. Worthing knew better than to push Emily too much for fear of hardening her heart, but Bridget cared not for her sister's qualms. An envelope appeared at their breakfast table which cinched Emily's status as nearly engaged to be married in Bridget's eyes.

"Who is it from, Papa?" said Emily.

"Miss Mary Wingrave. She invites us to dinner on Friday," he said. Bridget laughed to herself despite Emily's scowling.

"Thank them for my part of the invitation, but I shall decline," said Emily.

"What? Why?" inquired her father.

"I do not wish to leave Mama alone."

"Nonsense. Your mother has always insisted that we go out and live our lives while she is incapacitated. You will go."

"Is that an order?" said Emily.

"It is a firm suggestion to a stubborn young lady. Besides it would hurt your mother to hear you stayed for her."

"Yes, Papa," said Emily. She would not challenge him if he expressly wished it. He'd given her much independence as a daughter.

"May I go, Papa?" asked Genevieve.

"The invitation expressly states that everyone is invited, with pardons for Mrs. Worthing's well-being." Genevieve smiled, her joy warming the hearts of her family.

"Does it say if Emily should come ready to hear an offer?" said Bridget.

"Bridget Worthing, don't be ridiculous!" Emily said, too loudly for the table.

"If you two do not stop quarreling over Mr. Wingrave, I shall have your pocket money for the week. Must I bend to childish consequences? Or do my daughters possess enough presence of mind to behave in accordance with their age?" said Mr. Worthing. They bowed their heads in submission.

"Good. I have business out of doors today. Genevieve, to Ms. Pierce when you are finished with breakfast. Girls, tell your mother about our invitation and do not trouble her by carrying on your argument in her bedroom." Mr. Worthing pushed his chair in and left. The sisters finished breakfast, each giving Genevieve a kiss on the forehead before taking to the stairs.

"Why are you being so strange about Mr. Wingrave?" inquired Bridget.

"I'm not," said Emily. Bridget stepped in her way and faced her sister. She required a better answer, this time without humor.

"If you seriously desire an answer that is not for your own amusement, let us talk of this in our room instead of here in the hall where everyone is privy to the discussion," Emily hissed through her teeth.

"Now, what is different about this man? I have teased you countless times before, and I've never garnered this much reaction," said Bridget when Emily had closed the door. With a heavy heart and an even heavier sigh, Emily took a seat on their vanity stool.

"Most men are easily dissuaded, but even I cannot doubt Mr. Wingrave has an unusual regard for me. The escalation of this situation, if he is encouraged, can only mean embarrassment for both our families."

"Why must it mean embarrassment? Do you have no feeling for him whatsoever?"

"My feelings are unimportant. I will not allow myself to enter into a situation like marriage," said Emily.

"You mean, you are serious about your assertions? About never marrying?"

"Why should I marry? Why should I pledge to bow to a man?" Bridget stared open-mouthed.

"What kind of man would you choose that would make you bow? I do not see it in Mr. Wingrave."

"What about Mama?" said Emily, "I cannot leave while she is ill." Bridget paced in upset.

"You must know Mama may never get well," she whispered.

"I won't leave you all here while I set up a house of my own. Genevieve needs a mother, I can at least play at that until she gets older." Emily and Bridget allowed the discussion to trail off, neither sure of what path could be taken.

The view of Reddester from the carriage left nothing to be desired. Knots of trees and bushes with freshly trimmed paths made up the private grounds of the property, followed by a view of the farms on the horizon that had been in limbo without an owner to oversee the land. A lake came up beside the road, siphoned off from the Tripton Valley River that cut through the heart of the countryside.

"Mr. Wingrave must get people on those farms or he'll miss the best of the harvest," said Mr. Worthing. Charlton itself had many farms over which he presided. It made Emily proud to see her father so involved in the day to day work that supported his family, unlike some gentlemen that hired out the difficult work for a penny wage. It was beneath no one, she decided, to be able to perform the tasks they asked of the people who served them. Her father's loyal tenants and constant prosperity had driven off the criticism that came with such a revolutionary viewpoint, but that only relegated it to the mumbles of the arrogant landed behind the doors of their parlors.

"Perhaps he does not know the business of Tripton so well as you do," said Bridget. To Emily's puzzle she added another piece--Mr. Wingrave claimed no profession. With the state of his hands, he must have been doing something strenuous. The son of a Lord need not concern himself with hard labor, deepening her suspicions.

"Perhaps," said Mr. Worthing. Reddester Hall broke through the trees, crowning an expansive lawn. The gardens which had been a month earlier in shambles were now free of overgrowth and forming buds, as gardens should in spring. When the carriage stopped, Emily took a deep breath to prepare for the social onslaught coming forthwith. Mr. Wingrave appeared on the front walk to greet them.

"Welcome Mr. Worthing, Miss Worthing, Miss Bridget,

and Miss Genevieve. Your son is still away?" said Mr. Wingrave.

"Aye, Peter sends his regrets that he could not conclude his business before tonight."

"I understand. Let us join my siblings in the sitting room." His smile was no less warm than when he asked Emily to dance for the third time, a sign that time had not made him think better of being attentive to her. Emily kept her gaze on the floor.

Years ago, when last the Worthings had been inside Reddester, it had been decorated to the taste of old Mrs. Charles who favored a grand style in all things, even to the detriment of elegance. Whether it was Mr. Wingrave or Mary in charge of the house, Reddester had become a much more beautiful surrounding than Emily remembered. Simple, quality furnishings echoed around intricate focal points, drawing one's eye to the character of the house.

"My goodness this place has changed. Someone has fine taste," said Mr. Worthing.

"My sister and I both had a hand in it, though I insisted on many things since this is where I intend to stay," said Mr. Wingrave. Bridget nudged Emily and gave her a wink. Emily looked away and pretended to admire the art they passed.

"Mr. Worthing, so good to see you again!" said Mary as they entered the sitting room.

"Thank you, Miss Wingrave. You look in fine spirits

tonight," he replied.

"How could I not be? Oh, but where is Mr. Peter?"

"I've already accepted his regrets as he's on business," said Mr. Wingrave.

"Oh. Well, I shall get to know the Misses Worthing better then," said Mary.

"That would be an honor," said Emily, happy to engage the sister and not the brother. Miss Morley hung near the sofa, reluctant to join in.

"Miss Worthing! I've heard that I missed your performance at the ball, a great tragedy. May we entice you to play sometime this evening?" asked Mr. Sheridan.

"If my hosts wish it, I cannot refuse," she answered.

"I would hear everyone with an inclination play tonight," said Mary.

"Excellent. I'll begin," said Miss Morley, marching to the pianoforte. She played softly enough for conversation to continue, so the ladies took seats on the sofa and chairs while the men formed a circle near the fireplace. Genevieve, nervous about embarrassing her family, stayed near Emily and took her cues. Bridget and Mary conversed easily, both disposed to friendliness. Without an objection like Emily's, it was a mystery why Mary Wingrave had not married. She had the same good looks as her brother, and a charming personality, yet she must have been over five and twenty if not nearing thirty years old. When Emily caught up with their chatter, she found herself the subject.

"Emily has been taking care of us while Mama gets well," said Bridget.

"You are lucky then, to have such a sister," said Mary. A flash of sadness stole over her face, then disappeared. Emily glanced around, but no one else had noticed.

"They praise me in company, at least. When I'm doing the taking care of you would think I'd asked them to build me a pyramid," said Emily to good-natured laughter.

"A fair task master, then. My brother Jonah complains in the same way when I make him practice civility. He cannot always be hiding in corners waiting for someone to come talk with him," said Mary, casting a sly look toward the gentlemen. Jonah took notice of his name and colored most brilliantly. With trepidation, he approached them as if his feet stuck to the floor with each step.

"Are you making me seem foolish, sister?" he asked with a slight smile.

"Never, dear. I am proud of you for conquering some of your bashfulness, under my tutelage of course," Mary said.

"Some, I'm afraid, is unsatisfactory. One day I would be among people as easily as Elijah," said Jonah.

"That is hardly fair to yourself. Elijah had the benefit of being away at... on business," said Mary. Mr. Wingrave's happy countenance fell to a stern glare from across the room, just long enough to register before his face relaxed again. Mary continued, though visibly anxious, "He had many people to practice with."

Emily, all too aware of what passed though she could see everyone dismissing it as a slip of the tongue, pointed out her observation, "Are you well, Miss Wingrave? You seem suddenly dizzy."

"Oh, I am quite well, thank you. Just a spell, it's passed." Miss Morley's song finished to little applause.

"Miss Worthing, may I entice you to take a turn with me in the gardens?" said Mr. Wingrave.

"Oh, indeed! We should all go. Elijah has had over twenty men working on them since the ball," said Mary. He blushed, his head dropping as Emily took in the meaning of that.

"I would enjoy that," said Emily, taking his proffered arm. Freshly-cut greenery and damp, churned earth stirred the garden into a perfumed frenzy as the flora and fauna settled into their new homes. Owing to their new master, the vines had not been eliminated, but cut back, giving a wild look to the tame sections of delicate flowers. Walls and trees made a maze of the Reddester gardens, tempting onlookers to believe they might get lost.

The party broke off into twos and threes. Mr. Wingrave took Emily away from the others as soon as it was polite to do so. As an excuse to lean away from him and because she longed to, Emily reached out and let her palm glide against one of the vines, bits of ornate stone peeking out from underneath. The silky leaves gave no resistance. Emily drew her hand back only when the wall ended in an archway.

"I did not know that gardens were such a priority to you, Mr. Wingrave," she said.

"I will confess to wanting them suitable for our dinner tonight," he said.

"You have proven to be a conscientious neighbor." Amused with his obvious concealment of goodness knows what after he had promised to speak honestly, Emily was at ease.

"Hopefully I can be more so over the years." She felt the double-edged meaning of his statement and wisely kept quiet. Even if Mr. Wingrave was comfortable claiming familiarity with her, she could not build esteem knowing he silenced his own family on his past.

"You are thinking deeply, Miss Worthing. Can I trouble you to let me know the subject?"

"In truth?" he nodded, "You."

"What an answer to be so tacitly given! What pray tell, do you think of me?" he said.

"Though I am honest, I shall not concede all my thoughts, Mr. Wingrave, so do not expect full disclosure. I think you are a man of interesting talents and knowledge. One might wonder where you came upon those things," said Emily. Mr. Wingrave thought while Emily held her breath, waiting for answers to her worrisome query.

"Men of character seek out growth. With the resources at my disposal, you cannot imagine I had a lack of opportunity," he said. A vague, unfulfilling response. Emily resolved not to press him or volunteer more conversation.

"You are frustrated? You wish to know what school I attended? How I spent my time? Are those qualifications as important as the result you see before you?" he said with a touch of heat.

"No. I always seek to fill the gaps in my knowledge. If all we took was the present, we would never learn from the past," said Emily.

"I see. Then let me hold up my promise in telling you that I wish you to know eventually. But not yet." Emily colored at his devastatingly hope-inducing answer. Her feelings were getting away from her in his presence.

"Let us talk about you, Miss Worthing. I am fascinated by your friendship with Miss Barham and your 'pact.' How long have you known her?"

"Anne and I have been friends since childhood. Barham Park is a twin estate to Charlton, built by two friends who settled here to take advantage of the rich soil. Our families have always been close."

"And your pact? How did that come about?"

"As long as we are unmarried, we can assign our own

value," said Emily.

"And if you meet a man who values you as much or more than that?"

"Does such a man exist?" she wondered aloud.

"You think very little of the masculine sex," said Mr. Wingrave.

"In a world where women always come second, how could I not?"

"Perhaps you should judge individuals, instead of a large collection with nothing in common but what they were given at birth."

"Enough of them have come together to perpetuate their accepted superiority that I feel comfortable with my opinion. Or is your true point that I should not judge you by that standard?" said Emily. She stopped in a small courtyard where she could face him, the laughter of the others muffled by hedges.

"I suppose that is the only point I have left, for you've not had the experience I have of knowing many great men."

"You suppose me ignorant?"

"I do." Offense drew red splotches on Emily's cheeks.

"That is not very gentlemanly," she informed him, walking away without his arm.

"It is honesty," he replied, "Which is what you required of me." Her steps halted and she turned on him in suspicion.

"Why is it that you put yourself in my company? Is it an

examination of my opinions or do you find dismissing them a pleasurable pastime?"

"Neither. I think you are a lovely, intelligent woman. My opinion that you could benefit from being out in the world more does not hinder you in my esteem," said Mr. Wingrave. Frustration boiled up inside Emily's chest, and it took all her nerve to behave as a lady should.

"Thank you, Mr. Wingrave. I shall take it into consideration when I'm not needed at home." He flinched.

"I am sorry, Miss Worthing. I forgot myself. Please, let me take you back to the house," said Mr. Wingrave. Rather than let Bridget know they'd quarreled, she took his arm again.

"There you are Wingrave! I was wondering where you had got off to with the lovely Miss Worthing! I found a rose bush that I am sure she will appreciate," said Mr. Sheridan.

"A rose bush? Most fortuitous," said Emily, leaving Mr. Wingrave to stand on the other side of Mr. Sheridan.

"Wingrave, come over here! There is a buried sculpture you must rescue," called Miss Morley from where the other ladies gathered near an old tree. He left Emily and Mr. Sheridan to hunting down the rose bush.

"Shall we?" said Mr. Sheridan. He made no move to gain her hand, letting her choose how she walked.

"Yes, we shall," she said, in much better humor. Mr. Wingrave's insistence on closeness had made their encounter even more draining. Mr. Sheridan chatted on about many things, his acquaintance with Lord and Lady Wingrave, the parties he had attended in Endland's capital, Dunbarrow, and the education he had received there. If Mr. Wingrave was a foggy mirror, Mr. Sheridan was clear glass.

"Ah, here it is!" cried Mr. Sheridan. A fine rose bush leaned heavily on a back wall of the garden, new flowers forming now that sunlight could get through.

"Oh my, you shall have to let me know what color it blooms in. It will be beautiful," said Emily, truly admiring the elderly plant.

"Not so beautiful as you, Miss Worthing. Have I told you I have a house up north nearer to Landhilton?" Emily did her best to ignore any implications that might come with this information.

"No, you haven't mentioned it."

"It's an elegant property, Barkrum. I've often wished to have a lady for it," said Mr. Sheridan. Emily bit her tongue against her first response.

"Perhaps one day, you will," she said. Meandering away from the rose bush back towards company, Emily sighed. The Wingraves had caused her so much anxiety since arriving, it would not have shocked her to hear it was by design.

"Miss Worthing? Miss Worthing, may I have a moment?" asked Jonah before she could get to the others. He waved Mr. Sheridan on and took up walking beside her.

"Yes, what is it, Mr. Jonah?" said Emily.

"You are friends with Miss Barham?"

"Why, yes I am."

"Could I ask you the name of her younger sister?" he said, flushing.

"Oh, that would be Victoria," said Emily. Anne's younger sister, known for her shyness as well, made little impression on most.

"Thank you, Miss Worthing. I couldn't bring myself to ask at the ball."

"You know, Mr. Jonah, being bashful isn't the worst kind of flaw. Perhaps you should consider that as long as you act with sense, it is better to be remembered than to never be noticed." Jonah had the same look of thoughtfulness as his brother.

"That is sound advice, Miss Worthing. Thank you."

"Dinner is served," called Mary, ushering them in.

The Wingraves had chosen an intimate dining room for the event, a mark of their acceptance of the Worthings as close friends. Soft candle light shone on each face, giving everyone an ethereal glow. The night continued to go poorly for Emily when she found herself seated next to Mr. Wingrave. Mr. Worthing sat at the other end of the table with Genevieve and Mary whom he entertained with his special brand of storytelling.

"How was the rose bush, Miss Worthing?" said Mr. Wingrave.

"Quite pretty," she said.

"Told her it was nothing to her beauty," hiccuped Mr. Sheridan, who had, upon sitting, swallowed his wine and asked for another.

"I'm sure," said Mr. Wingrave.

"I'd not want to be compared to a flower," said Miss Morley to Emily's right hand.

"Oh, and why is that?" inquired Mr. Wingrave.

"It's delicate, and at times, thorny," said Miss Morley.

Feeling the pointed end of this remark, Emily said, "Thorns are a defense against the stupid and unwary. And no matter the weather, flowers always come back." Miss Morley sniffed and twisted to Jonah on her other side. Mr. Wingrave cleared his throat behind a napkin in what Emily would have called a veiled chuckle if it had not been entirely unsupportable to laugh.

"To the rose of Charlton!" said Mr. Sheridan. He held up his glass in a toast.

"I would share the honor with my sisters, if you don't mind. To the roses of Charlton," corrected Emily. Everyone smiled and drank. The dinner went on, as most do, until

Genevieve rose from her seat unexpectedly and went to Emily.

"Em, I am ill," she said. Emily rose immediately, took her by the shoulders, and made their way to the restroom.

"Please, hold it in until we get there," whispered Emily. Genevieve nodded. She did wait until Emily could get her over a wash basin.

"Too much wine for one not used to it. We'll clean you up and you will feel fine, my dear," Emily soothed her. She rubbed the poor girl's back until it was over, then entreated a nearby maid for some water.

"Oh Emily, how can I face the Wingraves?" said Genevieve as her sister put her hair back in place.

"Darling, you are young. They will understand," said Emily. The water arrived and Genevieve was put to rights.

"No more wine, tonight," said Emily.

"No caution needed," said Genevieve.

"Put on your best pitiable smile, it will stave off any cruelty," Emily assured her. Genevieve practiced until they entered the dining room, allowing her eyelids to droop in fatigue.

"Miss Genevieve, are you in need of a doctor?" said Mary.

"No, thank you Miss Wingrave, I..." Genevieve broke off, embarrassed.

"Genevieve is not allowed wine at our house. It

overcame her for a moment," said Emily, releasing the girl to her chair.

"Oh, that's all right. We have fresh juice from this morning," said Mary. Emily gave thanks and regained her seat.

"It must be difficult, mothering your sister," said Miss Morley. Genevieve's face fell with shame and Mary frowned at the horrid manners of her friend.

"Not at all, Miss Morley. She is a joy to our family. What you call mothering, I call caring," said Emily.

"Surely the added responsibility must keep you from pursuing the priorities of a young lady, marriage for example," said Miss Morley. Mr. Worthing and Mr. Wingrave shifted with unease in their seats.

"I assure you that I devote just as much time to that as it deserves," said Emily. Miss Morley smiled at Mr. Wingrave.

"Mr. Worthing," he said, ignoring Miss Morley's triumphant grin, "Do not let me forget to give you a package for Mrs. Worthing. I've had the cooks prepare her a special sampling of what we ate tonight, so that it would not need to be described." Emily looked up at him in infinite surprise.

"Oh, Elizabeth will be overjoyed with that. She bears it well, but she knows she misses the delights of company," said Mr. Worthing. His eyes shined when he spoke of his beloved wife.

"That is very thoughtful, Mr. Wingrave. Thank you,"

said Emily.

"It is my pleasure. Now, dinner has concluded, will you play for us? Genevieve, too, if she is well?" said Mr. Wingrave. Emily nodded and followed everyone back to the sitting room. The manservants, with Mr. Wingrave's help, rearranged the furniture for a concert.

"Genevieve, do you think you can perform?" asked Bridget taking stock of her sister.

"I can play, but Emily will have to sing," replied Genevieve.

"As you wish," said Emily. Genevieve thumbed through the available music and chose a song about a girl falling in love at her first party. As Emily sang and turned the pages, she absorbed the rapt attention of Mr. Wingrave. He appeared to be deep in thought. Miss Morley tried to converse with him in whispers which he quickly put down.

"Bravo, bravo," said Mr. Sheridan who had nearly fallen asleep in his chair.

"We won't tax Genevieve anymore tonight, but I do hope to hear music from you two in the future," said Mary.

"It's a wonder to me," said Miss Morley after the furniture had been put back and the party drifted into groups of men and women, "why you sing about love, Miss Worthing, when marriage does not interest you." The men's chatter died to a crawl as several ears leaned to hear the response.

"I am not without feeling because I do not believe marriage to be in my best interests," said Emily. Sensing why Miss Morley chose to goad her so, Emily kept calm and light-hearted.

"What is feeling if it is all for naught?" said Miss Morley. She did not look to Emily when she said this, but Mr. Wingrave. A curious anger rumbled through his mannerisms.

"No emotion is for naught if we are to remain of human soul. Love, forgiveness, sorrow, rage, these make up the blood of us while our logic and reason form the vessels," said Emily.

"And if one or the other becomes too strong?" inquired Mr. Wingrave.

"Then we may bleed out or be closed off."

"What if one is blind and does not know they are closed?" he challenged her.

"Hopefully, one they love will open their eyes," said Emily. Mr. Wingrave stood back, satisfied. Emily did not understand what victory he thought he had earned. If Elijah Wingrave expected every woman to be gratified by his attention, to stand by and wait for an offer, he was a fool in her mind. Refusing to indulge him did not make her closed.

"How about a game of cards?" suggested Mary. Emily accepted without hesitation.

3. NEW AND OLD

Emily hid in a stack of books for a week after the dinner at Reddester. Once, Mary and Mr. Wingrave came to call and she'd begged a cold. Mrs. Worthing had been so pleased with Mr. Wingrave's package that she had scarce stopped talking of what a nice young man he was ever since. Emily's time in hiding had run out, however, as a public dance in town required her presence.

"Papa, can't I stay with Genevieve? She, Mama, and I can have a pleasant time here," said Emily. She would rather hear her mother talk of the man than see him in the flesh. Catching her father alone at his writing desk had been tricky enough with Bridget's constant surveillance.

"Emily Worthing, what has gotten into you? If it is Mr.

Wingrave that troubles you, I must put forth that you may be fooling yourself. I've never seen you hide, fear is not in your nature. What has changed?" said Mr. Worthing. With his wife indisposed, he'd become more aware of the inner workings of the females he lived with, adapting to the dual role he had to fill.

"I feel as if everyone is staring at me because of the liberties he's taken. It is a point of drama to others, the maiden sworn not to marry and the dashing suitor, clashing on a field of battling wants. I am being pushed into a storybook, and expected to conform to the blushing bride one expects at the end of a tale."

"My goodness girl. May I never accuse you of not thinking things through. If Mr. Wingrave falls in love with you, I shall be the first to bless the match. He's a sensible, fortunate man," said Mr. Worthing.

"You would give me away?" she said. Tears formed at the corners of Emily's eyes, compound stress catching up with her.

"Don't be preposterous. I've seen you together, and if you don't fall in love with him equally I shall eat my hat." Emily gasped in fury and fled the room filled with Mr. Worthing's laughter. "Be ready for the party, Emily! I'm taking bids on your hand tonight!"

Bridget came from the parlor, and, having overheard her father, followed Emily outside.

"You know he jests," said Bridget.

"Oh yes, everyone jests," said Emily.

"If you are set on refusing Mr. Wingrave, then why does this matter? Where is my sister that faced any social danger with a brave smile and a sure remark on anyone's sense that disagreed?"

"I don't know," said Emily. Glad to be out of sight, she stomped along a path through Charlton proper until her anger subsided. "You are right, Bridget. I have let this dampen my spirits too long."

"Aye, a great soggy mess you've turned in to. Almost like when we first met Mr. Wingrave," said Bridget. Emily prepared a scathing retort, but instead she laughed. "There is my sister! Her humor returns!"

"I am sorry. I've been difficult, haven't I?" said Emily.

"Worse to some than to me. I was certain I would have to separate you and Miss Morley before someone lost an eye. Mary could have wrung her hands raw. But... Miss Morley deserved reproach. Her comments were unpardonable."

"She seeks marriage and Mr. Wingrave is right in her path. I won't take it to heart." They walked side by side.

"I wish someone were in my path," said Bridget.

"Perhaps when mother is well we might take a season in the city. Your prospects will be much better there."

"You would come with me?"

"Why not? I would go for the culture myself. See more of the world," said Emily. The words of Mr. Wingrave echoed back at her causing an inexplicable squint to confuse Bridget, until Emily smiled and talked more of what they might find in Dunbarrow.

"Who is that?" inquired Bridget of Anne Barham. A tall man with a stately air had slipped into the public dance almost unnoticed.

"His name is Mr. Edward Annesley, a visiting gentleman. His family are old nobility, very well-regarded at court. Mama has been after how long he plans to stay to no avail," said Anne. The Wingraves arrived, Mr. Sheridan and Miss Morley in tow. None of the women missed how Mr. Annesley took a keen interest in the family, since they watched him so closely.

"What was that about?" asked Emily.

"Maybe he knows them?" said Bridget. Mary and Miss Morley came over to them directly.

"Miss Worthing, Miss Bridget, Miss Barham, Miss Victoria, how are you all this evening?" said Mary.

"Quite well, I thank you. Have you settled in at Reddester since last Friday?" said Emily, but Mary Wingrave looked elsewhere. Upon perusing the room her gaze had fallen upon Mr. Annesley, which caused her no little upset.

"Mary?" said Miss Morley, following her eyes. She sucked in a breath and said, "Mary, Miss Worthing asked if you have settled in."

"Oh? Oh yes, quite settled. Excuse me, I am suddenly disoriented. Olive could you take me to fresh air?" said Mary, leaning heavily on her friend.

"Excuse us," said Miss Morley.

"Now that is very odd," said Anne.

"They must have an acquaintance, though I cannot say what would make her faint at the sight of him," said Emily. Mrs. Barham interrupted their speculation, dragging her husband and Mr. Annesley behind her.

"Anne? Anne? I must have you meet Mr. Annesley! He has told me the latest news from the city and it is just fascinating," said Mrs. Barham.

"Pleased to meet you," said Anne with a smirk, "Let me also introduce my dear friend Miss Worthing, her sister Miss Bridget, and my sister Miss Victoria." Mrs. Barham recalculated the wisdom of introducing Mr. Annesley to her daughter amid so many young ladies.

"Very pleased to meet you all," said Mr. Annesley.

"What news do you have?" asked Bridget, "Of the city?" Bridget's animated beauty stole Mr. Annesley's attention from her daughters just as Mrs. Barham had feared.

"I merely said that it was windier than usual, Miss

Bridget, nothing stupendous," said Mr. Annesley.

"What is more stupendous than the wind, Mr. Annesley? It is purported to carry the music of the ages on its back, or perhaps the voice of one's lost love," said Bridget. Faced with an unexpected answer, Mr. Annesley stared at the teasing grin Bridget leveled at him.

"That is... something I had not considered. Perhaps I have spent too many days huddled in my collar to notice any music," he said.

"What a shame, Mr. Annesley. Wind music is my favorite next to the creations of my sister," said Bridget. Mrs. Barham looked between the two of them, dissatisfied.

"Wind music? What nonsense! Anne can play a tune on the harp that would shame any frigid gust, isn't that so my dear?" said Mrs. Barham to her husband.

"I think it was meant in an extraordinary sense, love," said Mr. Barham.

"Oh Harold, do not speak if you cannot follow along," said his wife.

"Would you like to dance, Miss Bridget, when the music begins?" inquired Mr. Annesley.

"That sounds lovely, thank you, Mr. Annesley," said Bridget. Mrs. Barham took off for another corner of the room to sulk, taking Mr. Barham with her. Anne sighed in relief. Jonah approached Victoria Barham, giving Anne and Emily a superb opportunity to leave the couples behind.

The public hall rang with laughter and the clinking of glasses. Mr. Worthing himself had funded the rebuilding of the uncared for structure, insisting on a sturdier floor and a new balcony for romantic views of the night sky. Mary and Miss Morley were not on the balcony, leading Emily to think they'd gone out the front where the servants and drivers made their own merry.

"This is how it shall be, when we are old maids. We shall slip away from couples to talk about our adventures," said Anne.

Caught thinking about the Wingraves, Emily blurted out, "If your perfect man walked into this room and valiantly proposed, would you accept him?" as they took a turn about the room.

"That is a strange question. My perfect man... Barring the notion that he does not breathe air, but faerie dust, if he could make me happy and treat me as I wish to be treated, would I marry him? I--"

"Miss Worthing, Miss Barham," Mr. Wingrave interrupted Anne's answer, "Miss Worthing, would you give me the honor of dancing with you again?"

"I will, thank you," said Emily and he led her away. Anne pursed her lips, and shook her head.

"Your sister had a dizzy spell, do you know how she fairs?" said Emily.

"I have ordered the carriage for her. Apparently it did not pass," said Mr. Wingrave.

"Peter will be disappointed. He had planned on dancing with her."

"Send along her apologies, if you will," he said.

"Have you met Mr. Annesley?"

"I have. He's an old friend of mine."

"Oh. 'Tis a shame then that he does not stay at your house," said Emily.

"We haven't spoken in many years," said Mr. Wingrave. The subject was firmly closed, even to Emily.

"I see," she said.

"You seem in better spirits tonight than I've seen you before," said Mr. Wingrave.

"My sister reminded me what taking oneself too seriously can do to one's constitution."

"A splendid victory for your sister, though I must warn you, if Mr. Sheridan sees how much improved you are, he'll be quite taken in."

"Mr. Wingrave!" cried Emily.

"Do not be shocked by the honesty you ask for or I shall no longer give it to you, Miss Worthing." Mr. Wingrave smiled as she calmed her nerves. For his treachery, she decided to tease his own sensibilities. She put on a considerate frown as they stepped toward and away from each other with the music.

"Mr. Sheridan is a nice man," said Emily, "With jolly manners and a house fit for a lady."

"You... are correct." The confusion played across his face.

"What are you imagining, Mr. Wingrave? That the value of a secure husband is lost on me?"

"More that a secure husband is of no value to you, a daughter of fortune who cares for her own needs."

"That makes me sound rather selfish, Mr. Wingrave," said Emily.

"Not at all. I would call it self-reliance. As with all things, a virtue can be turned into a fault, however."

"Perhaps you are right. I should learn to depend on a nice man, someone with jolly manners." She relished the sight of his troubled stare, usually so unaffected.

"I think you would do better to depend on a different sort of man," he said at last.

"Oh? And what sort of man is that? My own definition caused us some difficulty, so this time I shall let you choose." The dance came to an end and Mr. Wingrave led Emily away, so engrossed by their interaction that neither realized how they seemed to others an involved couple.

"Intelligent, sensible, and with enough affection to overcome your prideful boundaries," said Mr. Wingrave. His frank description made Emily laugh.

"Did I tell you that such a man does not exist?"

"If he did, would you have him?" The query silenced her laughter, so awash with implications that any humor was caught in her throat. A shadow over Mr. Wingrave's shoulder broke the intense communication and saved her from answering.

"Wingrave, I would have words with you," said Mr. Annesley. Mr. Wingrave turned from her to face the one who addressed him.

"Our families have nothing to say," he stated, striding away from the man without disengaging Emily from his arm.

"You'll be pleased to know Mrs. Pratchett is well in Dunbarrow," said Mr. Annesley as he followed them. Mr. Wingrave whirled on him in such fury that Emily let go and stood back.

"Do not speak of it here!" he warned, startling nearby dancers. Mr. Annesley frowned, but relented, bowing his way back to Bridget. Mr. Wingrave settled and regained connection with Emily. The mystery surrounding him had gathered up into a storm in her head, the first raindrops now fell.

"I apologize, Miss Worthing."

"I accept," said Emily. Not even in her curiosity could she bring herself to ask about that kind of a reaction.

"I know not what to say after such behavior, I cannot explain."

"Another secret? Do I see the real Mr. Wingrave before me, or is it a doppelgänger?" said Emily. He smiled.

"All too real, my lady."

"Hmm," she sighed.

"This does not prevent you from answering my question," said Mr. Wingrave.

"After the reflection of a few moments, I cannot see why it is of any consequence. If I advertise my answer, how shall I surprise anyone? I am due a certain amount of anticipatory nervousness on the part of my suitor, as is any woman."

"I see that feminine wiles have not eluded even you, Miss Worthing. You would keep your suitor in just as much agony as the next woman, and with even less guarantee of success." Their walk slowed as they found a corner to stand in. The party went on around them, their body language throwing a shroud of privacy over the space they occupied.

"If anyone agonized over me I should be extremely surprised, considering my well-known views," said Emily.

"Love cares not for the decree of mortals." Feeling again the weight of his words, Emily cast about for another subject. Already they leaned too close to one another.

"Maybe if I could find a husband like Mr. Barham," she suggested. He had not left Mrs. Barham's side all evening.

"Mayhaps you marry a hound instead, they come trained already," said Mr. Wingrave.

"You do not believe in obedience to one's wife?"

"Obedience yes, but not at the sacrifice of dignity. Mr.

Barham does himself and his business harm by acting in such a way as to disrespect himself to please his wife," said Mr. Wingrave.

"You would displease your wife to further your image?" inquired Emily.

"I would hope that my wife would not ask me to belittle myself for her. I, however, have not sworn off marriage in the hopes that there will be one woman with the qualities I seek, instead of despairing that the majority of the feminine gender does not meet my requirements." His eyebrow arched in her direction.

"How impertinent of you to argue with me so!" laughed Emily. She and Mr. Wingrave found many more things to argue over before the night was through, every so often remembering that it was impolite to monopolize each other's attention. By the time Emily laid down on her pillow, she found herself thinking of Mr. Wingrave in different terms, as one who might belong to her if his secrets were not so obvious, and cumbersome to rationalize.

"He is amazing, Mama, so orderly and graceful," said Bridget.

"So I've heard. I have also heard from your sister that you spent most of the party talking and dancing with him," said Mrs. Worthing.

"I don't know how Emily came upon that knowledge. She herself was nearly wrapped in Mr. Wingrave's arms. Did you know I had people ask me if they are engaged?" said Bridget. Emily gasped.

"Who asked that?" said Mrs. Worthing.

"Anyone with a daughter in fifty miles," said Bridget, more smug than accusing.

"What did you tell them?" asked Emily.

"Don't be upset with your sister, love. Is your behavior not cautious enough?" said Mrs. Worthing.

"I thought, but I didn't know... We were only talking," said Emily.

"I told them that you were not, but did my best to hint at a solid friendship," said Bridget. Emily nodded her thanks, too ashamed of her impetuous fascination overriding her social finesse.

"Anyway, Mr. Annesley seems a good man, if the reports are true. Let your heart judge this one, Bridget, instead of your sharp tongue," said Mrs. Worthing, "Next week, the doctor wants me removed to the sitting room, to start building my strength. Then I can help you girls, by observation at least."

"That is great news, Mama!" cried Emily. The following Monday Mrs. Worthing did journey downstairs for the first time in two years. The entire family was overjoyed with having her in a common area where they could visit easily and see their mother normally dressed. That Wednesday, Mr. Annesley called on the Worthings.

"Welcome, sir, welcome!" said Mrs. Worthing, bidding him to sit down.

"I was told you were ill, Mrs. Worthing, but I am very glad to see you in better health," he said. Emily and Bridget answered the summons, entering the room just as he sat. Mr. Annesley hopped out of his chair and bowed to the ladies as they took their places.

"How nice to see you again, Mr. Annesley," said Bridget.

"And you, Miss Bridget. I am going to Tripton and hoped to be favored with your company," said Mr. Annesley.

"To Tripton? Aren't you staying at the inn?" asked Bridget.

"Ah, no. I have been staying at Reddester Hall since Saturday," he replied. Emily blinked at the new information. After Mr. Wingrave greeted him in that fashion, how did Mr. Annesley gain admittance to Reddester?

"I would be delighted," said Bridget.

"And you, Miss Worthing?" he asked.

"If the invitation is open, I will go as well. Mama, may I fetch Genevieve? Her lessons should be nearly over for the day," said Emily.

"That would grand, Emily. Do have fun!" said Mrs. Worthing.

"If you wait for me, in the front hall, I will find Genevieve," said Emily. Her youngest sister had finished her lesson and was more than grateful to go out of doors.

"I get to meet Mr. Annesley? The one Bridget had talked of?" said Genevieve.

"Yes, my dear, but don't tell him that," laughed Emily. They met the others in the front hall, Genevieve quite surprising Mr. Annesley by hiding behind her sister.

"Do I look frightening?" he asked, peeking around Emily.

"No," said Genevieve.

"I shouldn't. I am skin and bones, human through and through, not a bogeyman. See? My hair is even the same shade as yours," he persuaded her. Blushing, she came out and curtsied.

"Pleased to meet you," she said.

"Just as beautiful as your sisters," said Mr. Annesley. Genevieve's blush deepened.

"Thank you," she mumbled as Emily and Bridget giggled.

"Tell Mr. Annesley what you've been doing today," he said, giving Genevieve his arm. The four of them walked on, though at some point when Genevieve had exhausted her conversation, Bridget took her place.

Tripton itself was in high spirits that fair weather day,

and they came upon the carriage stand just as the travel coach arrived. From their position by a shop, Emily could see the passengers dismount. The first was a local woman, returning from Dunbarrow, accompanied by a man. The next passenger confused her, and she looked to Mr. Annesley for an explanation.

"He looks very much like you," said Emily, interrupting what he and Bridget had been saying. Mr. Annesley was the taller, but this man was more handsome in a manicured way.

"Do let us go in," said Mr. Annesley. He rallied Bridget and Genevieve, but Emily would not hide. The man spotted her, and quite pleased with what he saw, approached.

"Excuse me, Miss...?"

"A gentleman should introduce himself before asking a lady's name," she replied.

"Forgive me, I am Mr. Jude Annesley. Do you know of my brother? Edward?"

"I know of him," she said.

"Good, he is in this town?"

"As far as I know." Her shortness boggled him, so he pressed on with charm.

"Does a lovely lady like you know where the inn can be located?" Emily pointed across the street and bid him farewell. He gave her a haughty wave and went off to find his baggage. The last passenger stretched with fatigue, a man in uniform, decorated highly. She recognized the insignia of a Batteran and bowed her head in respect.

"Thank you, Miss. I would have you look at me," he said.

"Yes, Batteran?" she said.

"Batteran Phelps, my lady. Can you direct me to Fortcaptain Wingrave?"

"I'm sorry?" she said. Of all things he could have asked her, that was one of the last she expected.

"Fortcaptain Elijah Wingrave?" he asked again.

"Oh! Um, excuse me, he has a house, Reddester Hall, a few miles southwest of Tripton."

"Splendid. I've business with Captain Wingrave, so your help is much appreciated. May I ask your name?"

"Miss Worthing, of Charlton."

"Much obliged, Miss Worthing," said Bttn. Phelps, with a bow. Alone on the street, Emily could have fainted from the multitude of information she'd just received. She trudged into the shop, unaware of what they even sold.

"Miss Worthing?" said Mr. Annesley.

"Your brother?" she said.

"Not anymore." A deep sorrow filled him, crowding out the happiness he'd had just moments before.

"Fair enough," she said.

"Was that a Batteran I saw?" he asked.

"Oh yes, he'll be calling at Reddester," said Emily, "I'm afraid I need to go home, I feel unwell." Bridget and Genevieve picked through fabrics on the other side of the store.

"If it has anything to do with Jude, I apologize," he said.

"No, Mr. Annesley. I will not pry into your family business, he did not offend me."

"He is disowned. Please do not think the worse of us." It seemed more that he did not want Bridget to think worse of him, but Emily did not point this out. Whatever had happened was their own business.

"I will not, if you do not mention the Batteran to my sisters," she said. Bridget and Genevieve came closer.

"Agreed," he said, smiling at them.

"Emily?" said Genevieve taking in the distress.

"I'm sorry, darling. I do not feel well. You two may stay with Mr. Annesley, but I must go home," said Emily.

"Are you sure you don't want us to come with you?" asked Bridget. Knowing that Bridget could not be out with Mr. Annesley alone just yet, Emily insisted they enjoy the town. She began the trek back to Charlton.

Nothing had settled in her mind before she heard hoofbeats behind her on the road. Serendipity shined down on her with a mischievous taunt--Mr. Wingrave travelled to Charlton, too. He reined in his horse and dismounted.

"Miss Worthing! What are doing out here by yourself?"

he asked.

"Walking, Mr. Wingrave," she said, not bothering to stop for him.

"You will not greet me properly?" said Mr. Wingrave.

"I am upset, sir, you will forgive me if I do not stand on ceremony just now," said Emily. Mr. Wingrave walked his horse up beside her.

"Perhaps I shall, if you tell me what upsets you."

"I cannot say."

"Now I must know," said Mr. Wingrave.

"You have your secrets, and I have mine," said Emily.

"I would allow you those secrets if I didn't feel that you were upset with me specifically."

"And if I am?"

"I cannot make amends without knowledge of my transgressions." Mr. Wingrave's high spirits agitated Emily further.

"You are hiding things from me, and the friends you've made here."

"Why does that upset you now? I thought we'd discussed this already," he said.

"It was different when I didn't know some of what you've hidden," said Emily to an aghast expression, "It begs the question, how much can one hide of one's self before their character also becomes obscured?"

"I would have you tell me, Miss Worthing, what you have found out," said Mr. Wingrave.

"It is uncomfortable, isn't it, not knowing?" she said. She could not fathom why she was so angry with him.

"Miss Worthing," he said, voice harsh and miserable.

"You will know by day's end, what I know. Until then, savor this feeling and use it when next you make friends."

"Emily," he begged, "Please." Her given name rolled sweetly off his tongue, and her heart burst with sympathy.

"I would remind you that we are not family, Mr. Wingrave. Or is it Captain?" she said. His expression softened in pain.

"How?" he asked.

"Batteran Phelps arrived on the travel coach today, looking for Fortcaptain Wingrave. He asked a passing lady where to find you," said Emily. Silence filled their time until he could speak.

"I served for eight years on the border."

"Eight years! But you're so young! How did you become a Fortcaptain in such a short time?"

"I commissioned as soon as it was legal. I studied and I won battles, I advanced. By the end of my second contract, I had had enough of war," said Mr. Wingrave.

"Why do you not tell anyone?" Emily's respect for him surpassed even her resistance to forming a relationship, and she could not imagine being ashamed of his service.

"I did not enter the military with thoughts of glory. I do not want to remember I was there other than knowing our country is secure." Emily pondered him in the ensuing quiet.

"You would look handsome in uniform," she said to laughter.

"You flatter me, Miss Worthing. I never thought a uniform suited me."

"Your service is quite a secret, but it is not all, is it?" asked Emily.

"No," he said.

"And you will not say more?"

"No."

"I shall remember to hold myself back then," said Emily. It embarrassed her to acknowledge her rising esteem, and yet realize Mr. Wingrave failed to be open at every turn.

"That pains me, Miss Worthing," said Mr. Wingrave.

"Such is the nature of deception."

"I do not mean to deceive you." Emily scoffed.

"If I gave you a string, but did not tell you what was tied to it, would you not feel lied to when you pulled and it would not come? Perhaps it was tied to a tree, or a great beast, but you wouldn't know until you pulled, until you needed the string," she said.

"Are you in need of string?" asked Mr. Wingrave.

"Oh, you impossible man! Why do I bother arguing with you?" Charlton was on the horizon.

"I do not know, Miss Worthing, but I'm glad you do," said Mr. Wingrave.

"Mr. Wingrave..."

"Yes?"

"My sister has informed me that several people asked her if we had become engaged," said Emily.

"Surely you don't worry about the assumptions of others?"

"I do if it means I have behaved improperly."

"And have you?" asked Mr. Wingrave.

"I don't know," she said after some thought.

"We have become fast friends," he said.

"It's not so simple as that."

"Why not?" Emily bit her lip, hesitating to bring her true feelings to the fore.

"Nevermind, Mr. Wingrave. I merely think we should be mindful."

"As you wish, Miss Worthing." The pair made it in the doors of Charlton, and to the sitting room without more squabbling.

"Mama, Mr. Wingrave is calling," said Emily.

"Do come in! Have a seat Mr. Wingrave," said Mrs. Worthing. He thanked her and found a comfortable chair.

Emily took up her needlework so that she would not constantly look at him.

"I see you are downstairs, Mrs. Worthing, you are doing well?" said Mr. Wingrave.

"Very well, thank you. I've been up all day, but I am not tired yet. Why have you come home so soon, Emily? I expected you to be in town with Mr. Annesley most of the day," said Mrs. Worthing. The gentleman's eyes tightened at the mention of Mr. Annesley, but he didn't stir.

"I took ill and left my sisters in Mr. Annesley's company," said Emily. Mr. Wingrave relaxed into amusement.

"Did the road's medicinal properties cheer you?" said Mrs. Worthing with a sly wink.

"It was just a spell," said Emily, scowling at her.

"How did Genevieve like him?" inquired Mr. Wingrave.

"She hid from him at first! But then he charmed her into walking with him," said Emily.

"He is a charming man," agreed Mr. Wingrave.

"He must be, for I found out today that he stays at Reddester," said Emily.

"At Mary's insistence. She sees it as a way to heal the rift between our families. I have not heard Miss Worthing play by herself yet, Mrs. Worthing. Do you think we can persuade music from her?" he said, changing the subject.

"When Emily was small I could not stop her from

singing at volume, she can certainly humor me now when I ask,"
said Mrs. Worthing. Mr. Wingrave laughed at this different
picture Emily's mother afforded.

"Only if you spare Mr. Wingrave more stories of my
childhood," Emily said.

"On the contrary, I find them entertaining," he said. She
went to the pianoforte and played a piece of her own
composition. It was complicated, and without lyrics, but she
played it with feelings she had never experienced. As her fingers
wove the melody, things cleared in Emily's mind. She was falling
in love with Mr. Wingrave, despite his secrets and her intentions.
It was astoundingly simple in this context. Each note chided her
for neglecting her feelings. When it was over, Emily stayed bent
over the keys, unable to look up.

"Darling?" said Mrs. Worthing. Emily tore her eyes from
the instrument to see her mother, then Mr. Wingrave. She could
not doubt his admiration, pouring so openly from his being.

"Pardon me," she said, taking leave of the room. Her
insides ached with the rearrangement of every priority she held
dear.

"Miss Worthing?" called Mr. Wingrave. He caught up
with her in the front hall. Her face crumpled with the effort of
containing herself. When she did not turn to him, he moved in
front of her.

"Miss Worthing? Emily? What is the matter?"

"You came to Tripton, inserted yourself into my company, and you've been upsetting me ever since, Mr. Wingrave," she said with a weak smile.

"Emily, if I could…" Mr. Wingrave started until the door to Mr. Worthing's study opened.

"Mr. Wingrave! Glad to see you, I was just about to call on you to discuss the farms. Have you a free moment?" said Mr. Worthing.

"He does, Papa. I am going out to pick flowers for Mama," said Emily.

"She will love them! If you'll follow me, Mr. Wingrave," said Mr. Worthing as he went back into his study.

"Emily--"

"You are wanted, in the study," said Emily. Out the door she sped, away from his confusing affect on her. With great industry, Emily picked the best blossoms for her mother's vase.

When Emily could see her sisters in the distance and Mr. Wingrave had not yet departed, she went out to meet them.

"Hello dears! Did you enjoy yourselves?" called Emily.

"Very much!" said Genevieve, "But I worried about you."

"No worries, it was nothing. Bridget, what did you find?" said Emily. Bridget held books tied with twine.

"An adventure for you and Papa, a romance for myself

and Genevieve, botany for Mama, and a memoir for Peter."

"I have never seen two ladies with more of an interest in books. I am quite impressed," said Mr. Annesley. Mr. Wingrave came out of the house, and upon seeing the gathering, joined them.

"How was town this day?" he asked. He gave Emily a sidelong glance.

"Wingrave, may I speak with you for a moment? It won't take but a second," said Mr. Annesley. Mr. Wingrave excused himself and led Mr. Annesley a fair distance away. Emily kept a close watch on Mr. Wingrave's countenance as Mr. Annesley delivered whatever news he felt urgent. It changed dramatically when Mr. Annesley ceased speaking, going from anxious to a glimpse of the temper he'd displayed at the public dance. He came back to the group quickly.

"I must away, forgive my suddenness. I had a lovely day," said Mr. Wingrave. Emily felt the loss of his presence, even if she did not want to be directly with him until she could sort things out. Mr. Annesley left shortly thereafter, citing business at Reddester. Bridget gushed even more about him as the girls went inside. Emily reveled in thinking of her sister's romantic interest instead of her own. It seemed that Mr. Annesley was less complicated than Mr. Wingrave.

4. GROWING PAIN

The Worthings did not see either man at Charlton for several days. Emily took the time to meditate on what she had discovered. Had Mr. Wingrave been about to confess feelings for her, or would it be more smoke and mirrors? Regardless, she had to work through what she would do now. The end result of love was marriage. Logic and fledgling emotions told her that Mr. Wingrave was the man she didn't think existed, but fear held her back from relinquishing independence.

"I have to wonder why they've not come," said Mrs. Worthing, "I'm convinced they are both in love." The Worthing women gathered in the parlor when food for their thoughts had run out and the absence of any visitors except the Barhams left them lonely.

"There is much we don't know about Mr. Wingrave, and I daresay even Mr. Annesley," said Emily. Bridget bristled at the mention of him.

"Mr. Annesley has been perfectly open," she said.

"What is his business here then?" inquired Emily. Bridget flushed.

"I'm sure it's nothing scandalous," she said.

"Who mentioned a scandal? Even seemingly innocuous quests can define character," said Emily. For once, Bridget fell speechless, Emily was correct, though it would not be admitted aloud.

"I would be happy to see Mary," said Genevieve, "She knows everyone in Dunbarrow, tells the best stories."

"I agree. We are stagnating," said Emily. From her seat by the window, for she had been advised to get light sun, Mrs. Worthing exclaimed.

"Here comes the Wingraves' carriage. Thank goodness for I could slice the melancholy in here with a knife," sighed Mrs. Worthing. She rang for Peter, who arrived just before their guests were presented. Their housekeeper, Velma, entered the parlor.

"Mr. Wingrave, Miss Wingrave, Mr. Sheridan, Mr. Annesley, and Miss Morley, ma'am," she said.

"Thank you, Velma. Good day! Do come in and sit," said Mrs. Worthing. They filed in and greeted the Worthings.

Peter seated Mary between himself and Genevieve, while Mr. Annesley took up station near Mrs. Worthing and Bridget.

"How fare you Miss Worthing? It has been a week at least since last I saw you," said Mr. Sheridan.

"I am well, Mr. Sheridan, thank you."

"Mr. Annesley informed me that you took ill while walking through Tripton, I hope it was temporary," he said.

"It was. At least I thought so. I had a few episodes that day, probably fighting sickness," said Emily. She refused to look at Mr. Wingrave though he plainly centered himself in her field of vision.

"That is a wonderful notion," said Mr. Annesley, "Bridget has suggested we take a picnic outside, steal some bread and cheese from the larder."

"A magnificent plan," agreed Mr. Wingrave, "If the ladies are up to it."

"Mama, do you think you could come with us? I shall move a chair for you to sit on," said Emily.

"As long as I don't overexert myself I should love to," said Mrs. Worthing. It was settled and all of them made preparations, though Mr. Wingrave would not let Emily carry a chair without doing it himself.

"I am a gentleman's daughter, not a weak-limbed child," she said under her breath to him.

"I would never imply that, Miss Worthing, but you

would be just as offended if all these strong men let you carry your burden with no offer of assistance," said Mr. Wingrave.

"Apparently I am contrary, too," she said in a huff. Emily joined Genevieve in conversing with Mary and Peter, pointedly gaining distance from Mr. Wingrave. From there she could see quite a serious attachment forming between her brother and Miss Wingrave. She would be his senior, but Peter did not mind. His open, clever expression delighted Mary, and Emily applauded everything he did correctly. Peter supported her in conversation, but did not assume, instead allowing Mary to choose how intimate they were.

"I've heard a great many times about the Worthing Library. Is it as grand as the stories?" asked Mary.

"Grand? If you consider brimming with books grand. We are nearly out of space; Papa has been planning an additional wing," said Peter.

"An addition to the house for books? What dedication! And the whole family reads voraciously, a fantastic hobby to bind you together. I was also told that you make Genevieve play chess? I thought it was a gentleman's game?"

"Genevieve is as clever as any lad, there is no reason why she should not challenge her logic. Emily and Bridget were forced to oblige me until they grew old enough to win," laughed Peter.

"Your family seems a model of support. All your siblings

have turned out very well," said Mary.

"Only my siblings?" asked Peter. Mary blushed and chided him for for provoking her.

The friends picked a shady place to set up lunch, near patches of flowers and berries. Mr. Wingrave put Mrs. Worthing's chair at great advantage with a view of everyone. Genevieve begged Mary and Peter to join her in picking berries. Emily went off by herself with the excuse of checking the height of their stream, which fed directly off the river.

"Miss Worthing, let me join you. I've a great curiosity about the grounds here," said Mr. Sheridan. Emily allowed it, unable to reject a walking partner, but she did not volunteer conversation.

"I've heard from some people that you will not marry, Miss Worthing," said Mr. Sheridan.

"I am not inclined to do so, no," said Emily. He approached it as if it were merely an interesting fact about her rather than a philosophical statement, a thing which intrigued and repulsed her.

"That's just like Wingrave," he remarked.

"How is that like Mr. Wingrave?" said Emily.

"Oh, he has refused to become attached thus far, despite the wishes of his mother. Of course, she would see him with Miss Morley, which I do not believe he fancies."

"I think you are right, sir," said Emily. Mr. Sheridan

beamed under her affirmation, taking it as a compliment to himself. They strolled through a swath cut through the thin woods just before the stream.

"You are a fine lady though, Miss Worthing. I would hate to see you unmarried forever." Emily chuckled without humor, seeing no other appropriate response. "What about children? Do you not desire them?"

The striking turn of the discussion caught her off guard such that she answered more openly than she would have intended, "I do desire children, but I do not want my ability to have them to be my only asset."

"You do? Marvelous," he said, "I have always wanted children. I would not even mind if an heir was produced, I want them so." It was clear he thought this would placate her tendency toward equality.

"So much the better for your wife, since she cannot determine the gender of her offspring until they are born," said Emily. Mr. Sheridan had such a curious propensity to ignore whatever was said that did not fit with his thinking that Emily could not help but think he had gotten this far in society only by relation. They arrived at the stream, and Emily did her best to give off an aura of contemplation so Mr. Sheridan would not feel the need to talk. It was broken shortly by footsteps coming near. Mr. Wingrave and Miss Morley came down the path toward the stream. The pairs greeted each other.

"Ahoy Wingrave!" said Mr. Sheridan.

"Hello cousin, have you found the stream high or low?" asked Mr. Wingrave.

"I would call it high myself, you Miss Worthing?"

"It is just right after the storms we had a few weeks past. Everything flooded then," said Emily.

"Does it matter much that a stream is high or low?" said Miss Morley, quite vexed that her walk with Mr. Wingrave had turned into a meeting.

"Why yes, it does. This stream goes directly past the fields that Charlton estate oversees. No water, no crops," said Emily as Mr. Wingrave opened his mouth to explain.

"Perhaps it matters then, to the man of the estate, but why is the daughter so concerned? Do you not trust your father to monitor the water?" said Miss Morley.

"Of course I trust him, but I would also keep an eye on that which feeds my family."

"I am tired, Mr. Wingrave. I wish to go back," said Miss Morley.

"I agree, it is tiresome to walk all this way. I thought we were having a restful picnic?" laughed Mr. Sheridan.

"In that case, why don't you two walk back, and Miss Worthing and I will observe the stream?" said Mr. Wingrave. Miss Morley opened her mouth to object, but Mr. Sheridan happily stuck out his arm, which she then had to take or risk being rude. When they had gone, Mr. Wingrave smiled at Emily.

"I am confused, Miss Worthing. Earlier, did you want me to break my promise? About being truthful?" he said.

"No, but perhaps you should consider that your opinions are not always the truth," said Emily. Looking at him was awful, so she meandered along the bank, watching the fishes.

"Let me amend my promise then, to give you the true facts and my true opinions."

"Do you really think of me that way? That I cannot be pleased?" asked Emily.

"No, you took me too seriously. I do think it difficult to please you." She frowned.

"Mr. Sheridan has told me another secret, Mr. Wingrave, and I wonder that you've failed to mention it," said Emily. Mr. Wingrave took a deep breath.

"Yes?"

"He said that you also refuse to marry." He let the breath out.

"It may appear that way to some," he said.

"Hmm," she said, letting it hang in the air to tease him.

"I missed speaking with you the last few days. I had no one to debate philosophy with me," said Mr. Wingrave.

"Things must have been busy at Reddester for you to miss opportunities to spar over ideas," said Emily.

"Quite," he said and left it at that.

"We should get back, before more rumors about us start," said Emily.

"You would not want Mr. Sheridan to think you prefer my company," said Mr. Wingrave.

"That is not one of my concerns, sir," said Emily.

"Then what is? We are in front of no one but family," he said.

"I would have my family think well of me before any acquaintance."

"Your family will not think ill of you for walking with me." Emily laughed.

"How do you know, Mr. Wingrave? They might be wondering right now if you are proposing to me. We can't have that," she said. Emily strolled away without him until he insisted on escorting her.

"You are an unpredictable creature, Miss Worthing. Most females would be happy for anyone to think they warranted an offer of marriage, but you are horrified," said Mr. Wingrave.

"My value is based on the quality of my person, not the quantity of men I can induce to propose."

"Is there a quantity?"

"That would be a horrid thing to boast of," said Emily. Mr. Wingrave chuckled. The others had all gathered on a blanket surrounding Mrs. Worthing and awaited their return so that the picnic could begin.

"Emily, our plan to visit Dunbarrow is essential now, after hearing Mr. Annesley speak of it with so much affection," said Bridget.

"I agree. You should all visit by year's end," said Mr. Annesley.

"Genevieve and I shall have to wait until winter, for I will be better, and she will be older," said Mrs. Worthing.

"That is a fantastic idea, ma'am," said Mary.

"But the two eldest would enjoy it, would you not?" said Mr. Annesley.

"Indeed. It is my chief objective to see more of the world," said Emily with a sly glance at Mr. Wingrave.

"I would be thrilled to see the sights you've enumerated, Mr. Annesley," said Bridget.

"Perhaps I can persuade your father to take a winter house there," said Mrs. Worthing. They shared stories of town throughout their lunch--balls, masquerades, chapels, libraries larger than the Worthings'.

"There is another party in Tripton in less than a fortnight, shall you attend?" Mrs. Worthing asked Mary. She looked to her brother for assistance.

"Unfortunately, I cannot promise our presence there. Mary and Miss Morley are taking a short jaunt about the neighboring countryside and I have been beset with business, getting Reddester back up to function," said Mr. Wingrave.

"We will mourn your absence," said Peter, speaking chiefly to Mary.

"No worries! Jonah and I shall attend," said Mr. Sheridan. An awkward moment followed in which the sounds of chewing were all that was heard.

"You were lying, Mr. Wingrave," Emily muttered as the group picked up their lunch things.

"I was. I did not promise transparency to everyone," he said.

"You cannot think I wouldn't recognize falsehoods when I've been fed so much of the truth."

"No, but while you may know I excused myself falsely, I cannot explain any further." Emily said nothing in return, reaching the limit of her frustration with him for one day. The Wingrave party left shortly thereafter.

"Mr. Annesley is the best sort of man," Bridget sighed.

"I agree. His motivations have proven pure so far. What say you Emily?" said Mrs. Worthing.

"With the exception of his original design in coming here, I can find no fault. And he appears to appreciate Bridget's cackling like a mad hen." Emily flopped onto the sofa, dropping any ladylike pretense.

"He is kind and generous. Did you know he promised

Genevieve a music box for her birthday?" said Bridget.

"It is a fair approach, flattering a lady's beloved sibling to gain favor," said Peter, "Perhaps I should buy Mr. Wingrave a dolly." The women could not resist the image and broke into giggles.

"Oh, Peter that would be a sight!" laughed Emily.

"No, no, it just might work if I can have it fashioned after Emily's likeness."

"You heartless boy!" she shouted at him through tears of mirth.

"What diversion is my family about?" said Mr. Worthing as he stepped into the room.

"Your son is scoundrel, sir! I demand you lash him in my honor," said Emily. She wiped her cheeks of wetness.

"A scoundrel, eh? Takes after his father, isn't that right Elizabeth?" Mrs. Worthing blushed heartily, and waved her hand at him.

"You are both foolish tricksters, ever seeking the next joke you might play on someone," she said.

"My own wife would cut my legs at the knees. It cannot be helped, I suppose. I am glad to have you, Mrs. Worthing," said Mr. Worthing.

The Wingraves' absence was a great detriment to the Worthings at the dance in Tripton. Mr. Annesley was also not to be found. Ready to call her family and leave, for they were just as uninspired, Emily heard a hush fall over the room as Mr. Jude Annesley made a grand appearance, holding himself very high. It was like a shot at the beginning of a sport; his entrance sparked the social games and the contenders quickly jockeyed for advantage. When he had been introduced to everyone's daughter and invited to the Ball at Barham Park in two month's time, Mr. Jude Annesley could finally move about unhindered. Emily observed him taking her in, the light of recognition glowing in his eyes.

"My fair lady, my director, will you at last tell me your name?" he inquired, stopping in front of her and Anne. Emily could have spit at him if it weren't lowly and terrible, for she had seen, from across the room, Victoria Barham slight Jonah Wingrave to pay heed to Mr. Jude's progress. She and Anne had had a fit of misery over Jonah's anguish.

"Miss Worthing, and this is Miss Barham," replied Emily.

"Delightful. Miss Worthing, may I have a dance?"

"I... Yes, Mr. Jude, you may."

"I'll see you when next the music starts," he said.

"My word, he has charisma in spades," said Anne.

"Were charisma all that makes up a man, he would be set," agreed Emily.

"You are not pleased with him?"

"He has the air of one used to having the attention of everyone in the room. I am pleased by those who are satisfied with just mine."

"Like Mr. Wingrave?" countered Anne.

"Did I not forbid you from speculation?"

"Come Emily, I have seen you together. I would not have you break our pact for anything less than the other half of your very soul. I am not insensible."

"Anne... It is all so confusing," said Emily.

"You are not a vain nor vapid creature. I trust you to judge his sincerity and weigh it against your instincts," said Anne. The musicians took their seats again, and Mr. Jude came for Emily's hand.

"I think you may be the loveliest woman in Tripton tonight," he said as the song covered his words from eavesdropping.

"Thank you, sir. I wonder who it shall be tomorrow?" said Emily. Jude recovered from the comment with bravado.

"If you are not here, then no one, for my eyes will still be blinded from your radiance."

"If I am so bright, it is a wonder you can see me at all."

"I have been warned, Miss Worthing, that you are not friendly to strangers. I don't take any offense."

"That is well, no offense was meant," said Emily.

"I am offended that you are yet unmarried. Have the men in Tripton gone mad?" said Mr. Jude.

"That is plain talk for one you just met, Mr. Jude. Sanity keeps the men in Tripton safe from embarrassment, as most know I would refuse any offer of marriage." He smiled on her with the manners of a predator.

"In truth, a woman that marries does give up her self in the process. I would have a woman that thinks better of her own value than that."

"I am surprised to hear a man say that, Mr. Jude."

"Don't be. I am a progressive thinker. I would ask though, Miss Worthing, if you think it unsupportable for a woman to fall in love. There is nothing more beautiful than a woman in love, especially one who may also defend her independence." Confusion filtered through Emily's thoughts, detracting from her attention. Who on earth was this man?

"Love is common to all people, women included."

"So what would a woman do with love if marriage was her bane?"

"I... I... do not know." The heat of the dance and Mr. Jude's continual use of his handsome features and sensual logic to engage her left Emily reeling with disorientation. She wished to see Mr. Wingrave, his strong and steady presence could solve this for her.

"Miss Emily, will you accompany me on the balcony?"

he asked when the dance was over. Wanting nothing more than
to be away from him, Emily did not even catch his liberal use of
her name.

"Forgive me, I promised Anne we would finish our
conversation."

"Another time, then," he said, before bending to kiss her
hand. She spluttered with offense as he turned to other pursuits.
Anger replaced all of the mystique he shrouded himself in.
Emily marched over to Anne and related their discourse
immediately.

"How forward! Why did you allow him to kiss your
hand?" said Anne, "I would have been tempted to upbraid him."

"I could not react, he had said so much that was
unsolicited. I want to know where he got his information. He
seems to know more about me than one meeting could confer."
She spotted him, using his charms on Victoria again as Jonah
watched on. "Oh! I think I have a handle on it now," said
Emily, gesturing for Anne to look. Anne gasped.

"That girl. I always knew she would fall for the first
slick-tongued lizard that crossed her path. She is so buried in
romantic ideas because of Mama. Trust me, Emily, she will say
nothing of you after tonight," promised Anne.

"Poor Jonah. He is heartbroken," said Emily. She
excused herself and made her way to him.

"Mr. Jonah! How handsome you look this evening,"

said Emily. He started and colored.

"Thank you, Miss Worthing."

"Have you danced at all tonight?"

"No, Miss. I cannot endeavor to ask."

"There might be a young lady, looking for a partner, just in front of you. Once a lady knows a man can ask, she will be more willing to say yes," said Emily. He smiled at her hints.

"Thank you, Miss Worthing. Would you honor me with a dance?"

"That sounds perfect," Emily answered. She took great pains in strutting past Victoria with her new partner. Even Mr. Jude could not keep her from noticing that Jonah stood up with another woman. Emily winked at both of them.

"All right, Mr. Jonah. We have her watching. If ever you were light on your feet, make it tonight," whispered Emily. He nodded and gave the performance she asked of him. After he struggled with not falling over in nerves, Jonah relaxed and laughed as they swirled in a fast-paced jig.

"Thank you, Miss Worthing. I see why my brother dances with you so often," he said as he led her to where Anne had been lecturing her sister.

"You are very welcome," said Emily, clearing her throat to throttle any noise of surprise.

"Hello, Mr. Jonah," said Anne.

"Good evening, Miss Barham. May I steal your sister

from you for a dance? If she is willing?" inquired Jonah. Victoria nodded her acquiescence, joyful to find that he still noticed her.

"That will teach her to let vanity spoil purity," said Anne, "She almost cried to see you two dance together. Foolish girl."

"Foolish," said Emily. She carefully avoided Mr. Jude for the rest of the night, taking great pleasure in seeing Jonah and Victoria dance several more times.

The next day, Mr. Wingrave besieged Emily on horseback as she took her exercise around Charlton, before it was suitable for anyone to call.

"Good morning, Mr. Wingrave. Have you business with Papa?" Emily greeted him. A black shadow rested on his brow, pushing his face into the darkest of states. He landed on the ground with a thud.

"No, I have business with you."

"How so?" said Emily, offended by his tone.

"You will never dance with that man again," said Mr. Wingrave.

"Your voice is unfit for talking to me in this manner, sir. Shall I go to the house and fetch my father?" Mr. Wingrave cooled his temper.

"Pardon me. I am pained to hear that you stood up with Jude Annesley last night. As a friend and as a man, I would advise you to think of him as an escaped convict."

"That is strong language. He has wronged you?"

"He has wronged himself and his family more than you will ever know. Promise me you will not touch him again."

"I want to know why, before I promise," said Emily.

"Emily," he growled, narrowing his eyes at her persistence.

"I will not make a promise in ignorance." Mr. Wingrave breathed out.

"I will not betray Edward's confidence by slandering his brother openly."

"Then we are at an impasse," she said.

"You don't..." he stopped, "I care... This is of utmost importance."

"I believe you, but until I am given an explanation, you shall have to trust my judgement," said Emily. He looked on her in exasperation.

"You ask everything of me that I cannot give you," he said before mounting his horse, and riding off toward Reddester Hall.

"Good lord," said Emily.

"That is most peculiar," said Bridget. Emily found her gardening behind the house. "And he just rode off? Like that?"

"With the proper encouragement I could believe it was a specter," said Emily.

"I cannot deny the growing facts, sister, and I fear the estimable Mr. Annesley may at least have a part in it."

"Who could deny them? When every time I see the Wingraves I learn of something suspect? Does Peter have any idea?" said Emily.

"No, I think not. Mary is much better at hiding whatever troubles them." They puzzled about it until dinnertime, and then on into sleep. Emily received no answers to her many questions for close to a week. It seemed every time Mr. Wingrave found something upsetting he would not visit them until his temper could bear it. Peter called on Mary at Reddester, and took Bridget along with him, but Emily would not bother Mr. Wingrave if he was that angry with her. Instead she took to teaching Genevieve new songs.

"Emily, when I get older, do you think I will find love?" asked Genevieve as they looked over music in the sitting room.

"Goodness, what a question. What made you ask it?"

"Seeing all of you with someone. It seems difficult."

"Peter and Bridget don't seem to be having any problems, so that makes me think you are referring to myself," said Emily.

"Well, yes," said Genevieve.

"When there are other things to consider besides one's self, love becomes more complex."

"Do you love him? Mr. Wingrave?" A knock at the door made them jump. Velma introduced the man himself.

"Good afternoon, Mr. Wingrave," said Emily.

"Good afternoon, Miss Worthing, Miss Genevieve," said Mr. Wingrave.

"I have to help mother, with my... bonnet," said Genevieve, smiling at her sister. Emily glowered at her, but excused her.

"Peter and Bridget are at Reddester. I am calling to check on your health since you have not accompanied them this week," he said. Emily gestured for him to sit. He chose a seat across from her needlework chair where she picked up the latest project.

"I am in good health, thank you Mr. Wingrave," said Emily. She had spent the days between their squabble and the present distancing her feelings from the surface, and it did not escape him.

"I apologize for my behavior when last we met. I was overcome by hatred and anger. You did not deserve the retribution you received," said Mr. Wingrave.

"No, I did not," said Emily, frowning into her stitches.

"Would you look at me, please? I cannot read your expression." Emily arched her eyebrow and did as she was asked.

"Thank you," he said.

"Mr. Wingrave, I do not understand you, and I will never understand why you seek my friendship above both our comforts."

"Don't be obtuse," he laughed, "If I were capable of relieving the discomfort which my company brings you, I would."

"One of the reasons I don't understand you, demonstrated by yourself just then--cryptic communication," said Emily.

"You do not want to believe it, the real motivation behind why I come here and invade your peace, so why should I be forthcoming?" said Mr. Wingrave.

"Because you promised."

"I promised I would speak always honestly, not that I would always speak." Emily resumed staring at her needlework. Mr. Wingrave huffed and moved to a closer chair.

"You are supremely frustrating, Emily Worthing. Even now you sit with your graceful hands barely plying that needle instead of meeting my eye. I have watched every sharp look you've given me since we met with amusement, at you for not realizing, and at myself for warranting each of them. I will not be denied your gaze of accusation," he said.

"You have little say in the matter, Mr. Wingrave." He stood and paced in front of her.

"You so effortlessly agonize me!"

"It is without effort or intention. It seems I can please only one of us," said Emily.

"Humor me with the constancy of your face turned in the direction of my own," said Mr. Wingrave. Emily carefully lifted her eyes to his, unsure of what she would see there. Streaks of desperation contained the earnest feelings exuding from him.

"There, you see, the confusion I've caused is just as much an accusation as any suspicious glance you've bestowed on me," he said.

"If I torture you so, why did you come?" asked Emily, tears forming and sliding down her cheek, devoid of premeditation. Mr. Wingrave knelt before her chair and wiped at them.

"No, Emily, don't cry, that is too much for me to bear. I can stand your confusion, and suspicion, but not your anguish. You destroy me with every drop." She blinked, and dabbed at her eyes until they dried. Mr. Wingrave stood when he was assured of her composure.

"I must go," he said.

"So soon?"

"Immediately, before I make promises I cannot keep. Farewell, Miss Worthing." He was gone before she could reply. Were it within her power, Emily might have run him down and demanded an explanation, but her legs and arms had gone weak.

Her little sister rushed into the room, eyes alight with
conspiracy.

"Did it go well? Did he propose?" said Genevieve.

"No, dear. Do not assume that he will."

"It is complex?"

"Quite."

Everyone in Emily' acquaintance looked forward to the ball at
Barham Park with intense anticipation for there were no parties
planned in the meantime. The Worthings and the Reddester
Hall friends took turns calling on each other, though Emily
would not go to Mr. Wingrave's house. She took those
opportunities to visit and walk with Anne.

"Mama informed me this morning that I will soon be
walking with a Lord's daughter," said Anne as they rounded a
hill in Barham Park.

"Aye, Papa was visited last week by a bookkeeper for the
court. Apparently, he's purchased enough land between
Charlton and the investments Peter handles to make up an
entire tract in Marian County," said Emily, "I am proud of
them, though we are all a bit skittish about the distinction."

"Skittish? Why so?"

"It changes little for us, though many will expect it to
mean we shall put on airs."

"That will pass with time."

"I hope. I've enough worries. I see that Jonah visits
Victoria again. Have they spoken of more than the weather
yet?" laughed Emily. Anne rolled her eyes.

"'Tis an achingly slow romance. At least, I have gotten
her to admit that she likes him," she said. On the horizon, a
horse galloped up the road.

"Who can that be? Jonah is already here," said Emily.
The figure grew closer, eliciting groans from both women.

"Jude Annesley? I hope he comes to see Mama, Victoria
is adequately occupied," said Anne. He changed course when he
noticed the ladies watching him.

"Miss Worthing! Miss Barham! How are you today?"
Jude greeted them.

"Very well, thank you, Mr. Jude. Have you come to see
Mrs. Barham? She may be inside, visiting with Jonah
Wingrave," hinted Anne. He frowned.

"Oh, I will not interrupt them. May I join you on your
walk, since your family is otherwise entertained?" said Jude.
Emily thought he should have acknowledged they were having a
private conversation, but they would not be rude. He talked of
himself mostly, an amusement not lost on Anne and Emily.

"Where do you go after Tripton, sir?" asked Anne,
hoping to draw out more for them to giggle over later.

"Once my business with my brother is concluded, I will

go in search of more adventure."

In a most unfortunate turn, the three of them ran across Jonah and Victoria just as they rounded a bend in the path. The shy lovers panicked at being discovered together, though they stood an admirable distance apart. Mr. Jude smoothed out a toothy smile into a grin as he approached Victoria.

"Miss Victoria! I cam to visit and am pained to hear you are otherwise occupied," he pouted. To Emily's astonishment, Victoria actually seemed worried that she'd hurt him.

"I'm so sorry, Mr. Jude, but I have already promised Mr. Jonah a walk about Barham today," she said, working her fingers together.

"Perhaps tomorrow then?" he countered. A flicker of satisfaction in Mr. Jude's eyes as he watched Jonah bristle made Anne and Emily sick to their stomachs. They stared hard at Victoria. She fidgeted and flushed with stress.

"I... I have promised Mr. Jonah lunch tomorrow," stammered the poor girl.

"Oh, well, some other time then. Enjoy your walk." Mr. Jude gave her a pitiful wave as Jonah bravely took her arm and marched away. Any pretense Jude had conjured fell when he returned to Anne and Emily. Without missing a step he said, "I've often thought of traveling to Tadoros and tasting the spices across the Bay."

"That is an adventure," muttered Emily, still disoriented

by his change in tone.

"Would you ever want to see a foreign country, Miss Worthing?" he asked. His question was only a few handsome smiles from a suggestion.

"I may one day, when my family is not in need of me," she replied. Anne hid her shock by intently watching birds fly overhead.

"It is very interesting that you will not give up your independence for marriage and yet allow yourself to be tied down by obligations of that sort. What is the point of guarding it from one and not the another?"

"That is a rather impertinent question," said Emily, flushing.

"Is it? Is it impertinent or uncomfortable? I am attempting to understand your declarations from every angle. I assumed that since you talk of your prejudice against marriage publicly that it was open to discuss," said Jude.

"I will give you that I have invited discourse by daring to give my opinion openly. It does not follow that my familial loyalty or obligation hinges at all on my signing over the rights to my property to a man."

"Loyalty I grasp, but obligation? Your family has the resources to get on without one daughter." Mr. Jude relished the state of unrest he caused, every new shade of red was a layer of emotion, good or bad.

"Perhaps they could 'get on' without my physical help, but how would it seem for me to abandon them in feeling? To tip my bonnet and wish them well as I went to enjoy myself?" said Emily. Anne watched them in fascination, having no interest in calling attention to her observation by speaking.

"A woman such as yourself would never abandon them in feeling, but feelings are not in the body, they are in the soul, which is at once nowhere and everywhere. Your body need not be present for your family to know you love them," said Jude. Flummoxed with too many objections to make instantaneously, Emily glared at him until he laughed.

"Do not take me too seriously, Miss Worthing. I am a philosopher who prods every idea with great care. All this thinking has made me peckish, however. I shall leave you to search out my lunch. Good day, Miss Barham, Miss Worthing," he said. Emily barely curtsied to see him off. When he had gone and the sound of his horse could be heard in the distance, Emily let out a enraged shriek. Anne laughed through her disbelief.

"I am very glad you are the prettier, dear Emily. If it means the attention of every cad that comes through town, positing their selfish ideas about my responsibilities, I pass on any scrap of beauty."

"What nerve! I can hardly see!" huffed Emily. It took three swift loops around Barham Park to calm her.

"I think it is for the best if every woman in Tripton

ignores Jude Annesley, especially Victoria. From what I've
heard, when he was disowned, the family cut him off from any
fortune owed to him as the eldest son," said Anne.

"Mr. Edward is the younger? That is odd. He is much
more gentlemanly," said Emily. They agreed, and spent the rest
of the visit dissecting Jude Annesley's moral fiber.

Three weeks passed. Emily and Mr. Wingrave shared the idea of
avoiding another sensitive meeting, and did not join in the
reciprocal visits of Peter, Bridget, Mary, and Mr. Annesley. Jude
Annesley visited Charlton one day, just long enough to make an
enemy of Mr. Worthing by suggesting he hire someone to
handle the farms once his title became official. After a speech
from the good Mr. Worthing, Mr. Jude did not reappear at their
manor, much to Emily's relief. As she watched him leave, Emily
took note of the Wingrave carriage approaching with Peter on
horseback, trailing behind.

"Miss Emily, I've come to ask a favor," said Mary once
she'd settled in the sitting room, "I've found an old instrument
in the attic and hoped you could evaluate it for me." Loathe to
chance seeing the master of Reddester, Emily balked.

"Cannot Mr. Wingrave tune it? Or at least determine its
worth?"

"He has been gone from the house of late, taking a keen
interest in the intricacies of his estate, constantly galloping to this

farm and that," said Mary.

"Very well. When shall I come?"

"Tomorrow, if you are not otherwise occupied. It will be Elijah's private instrument if it has survived storage. He asked me to order another if it did not," said Mary. Peter stole Miss Wingrave away to show her the library, and the date was set.

"I had Jacob move it in here so that you would not have to stoop in the dusty attic," said Mary the next day. The room was on the top floor of the house, away from the activity down below.

"Thank you," said Emily. She had never been alone with Miss Wingrave, but found it a peaceful experience. Mary had a weathered serenity that younger ladies did not possess. The keys of the pianoforte had been cleaned, as had the bench, so Emily sat without hesitation, despite the possibility of spiders still inhabiting its depths. She ran her fingers from the tinkling highs to the booming bass lows. The instrument itself was loose, but not without redeeming pitch and tone.

"Do you not play?" Emily asked as she continued her work.

"I do, but with no expertise," said Mary. With a nod, Emily transitioned into the same piece she had played for her mother and Mr. Wingrave, attempting to bring back that feeling of clarity.

"I have an odd question, Miss Worthing," said Mary.

"Oddities are gems among the sand, Miss Wingrave," replied Emily.

"You seem very secure in not marrying which leads me to believe your father has settled part of the Charlton estate on his daughters specifically. Is this so?"

"He has made it plain in legal documents that we would be compensated upon his death, though I do believe Peter inherits the land. He is a clever man, handles Papa's investments in town. I would not suffer," said Emily.

"That is well. I am glad you are all taken care of," said Mary. As if called by the music, Mr. Wingrave appeared in the doorframe, listening to Emily's song. She closed her eyes to resist examining him.

"How does it sound, brother? If I had known you would be back today, I would not have troubled Miss Worthing to test the pianoforte," said Mary.

"No, no, she is by far the superior musician. It is perfection," said Mr. Wingrave. Emily rose, ending the piece abruptly.

"This instrument is quite satisfactory, Miss Wingrave. A minor tuning and it would be fit for a king," she said.

"Excellent, thank you Miss Worthing. Let us rejoin the others then," said Mary. Emily obeyed, walking past Mr. Wingrave, keeping her eyes hidden. Downstairs, Peter reclaimed the attention of Mary and Emily was free to stare out the window as Mr. Wingrave awkwardly stood without purpose in the middle of the room.

"We are all looking forward to the ball at Barham," said Bridget.

"I only hope certain people do not attend, unless of course, Miss Worthing wishes to dance with them again," said Miss Morley. Emily looked over her shoulder at the insolent girl. Miss Morley had the surety and smugness of youth in her sneer, and Emily could not rise to occasion that day, so drained from making her expression behave. Rather than crafting a poignant, elegant rebuttal, Emily told the truth.

"I would not dance with certain people again if it would save me all the impolite comments in the world," she said. Miss Morley scowled mightily.

"I, for one, hope to dance with Miss Worthing, and all her sisters," said Mr. Annesley.

"Me, too?" said Genevieve.

"Especially you, Miss Genevieve." She smiled enough for all of them.

"Miss Wingrave, will you do me the supreme honor of reserving a dance?" said Peter.

"Do you need to ask, Peter? Of course, I will dance with you," laughed Mary.

"I will always ask," he replied. Mary blushed and giggled at his intentional statement.

Unable to stomach the romantic mood permeating the room, Emily spied the garden in full bloom below her.

"Bridget, I have not yet walked in the garden since the flowers blossomed, I shall not be gone long," she said. Everyone in the room had paired off with the exception of Genevieve who amused herself with sketching Jonah. Even Mr. Sheridan had gained the notice, if not the regard of Miss Morley.

Emily breathed in the fresh scent of summer flowers as soon as she stepped out. She wandered here and there, finding fallen petals to press. Next to flowing water, gardens were the best place for contemplation. Nature had the unique effect of bringing reality and fantasy together. Behind every lush curtain of vegetation it could be imagined that a magical kingdom rests, though it was not disappointing when the scene turned out to be a fountain or fallen log covered in moss because those could also hold secrets. Around that next vine ridden wall, Mr. Wingrave could be waiting. When he was not, Emily felt more hopeless than ever, that the fantasy of nature might be an illusion.

"Emily?" She whirled in the other direction.

"Mr. Wingrave?" Magic replaced flesh and there he was, though not as joyful as she conjured.

"You did it again," he said.

"Did what, sir?"

"You would not accuse me with your eyes of keeping things from you."

"Then you are more concerned with what I did not do."

"It is what you did do, by keeping my punishment from me," said Mr. Wingrave.

"Why would I punish you? You have done nothing wrong," said Emily.

"But I have, can you not see that?"

"No, I cannot. However much of yourself you choose to conceal is your business. You've made me one promise, and last I counted it remained unbroken."

"One can promise without using words, by their actions," he said.

"That is the fault of the observer if they assume an obligation that has not been verbally given," said Emily. He advanced on her, gaining admittance to the personal sphere in which no one ventured unless they could be certain of acceptance.

"That is all well in theory, but once again your naiveté shows through the hard and fast principles which you hold." Emily saw movement from the window, curtains moved, and she caught a glimpse of Miss Morley's dress before it vanished.

"Have it your own way, Mr. Wingrave. Feel all the accusations you think I should be giving you, I give you leave to speak for me in this instance," she said.

"That will not be enough." Mr. Wingrave wavered, leaning forward, then back.

"Elijah! Miss Worthing! I would have you play a song for us," called Mary, "I'm afraid poor Genevieve's fingers are exhausted from sketching."

Emily did not allow herself to be alone with Mr. Wingrave after that, but always he watched her, dark eyes cataloguing her movements and expressions. She relented and visited Reddester with her siblings under the stern command of herself to keep him at a distance. His frustration was at times, visible and heart-wrenching, but Emily had no other options. Without a proposal, their friendship has reached its plateau.

5. The Barham Ball

"Elijah, I would speak with you privately," said Mary after seeing the Worthings off. She had seen more affection today than she had ever witnessed on her brother's part.

"Is it very important, Mary?"

"Yes, to the library, where we can be alone." She led him, weary and impossibly unhappy, to the book-lined room. The collection did not come close to rivaling the Worthings', but it had a respectable selection. Through the pain, Mr. Wingrave noted that he should go about improving it for the pleasure of Emily.

"I fear you are getting too close to Miss Worthing," said Mary, "You know that is not wise."

"Then why are we here, sister? Was it not to see the

Worthings?"

"Yes, but too much intimacy is unadvisable, given our purpose here."

"I did not see you exercise restraint when familiarizing yourself with Peter Worthing," said Mr. Wingrave. Her face glowed bright pink.

"I know. I am sorry."

"Do not worry about me, sister. Miss Worthing and I understand one another."

"You cannot be good friends with her. We will always have to keep our distance. You do know this?"

"I do not see the harm in friendship," said Mr. Wingrave.

"I know, brother. It would not stay a friendship," said Mary.

"You ask too much," he said. She closed her eyes against the flow of saltwater, but sadness prevailed and it splashed on her dress. Mr. Wingrave cursed at himself and held her until she could cease crying.

"A few more weeks and I feel Mr. Annesley will ask me to marry him," said Bridget. She and Emily arranged each other's hair the day of the ball, and made endless changes to the accessories of their gowns.

"That is definitely the course he's on," said Emily.

"I am frightened, Emily."

"Why? Do you not love him?" Alarmed, Emily leaned to the side so that she might see Bridget in the mirror.

"I do. He laughs with me and delights in the same things. I miss him terribly when he is gone. His family is so high in social circles though, how will I cope? I hate pretension," said Bridget.

"There will be some that dislike my dear sister no matter the effort she puts forth, they will not be pleased. Your objective would be to please Mr. Annesley and no one else. Though you are so charming, I cannot think that the majority of the Annesley family will not fall in love with you in much the same way their son has," said Emily. Bridget sighed.

"Thank you. I forgot my priorities. What of you sister? What of Mr. Wingrave?"

"What of Mr. Wingrave..."

"Yes, you cannot fool me now. I know you feel something for him. Would you marry, if he were the one asking?"

"I've asked myself that question without any success, so it does not astonish me that I have nothing to tell you," said Emily.

"You falter on your mission! That is a good sign indeed."

"Only you would celebrate the downfall of my

principles." Bridget turned full round to accuse her sister.

"'I celebrate the downfall of your fear. I believe you and Anne have agreed on this too long. It may be her way, but I do not think it was yours. I think you used it as a shield until the right man came along because you did not know how to deny the ones who coveted your beauty."

"What a speech! Have I been figured out, dear Bridget?" laughed Emily.

"You have. That prickly demeanor you so often don is a mirage, hiding the sweet, loving woman underneath that would sooner cut off her arm than pain her loved ones."

"Enough of this, silly girl, hold still that I may finish your curls. Be happy with your own triumph and do not take up matchmaking to spread your joy. We can all see it shine from you," said Emily. Bridget twisted in obedience.

"You can fend me off no longer. I know the truth." Emily was not so careful with the pins after that, earning her several suspicious glares.

With a thudding heart and wild eyes, Emily weaseled past the greeting line after paying her respects to Anne. Miss Barham easily released Emily as she was in deep conversation with a new gentleman neighbor. Barham Park was equal in grandeur to Charlton with the exception of Mrs. Barham's penchant for art depicting violence, scenes of womanly figures wielding weapons stuck into the chests of their adversaries, usually men. The part of Emily that was not searching for the Wingraves wondered why Mrs. Barham had not taken the same stance as her daughter and refused men altogether.

She spotted Jonah and Mary conversing with Mr. Annesley by the refreshments, but before Emily could capitalize on this knowledge, a voice sounded too near her ear.

"It is a pleasure to see you here, Miss Emily," said Mr. Jude.

"Miss Worthing, if you please, sir," she replied, backing away. His arrogant grin did not give way under her reproach, a frustrating defense he had perfected.

"As you wish, Miss Worthing. Do let me know when the other is acceptable to you, for I much prefer your given name. It rings like church bells," he said. Emily kept more than a proper distance from Mr. Jude, though he constantly sought excuses to move closer, which continued until she bumped into a wall. "I do hope to have the pleasure of dancing with you again."

His proximity became alarming to her then. Mr. Jude did not know boundaries, did not respect signals given. Though she had to agree he was handsome, ugliness shown through his features, a want of propriety and character. Emily scowled into her hands.

"I have already promised several dances to another gentleman, sir," said Emily.

"That is inhumane of you, Miss Worthing! To come to a ball already spoken for? Who, pray tell, has taken such measures against me?" he asked.

"I have." Jude Annesley could have shivered out of his clothing at the sound of Mr. Wingrave's voice.

"Pardon," Jude whispered, then made haste away from them. Emily took in many upset breaths. Mr. Wingrave lifted her face so that he could see into her eyes, ignoring the raised eyebrows around them.

"Are you well?" he asked. Emily shook her head. "Let us take in some fresh air." He led her out into one of the courtyards, lit for the ball.

"Thank you, for refusing him. Even if he made you suffer for it," said Mr. Wingrave.

"Even before your request, I had already decided that Jude Annesley was not a good sort of man." They were virtually alone outside; the rest of the guests had begun dancing and weren't yet intoxicated enough to need the cool night air. The silence became weighted with the thoughts neither dared speak aloud.

"I need to explain myself and my behavior to you."

"I don't know if I can hear what you have to say," said Emily.

"You will hear it, Emily Worthing, or I will drop to my knee this instant and horrify you further," he said. She gasped, uncovered emotions rippling through her heart.

"That is cruel." Emily bit her lip against tears.

"Not as cruel as what I must tell you next."

"Why say anything then? Why do you toy with me?" she accused.

"Does not my voice give me away? Am I not clear in every instance? I ache for the day when I might hear you say my name with affection. I go mad imagining you around every corner of my house, making it your own, but I cannot ever, under any circumstances, propose to you. It would be the ultimate sacrifice of my family to do so," said Mr. Wingrave. His expression pleaded with her to understand.

"You must know then, what I have said without speaking. Leave me," said Emily. She hugged her arms close to her torso, holding herself together with the last of her strength.

"I will not. I would stay your friend forever before I wed another."

"A lifetime of of restraint? This is what you offer me?" Anger overshadowed hurt.

"It is all I have to offer," said Mr. Wingrave.

"I cannot promise to accept this always. It is unfair," said Emily.

"I am ashamed to have brought these feelings upon us

knowing that I could not deliver on any expectations. I could not keep myself from you from the first, and now I bring you misery instead of joy, but do you believe me, when I say that I love--"

"Don't say it. Please. Let it be understood. No broken promises. Friends forever?" said Emily.

"Forever," he whispered, caressing her cheek with the back of his hand. She blushed and he lost his composure, for a moment showing every wretched feeling he hid under a tormented smile. "I'm so sorry."

"Don't be. I can keep my principles now with no lapse in judgement. Old Miss Worthing, they'll call me," she said. Mr. Wingrave shuddered with the understanding that she would have said yes to any question he asked her.

"Let us go back, before the rumors start again," he said.

"I imagine now that there will always be rumors, Mr. Wingrave."

"Eli, when we are alone."

"Elijah," said Emily. Mr. Wingrave savored the word.

"A bittersweet day," he said.

They strolled back inside, arms linked, eyes adoring each other. She bid him farewell to stave off suspicion and censure, and found her friends. They watched one another across the room, never going long between glances. Emily and Bridget talked with Mary Wingrave of the Tripton dress shop when Jude

Annesley made a reappearance.

"Miss Worthing, Miss Bridget, Mary," he greeted them. Miss Wingrave flinched in pain.

"How can you speak to me so..." Mary mumbled.

"Our acquaintance is long, Mary. I've the right to use your name." Mr. Wingrave started across the room, held up by dancers.

"Mr. Jude Annesley, this is a gentleman's house. We would all prefer if you would act in accordance with the behavior expected here," Emily reprimanded. Her stern tone, so far from the girl he had cornered earlier startled him into offense. Jude Annesley advanced on her, counting on his closeness to embarrass Emily. His breath, thick with sweet wine, could be felt on her cheeks.

"Who are you but a rich daughter for the taking? Silence your objections in my presence!" Several people nearby became aware of what transpired between Miss Worthing and Mr. Jude. She refused to back down, though being so near him made her ill.

"No sir, I will not! You have shamed yourself by approaching us this way," said Emily.

"I do not feel shame, a useless emotion!"

"Shame would suit you much better than open deception! She who cannot see through the camouflage of a snake shall be bitten!"

Jude Annesley raised a hand to strike her, and with all the courage of an innocent never before harmed, Emily offered up her cheek such that the entire room would see the reality of the man before them. Mary looked on the bravery with eyes and heart split open.

Just into the swing, not softened by any guilt or second thoughts, Jude's arm was caught, by none other than Mr. Worthing. The rush of noise, curses from Jude and anyone he happened to strike in his attempt to get away, shrieks of fear from ladies who'd never thought someone could be so violent, and exclamations of disbelief, all collapsed into Emily's ears causing a distortion of sound and movement. All was slow and loud.

Mr. Worthing and Edward Annesley manhandled Jude outside and threw him down the front steps. From where he was, Mr. Wingrave admired the woman that could not be his bride. He had not reached her in time, and she had not lost heart. Their eyes met, and each feeling of respect and admiration passed between them, an admission of love where there could be none.

Mary cried, sobs choked with misery, and Emily folded her into the safe enclosure of an embrace.

"Shh, now he's gone. Abominably coarse man," said Emily. Mary cried harder.

"Miss Wingrave? Miss Wingrave?" said Peter, coming to

aid her somehow.

"A moment, Peter. True ladies do not wish to be pitied," said Emily. Mary hugged her and allowed herself to be taken to the powder room. Peter paced outside despite numerous assurances from Bridget that Emily was the one who had almost been struck. Mr. Wingrave shortly took after him and between the two, Bridget looked for wear on the rug.

"Thank you, Miss Worthing. Your family is truly a safe haven," said Mary. She had flooded two handkerchiefs before speaking.

"You are welcome, Miss Wingrave. I could not stand by and allow him to continue so without argument, though I did not expect my statements to work that well on his temper," said Emily.

"If one plays along with him, Jude is harmless. Once his discrepancies are pointed out, the facade crumbles and the serpent is revealed," said Mary.

"I hope he slithers all the way to another town and never bothers us again," said Emily.

"Don't we all," Mary muttered, "I am well enough. Let us go." Mary and Emily came out to several sighs of relief.

"Miss Wingrave, can I fetch you a glass of punch?" asked Peter.

"No, thank you, I do wish to dance," said Mary.

"It would be my honor," he said. Bridget coyly slipped

out of the sitting room, leaving Emily and Mr. Wingrave alone.

"That was brave," he said.

"Don't be ridiculous. Coming from one who has seen battle, it is a disingenuous compliment," said Emily.

"In battle one expects to be hurt. You did not volunteer for the infantry, you simply showed courage when it was needed." Emily smiled. "And thank you, for tending to my sister. She gives meanness more weight than it is due."

"You're welcome." Mr. Wingrave paused for an awkward second.

"May I have this dance?"

"You may have every dance," said Emily. He smiled brilliantly and kept her to himself for the rest of the night.

"Tonight is proof, Elijah. You love her," said Mary once everyone else had gone to bed that night. She sat at the table in his room, beseeching Mr. Wingrave with her wide eyes.

"I do," he said.

"I understand why. She is exactly like you, caring and headstrong. Were it within my power, I'd give you my blessing. But this proves to me that action must be taken. I am inviting the Worthing sisters to Landhilton for a fortnight. While we are gone, I demand that you wrest yourself from her affection. Whatever it takes to hide your heart away," said Mary.

"If the Worthings knew, would it be so bad?" Mr. Wingrave asked.

"Too many people know already. I will not let this ruin our family." Elijah clenched his fists and slammed them into his bedroom door.

"This is my life, Mary. You expect me to live it without joy?"

"I owe you a great deal, brother. I know. This is not a selfish act, even if it was caused by one. If people knew the truth, it would disgrace us. There would be no redemption."

"You do not believe in redemption through love? Through atonement? What about Peter?"

"I plan to use our time apart in the same way, to harden my heart if I can. It murders my soul to know we will be a source of hurt for the Worthings," said Mary. She wept thinking of Peter Worthing and his smiles while Elijah paced around his room, knocking over chairs and cursing.

The following Tuesday, a card party was called together at Reddester Hall.

"Are you certain, my dear?" asked Mr. Worthing.

"Yes, I need to get out of this house and feel like a human being again," said Mrs. Worthing.

"It is only to Reddester, Papa," said Bridget.

"That's far enough until I may be assured of her strength," Mr. Worthing replied.

"Oh Roland, don't be cross. I want to enjoy this evening," said Mrs. Worthing. Emily conspicuously stayed silent during this exchange, lost in her own quandaries. She helped her mother dress with the same taciturn aura hanging over her head.

"Emily, something is bothering you," said Mrs. Worthing.

"It's nothing, Mama," said Emily, pressing her lips into a line.

"I may have been in bed for two years, Emily, but I am still your mother. Your expressions are as plain to me as words on a page." Emily slumped onto the bed.

"I know. Promise me your confidence and I shall tell you some of what ails me."

"You have my word."

"The Wingraves are keeping secrets essential to their make-up from all of their acquaintances, even our family who has bonded closely with them. I know one of them, and it does not detract at all from Mr. Wingrave, if anything it raises him in my opinion. He is a Fortcaptain, retired from the border," said Emily. Mrs. Worthing sat back in astonishment and blinked rapidly.

"How did you come by this knowledge?"

"A Batteran troubled my assistance in locating Captain

Wingrave just after arriving in town. This is what made me take
ill and leave my sisters with Mr. Annesley."

"You have kept this to yourself this long? Why?" asked
Mrs. Worthing.

"He does not want society in general to know because he
doesn't want to remember it himself. Captain Wingrave served
for eight years, I can only imagine he witnessed terrible losses."
Mrs. Worthing nodded.

"I can understand that feeling on his part, and yet
perhaps he should remember. Such things cannot be forgotten,
only locked away where they fester. You say this is one secret,
there are more?"

"Yes, but I have not discovered them. It has come to a
point where he chooses the secrets over..." Emily left off,
blushing.

"Over you?" Emily frowned.

"I know not how I can earn his trust if I have not
already."

"Perhaps he needs more time in your confidence," said
Mrs. Worthing. Emily shook her head, not in disagreement, but
in confusion.

"I have given him reason to believe I would abandon
guaranteed independence and trust him with my person and the
fortune that accompanies me," said Emily.

"That is quite a sacrifice on your part. Let time work, my

dear. Secrets are like pebbles in a sugar bowl, they sift out naturally."

Trusting to her mother's advice, Emily looked forward to being at Reddester again. When her family filed out of the carriage and she laid eyes on Mr. Wingrave, Emily focused on light-hearted banter. They broke into groups of four, with three sitting out. Genevieve, nervous again, declined to play until she was better acquainted with the rules, while Mr. Wingrave persuaded Emily to look over new music just arrived from Dunbarrow.

"These pieces are interesting. I should like to know how they sound," said Emily.

"Then you should sit and we will muddle through them together," said Mr. Wingrave, patting the bench beside him. She obeyed his request, taking the higher octaves.

"Miss Worthing, it would please me if you did not leave my side tonight," said Mr. Wingrave once the music covered their conversation.

"This is your house, sir. I can scarcely go where you cannot follow," said Emily, smiling.

"Good," he said. They finished the first song, and on impulse Emily played a short burst of notes, then challenged Mr. Wingrave with a grin. He countered with his own set of mellow tones. She increased the complexity, gaining the attention of their audience. Mr. Wingrave met her, and gave a wink. Back and forth they played to laughter at the speed, and impressed sighs at the rhythms they battled with. Finally Mr. Wingrave's fingers stumbled over the keys and Emily achieved victory, though to her it seemed pyrrhic, for when he did falter an expression loud with misery shown on his face, quickly collected back into the good humor of the room. The others went back to their card game as Mr. Wingrave breathed heavily to regain composure.

"Mr. Wingrave? Do you want to play another?" said Emily. He nodded and chose a slower, easier tune.

"Forgive me, I have a competitive spirit," he said.

"You are doing it again, sir. It was not a spirit of any sort. Is something the matter?"

"My supreme happiness is barred from me, I can only glimpse it in moments like this, when I forget that you are not mine." Down on the keys, where no one else could see, Mr. Wingrave took her hand in his and continued to play with the other. Emily flushed as he caressed it with the finesse of a worshipper, opening her palm and tracing the curves. However highly improper it was, she allowed the intimacy to continue until one card group completed their game and Mary insisted they change out with Miss Morley and Mr. Sheridan. The unlikely pair wanted a turn in the garden and could not be prevailed on to continue with another game.

"Miss Worthing, I was just discussing with your mother

a trip to my parents' estate. Do you think I could have the pleasure of your company?" said Mary as she dealt the cards.

"Is it soon?" asked Emily in surprise.

"I leave at the end of the week. Mr. Sheridan and Miss Morley are coming with me, but Elijah and Jonah will remain here." Emily looked at Mr. Wingrave who refused to meet her gaze, instead staring at his cards as if they held the knowledge of the universe.

"Mama, would you go?" said Emily.

"No, darling, I'm not yet well enough for that. Bridget has already promised Mr. Annesley a picnic next week, but you and Genevieve are free to travel with Miss Wingrave," said Mrs. Worthing.

"Oh please, Emily, can we go?" asked Genevieve.

"Well I... How long would we be gone?"

"A fortnight only. 'Tis a short visit," said Mary.

"Is Peter coming along?" Emily asked.

"I have some business that cannot be left unattended," called Peter from the other table.

"It would be just us females. Miss Morley will be returning to her family home as well, so you, Genevieve and I would be the party," said Mary.

"I do want to go Emily, please! I've heard so much about Landhilton from Miss Wingrave," said Genevieve. At almost fourteen, Genevieve could not go alone. Emily sighed.

"I suppose it has been awhile since I left Tripton," said Emily.

"Then it's settled. We shall come for you on Friday morning," said Mary, "Elijah don't bend the cards!" Mr. Wingrave dropped them on the table in shock.

"Sorry, I was thinking of something else," he said, endeavoring to straighten them. Allowed by virtue of being his partner to watch him, Emily noted every change in body language he afforded, from stiff anger to sluggish resignation.

"You are not at all paying attention tonight, brother," scolded Mary when he gave up the winning point. He glared at her until she changed the subject. Mr. Wingrave left the card table and took Emily with him, despite the protests of his sister at losing their even number.

"There is one more song I wanted to play before night's end," he said, "You will have to listen instead of perform, if that is to your liking." Curiosity stoked Emily's enthusiasm.

"Absolutely. Let us hear it," she said. Mr. Wingrave adjusted on the bench and played without notation. The melody drifted around Emily, infused with a sense of something she couldn't define. Wrongness? Sorrow? Every word required her to listen with more attention.

"A woman moved across the room,
Her eyes broke my heart in two.
Of late, I've been wondering,

If she is the very thing,

Keeping me from leaving.

Time goes on, duty calls,

I can't have her after all.

I will take up sword and shield,

Ride out on the battlefield,

'Til my enemy doth yield.

Courage taken to go on!

Courage taken to go home!

There she is in light of day,

Smiling only for me.

Blessed I am to be set free,

I was kept in memory.

Only she could make me whole,

Only she could mend my soul." In light of the happy
ending, Emily expected more mirth on the faces of her family
and their Reddester company, but Mr. Wingrave's performance
had been so mournful that no one applauded. No one moved,
but to blink. If his feelings for Emily had not been clear to all
before, they were evident now.

"If this silence continues, I will be forced to play a dirge,"
said Bridget seeking to take the attention away from Mr.
Wingrave.

"Everything you play is dirge," said Peter. They
successfully diverted the conversation with bickering.

"Mr. Wingrave?" said Emily. His eyes had not left the pianoforte, but now he looked at Emily with a smile.

"Thank you for hearing it," he said. She nodded, very much disoriented. Mr. Wingrave closed the lid of the instrument and leaned on it to talk with Emily. He asked her opinion on everything, debating literature and philosophy as they arose.

"I don't think I've ever heard you speak with such verbosity, Mr. Wingrave," said Emily as her family prepared to leave.

"You will be away for a fortnight, I have to get my share of arguments before you go," said Mr. Wingrave.

"A fortnight is not so long," she said. Mr. Wingrave looked deeply into her eyes.

"No, I suppose not. Goodbye, Miss Worthing."

"Farewell, Mr. Wingrave," said Emily, dazzling him with an adoring smile.

6. Landhilton

Emily's trepidation about traveling to Landhilton multiplied when she did not see Mr. Wingrave before they departed. Mary arrived as planned and the three ladies journeyed in discomfort across from Miss Morley and Mr. Sheridan, who simpered at each other with great industry. That Miss Morley's carried an obviously deceptive ring to it, Emily did not think Mr. Sheridan grasped nor cared. The eldest Worthing daughter instead turned her attention to learning more about her future host and hostess.

"I've been told Landhilton is an extensive property," said Emily.

"It was a beautiful place to grow up," said Mary.

"Tell me about your parents. They must be kind to turn out such children."

"Indeed. They are forgiving, generous, and most kind. They will be exceptionally pleased that I've brought them two songbirds to replace Elijah for a time." Mr. Sheridan and Miss Morley exited their company at the town of Marchwood to take another carriage, leaving them the room to breathe.

"Now we shall have peace," said Mary, closing the door, "You may want to sleep. We will not arrive until almost midnight."

"I do not think I can sleep," said Genevieve.

"Rest then, love. Do not spend all your energy staring out the window, for you will need some to find your bed," said Emily. Genevieve settled into a restless meditation, laying her head on Emily's shoulder. Eventually the night overtook her, and she fell asleep.

"She is a precious child," said Mary.

"Too close, I'm afraid, to not being a child anymore," said Emily.

"I believe her transition to adulthood will be relatively untroubled, with her siblings to watch over her," said Mary. Emily smiled in satisfaction for she hoped the same thing.

Black iron lamps illuminated the first of Landhilton, globes of light sparkling off windows that moonless night. Servants and stablehands waited for them, dwarfed by the building behind them. They stood in a line at a sort of parade rest, only one man moved, presumably to call for his master.

Genevieve woke up in a panic when the carriage stopped.

"Why did you not wake me?" she cried.

"For what reason? So that you could fidget endlessly?" said Emily. Genevieve frowned, but held her tongue. Lord and Lady Wingrave made up the perfect picture of nobility in their expressions and presence, until Emily and Genevieve descended from the carriage. Then, panic arrested their civility.

"Mama! Papa!" cried Mary. She kissed them, either unaware of their change in demeanor or ignoring it.

"Mary, you did not inform us that you invited guests," said Lady Wingrave. This sounded to Emily more like, "you did not warn us."

"A few friends of mine are not a reason to trouble you. Mama, Papa, allow me to introduce Miss Worthing, and her youngest sister Miss Genevieve," said Mary. Lady Wingrave might have fainted were it not for the strong arm of her husband. Lord Wingrave resembled his sons enough to bring Emily an embarrassing stab of pain.

"Mary's friends are welcome here. I am Lord Wingrave, and this is my wife and Lady. Pleased to make your acquaintance," he said. Their anxious stares revolved around the three females who had come to call. Emily knew not what to say in light of such an awkward greeting, while Genevieve fluttered and squirmed under their scrutiny.

"Well, let us not stand out in the mist of night lest we

catch cold," said Lord Wingrave, calling out instructions for additional rooms to be opened near Miss Wingrave's suite.

"Please, wait in here a moment while your rooms are readied. We'll call for you," said Lady Wingrave. Mary attempted to join them in the sitting room, but Lady Wingrave took hold of her arm and steered her into a room nearby along with the Lord. Emily gestured for Genevieve to sit and wait for her in the dark room while she listened at the door, straining to catch some of what passed between the Wingraves. It was impossibly rude to eavesdrop, and set a bad example for Genevieve, but curiosity overwhelmed Emily's propriety. In their haste, the door had not been shut fast to what looked like a small writing room on the other side of the hall across from a wide set of stairs. A candle flickered violently in the room, and voices came through the crack.

"What were you thinking, Mary?" said Lady Wingrave.

"I want you to know them," pleaded Mary.

"The association is not wise, we've said as much from the beginning. You should have told us, at the very least," said Lord Wingrave.

"Now we will have our very--" A servant rushing up the stairs muffled the Lady's words. Emily cursed at the inopportune noise. "Do you ever think of this family first?"

"I thought, that maybe... If we could just... It is not only myself that I think of. Elijah... He's in love with her. And I, with Peter Worthing," said Mary.

"Elijah? In love? What a brilliant mess, Mary. What do you suggest? Are you yet willing to acknowledge your mistake? To allow the world to know?" asked Lady Wingrave. Emily could barely hear over the pounding of her heartbeat, so close to finding out what plagued Mr. Wingrave. Mary sniffled.

"I cannot bear thinking of it. I would hide forever before I saw the censure in Peter's eyes," she whimpered.

"Then by your hand, you've created a situation in which the Worthings cannot prevail. Is this how you would repay them?" asked Lord Wingrave. A strangled sob slipped out of Mary's throat.

"We will speak more of this in the morning," said Lord Wingrave. He swung the door so hard it bounced off the wall, and Emily had to stifle a gasp. She tiptoed to the sofa where Genevieve sat confused.

"My word, did we leave you without a candle? I apologize, ladies," said Lord Wingrave, "Please, follow me, so we can all get to bed. It has been a long night, for everyone."

"Yes, sir," said Emily, too bewildered by her stolen knowledge to create friendly chatter. Even by candlelight, Landhilton impressed the visitors, and the sisters found themselves wanting to see more by day. Their room and bed were too comfortable, even for nerves and scandal, to keep Emily awake. In her last moments of consciousness, her mind touched

briefly on the discomfort that had settled in since the card party
at Reddester. With a shock that she would forget by morning,
Emily realized that Mr. Wingrave had been warning her, though
of what, she still couldn't discern.

A timid knock on the door roused Emily and Genevieve from
slumber the next day.

"Who is it?" called Emily, hastily donning her robe.

"Come to see if you'll take breakfast in your room,
Misses," replied the maid.

"Yes, please. We are not yet fit to be in company. Do
come in," said Emily. Quick and quiet, the graying woman
entered and closed the door.

"I'll be in charge of your room, Miss Worthing. If you
need anything, call on me. My name is Katherine," she said,
dragging the trunks closer to the wardrobe and putting their
dresses away. "I hope you'll forgive the servants, Miss. We
haven't had any guests at Landhilton in over ten years. They
may be a bit unused to company manners."

"Thank you, Katherine. But, that does make me curious.
Ten years?" said Emily. Katherine grimaced into the clothing.

"Aye. Not since... Well, not since Miss Wingrave was
young," said Katherine. Sensing the maid did not wish to spread
gossip involving her master and mistress, Emily allowed the

subject to change. After they ate and dressed, Emily and
Genevieve were shown to the parlor where Mary and Lady
Wingrave silently did their needlework.

"Good late morning, Miss Worthing. I hope you do not
mind that we let you sleep in. I myself am still sore and weary
from traveling yesterday," said Mary.

"No, no, I do not mind. Is Lord Wingrave out today,
my Lady?" said Emily.

"For the morning. He shall return for dinner," said
Lady Wingrave. Her ladyship gave the curious impression of
being at once bashful like Jonah, and at ease with herself when
no one addressed her specifically. Genevieve peeked over Mary's
shoulder at her work, an embroidered scene of the night sky.

"Do you like it? I think I shall hang it in my room at
Reddester," said Mary.

"Oh yes, the stars are very well done," said Genevieve.
Lady Wingrave appraised her young guest.

"Have an eye for threadcraft, do you?" she inquired.

"I am basically educated in it, but Emily and Bridget
have just begun teaching me more complicated stitches, my
Lady," said Genevieve.

"If you would like supplies for your own project, there
are notions in the table, over by the fireplace. This room has a
small selection of books, and I can show you the library later, if
you desire. Don't be afraid to practice your music. That

pianoforte is well-cared for," said Mary. Genevieve availed herself of the mentioned supplies while Emily gingerly ran a finger along the side of the piano. Lady Wingrave watched both of them as if they'd grown devilish horns and could set fire to her manor at any time.

Emily sat on the bench, but did not lift her hands to play. Her imagination went wild, conjuring Mr. Wingrave to sit beside her and duet as they had at Reddester Hall, when he had taken her hand as a lover would, and given her the only intimacy they could afford. How had her feelings taken such a turn? From the beginning, Mr. Wingrave had refused to take any answer of hers at its surface value, always digging deeper, asking questions that she dared not ask herself. She gritted her teeth as her own traitorous mind admitted that she had grown from knowing him and pondering his questions. To sit here and view the room where Mr. Wingrave must have played on countless occasions might have been her undoing if Emily did not know he loved her. Yet another question came to her though, but not from him. Miss Morley had once asked what feeling was for if it was all for naught. Heading heart first into the consequences of that hypothetical question led Emily to extreme dissatisfaction. Love had conquered her reservations, but none of his. Never had Mr. Wingrave volunteered his personal history.

"Miss Worthing? Do you need sheet music?" inquired Lady Wingrave.

"Oh no, I was lost in thought. Forgive me, my Lady," said Emily. On command, she chose a piece in her repertoire that did not involve lyrics. The ivory did not lend Emily any of the usual comfort, so stricken was she with loneliness and longing.

"Miss Worthing, you have a great musical talent," said Lady Wingrave.

"Thank you, my Lady," said Emily.

"Oh yes, Mama, you should have had the pleasure of hearing her play with..." Mary swallowed as the near mention of Mr. Wingrave caused upset for reasons unknown, "enthusiasm, at Reddester." The Worthing sisters shifted in discomfort as Lady Wingrave let the discussion fall quiet. Emily rose and addressed her hostess.

"If I shall not be needed, might I walk about your property, my Lady?" she inquired. Lady Wingrave blinked.

"You are the walking sort?"

"I am the nature sort, my Lady," said Emily.

"Very well. There are many delightful areas to view," said Lady Wingrave.

"I would like to go with you, Emily," said Genevieve. Emily nodded her agreement and they set off. Whether Mary did not join them because she was not disposed to walking or because her feelings were even less calm than could be guessed, Emily did not know. When they were alone, Emily and

Genevieve let out breaths they were not aware of holding.

"This house is ill, Emily," whispered Genevieve.

"An interesting observation, my dear. We knew the children kept close and secretive, but I did not imagine the parents this cautious. I've never heard a house full of people so quiet," said Emily.

"Em, do you think we ought not have come?"

"Since our arrival I have gotten the sense that we should not be here. I hate to think this way of the Wingrave birthplace, but the evidence grows daily against our forming a serious attachment to this family."

Genevieve blurted out, in a fit of temper, "But I like Mary!" As if Emily had said the most unfair thing in the world.

"Calm yourself, you know I would not have it this way," Emily chided her, "But consider that what we know and cherish of the Wingraves are only pieces of the whole. I would have greater knowledge before declaring my devotion."

"Bridget said you are in love with Mr. Wingrave, is that not a declaration?"

"My you are in bad humor over this. Mind you are speaking with your beloved sister."

"I'm sorry, Emily."

"I accept. To answer your question, no, being in love guarantees no security. I have affection for what I see of him, but..." Emily broke off with a lump in her throat, "Well, not all love stories have a happy end."

"I think this one will," said Genevieve. Her certainty made Emily smile.

"Will it?"

"Yes. I know very little of men, but I have never seen anyone look at you the way he does. And he's so handsome!" They laughed.

"Sometimes the more handsome they are, the more troubles they bring," warned Emily.

"Is that Jude Annesley's fault? Too handsome?" inquired Genevieve. She frowned deeply thinking of his exit from the ball at Barham.

"Jude Annesley? I had hoped never to hear of him again. Yes, I suppose that may be one of his greatest faults, but I cannot help suspecting an error of upbringing, my pardon to Mr. Edward."

"Adults are very complex in more than love. I do not want to be one." With a petulant jut of her chin, Genevieve halted to look in her sister's eyes.

"You cannot stop the flow of time nor the growth of your bones. What you can do is keep your mind balanced with logic and feeling."

"Like you said at Reddester? About life's blood and vessels?"

"Good heavens! I am making headway with my two

wonderful sisters. You listen after all!" cried Emily.

Genevieve shook her head, "Of course, we listen. It is simply more fun to tease you."

"Oh you have followed in the tormentor Bridget's footsteps. All that hard work and snark wins out," Emily lamented, "I will congratulate her when we get back to Charlton."

Lord Wingrave did return for dinner and begged that Emily sit near him so they might converse.

"How have my children been behaving in Tripton?" he asked.

"Papa!" cried Mary, quite embarrassed.

"You will always be my child," laughed Lord Wingrave, "Or am I to assume you don't wish Miss Worthing to answer?" Mary blushed.

"Their behavior has been quite amiable. They are all well-liked amongst my acquaintances," said Emily.

"As expected. Hardly any trouble to get into in the country. It's the city you need worry about," said Lady Wingrave.

"We would not get into trouble anywhere," said Mary.

"No, not all of you," muttered Lady Wingrave. Lord Wingrave coughed and gave his wife a look of warning. He had recognized the wit of his guests and that Emily looked to him with questions.

"Excuse my Lady, she thinks Dunbarrow to be full of smoke and scoundrels, prefers the country. Tell me, Miss Worthing, of my sons. Have they found any charming women to dance with?" Lord Wingrave measured her glowing countenance, and Emily gathered that he was, at least in part, teasing her.

"Mr. Jonah has danced many times with Miss Victoria Barham, and visits her often," she said to distract them. The Lord and Lady did express surprise at Jonah's having the courage to visit a woman, but Lord Wingrave did not let Emily slide past without the other half of the answer.

"And Elijah? Who does he visit?"

"Papa, you cannot expect Miss Worthing to sit here and gossip all evening," said Mary.

"It is fine, Miss Wingrave, I do not mind giving him news of his sons. Capt. Wingrave has only danced with friends to my knowledge, and has no permanent designs on anyone, your Lordship," said Emily. She had said it to be vague, but the truth in the words struck her so roughly that Emily had to lean on the table.

"Miss Worthing? If my questions bother you, we can speak of other topics," said Lord Wingrave. His brow creased in concern that he might have caused her affliction.

"A passing stomach pain. Nothing more. Please, tell me

of your library," said Emily. The dinner guests relaxed as much as they could, now that the most difficult subject had been banned by mutual agreement.

"Olive, who has come with Mary?" said Miss Jones to Miss Morley. She gestured with her eyes. The Wingraves had just arrived at a neighbor's party.

"That is Miss Emily Worthing. Unpleasant girl," said Miss Morley.

"I should have guessed. She is so beautiful, she must have gotten Elijah's attention," said Miss Jones. Miss Morley leveled an ominous stare at her.

"How do you know that?"

"The servants are all abuzz with it, Olive. It's all the Landhilton crowd has had to speak of in years. I do not see her as unpleasant though, are you certain? Surely, Elijah would choose more wisely."

"One would think," Miss Morley muttered before smiling, "Good day, my Lady. How have you been?"

"Very well, thank you, Miss Morley. Miss Worthing, this is my niece, Miss Jones. Jill, Miss Worthing and her sister have blessed us with a short visit," said the Lady. To Emily the only blessed part of this excursion was that it would be so brief. In the week since their coming to Landhilton, she and Genevieve had taken turns being out of sorts and frustrated. Emily because

every nook of the county held a story of Elijah Wingrave and
hearing of him instead of seeing him tore at her heart.
Genevieve, because the air and questions that filled Landhilton
to the brim stifled her joyous spirit. Not only questions of the
true nature of their host family, but the constant quizzing from
Lady Wingrave. The Lord of Landhilton seemed content to
know their names, but the Lady sought out every flaw in the
Worthings' education and upbringing, of which there were few.
Discontented with this conclusion, Lady Wingrave had settled
on the siblings being allowed too much freedom and
independence. The inquisitor had also discovered that all of the
Worthing children were expected to be aware of the chores the
servants routinely did by experiencing them firsthand.

"You mean, you've milked cows? In your dresses?" she'd
said. Emily and Genevieve exchanged glances.

"Yes, my Lady," Emily had said. It put Lady Wingrave
in a sour mood for the rest of the day to think of a gentleman's
children "subjected" to such an education.

When her mother was present, Mary barely ever spoke, a
stark departure from her manners in Tripton. Lady Wingrave
did not possess any malice for her daughter or the guests brought
to Landhilton, but Emily guessed Mary had made her
uncomfortable enough to warrant poor manners. Emily wished
that the Wingraves would keep her and Genevieve out of their
machinations regardless of any gratitude she might be compelled

to feel for Mary's invitation.

Lady Wingrave left the young women to socialize with Miss Jones while she mingled with a crowd of matriarchs such as herself. Miss Morley could not bear Miss Worthing's company now that everyone in her own sphere knew she'd been thwarted by an unknown. She slunk away as a cat drenched with water escapes into the shadows. Miss Jones, being of good breeding and a genuinely curious demeanor smiled at Emily.

"How fares your visit?" said Miss Jones.

"It has been new and different from that which I am used to," said Emily.

"I can imagine. Landhilton must be astir. I have heard that you are quite familiar with my cousins. How are Elijah and Jonah? I've already had news of Frederick from Miss Morley, but she did not have much to report on other fronts." A slow creep of rosy color spread across Emily's face which satisfied many of Miss Jones' questions without the asking.

"They are in good health, and last I spoke with them, quite happy with Reddester Hall."

"That is good to hear. When Elijah commissioned in the army we were all worried about his future happiness, going in so young, you know. I am happy that it was not to his detriment," said Miss Jones. Perceptive as always, Genevieve squinted in confusion and looked between the two women. Not apt to speak, she gathered that Emily was not surprised by Miss Jones' statement, and did not refute it. Emily cleared her throat.

"No, I do not think Captain Wingrave was injured by his experiences anymore than had he waited until a later age. I think, in fact, it was for the better," said Emily.

"And Jonah? Have you yet heard him say a word?" Miss Jones smiled in remembrance.

"I think he has quite blossomed since arriving in Tripton. A kindred soul may have helped him to feel secure." Miss Jones nodded.

"Very good! He was always a sweet boy."

"I confess to aiding him a bit. Certain persons of a more flamboyant nature may have stolen the fancy he deserved," said Emily.

"I know exactly of who you speak. It is sad that he followed Mary, considering the history there," said Miss Jones.

"I was not aware they had history. I was told the two families did not get on." Emily resisted asking questions, letting only what was common knowledge float to the surface. Miss Jones took Emily into confidence, taking her arm and leaving Genevieve to seek out those of her own age.

"They don't get on because he broke their engagement years ago. Everyone knows that, but the Wingraves won't speak of it. I would not be around them without knowing, for fear of saying something that might kick the proverbial hornet's nest. My mother, Lady Wingrave's sister, was shunned for months for daring to bring it up. Since, she has not spoken of that business even in passing. Mary has turned down at least two proposals since then, from very fine gentlemen," said Miss Jones. Emily quieted her panic for Peter by assuring herself that Mary had not been in love with those men. If Elijah would not propose to her, then it followed that Mary would not accept an offer from Peter, but Emily's attention was wrested from these thoughts by more conversation with Miss Jones.

They became fast friends, though Emily stayed clear of admitting any feeling for Captain Wingrave. She found through Miss Jones that not everyone agreed with Elijah's choices, thinking it a lesser son's duty to take part in the military, certainly not the heir. Others were prodigiously proud of him for becoming such a decorated officer. No matter their position, every friend and relation had another story of him to tell, and since Emily and Genevieve were the freshest ears in the room, they were tugged this way and that to hear the tales.

"He's a crack shot! Killed a score of pheasants on my property for a party before he turned sixteen," said a portly gentleman whose name Emily didn't remember.

His wife chimed in, "And what a musician! You must have heard him play? Charms the birds right out of the trees."

"A thunderous temper though! I'll never forget when that Annesley chap visited the town after... well, right before Elijah left for the border. The constable broke them apart, but no one recognized the Annesley lad afterward, had to take him on his word!" said the large man, who Emily now gathered was an uncle to the Wingraves.

"Sir Sheridan, are you smearing my brother's name or commending him?" inquired Mary. After the whirl of storytelling, Emily looked on Miss Wingrave with gratitude.

"I think very highly of your brother, Miss Mary. I was only amusing Miss Worthing with a little history lesson," said Sir Sheridan. His boisterous nature, drink in hand, made all the more sense after Emily connected him to his son.

"Let us remember that some history must remain mysterious," said Mary. Emily frowned.

"History that is mysterious cannot be learned from, as is the purpose of taking it down," said Emily.

"I merely meant that you may not wish to hear about our childhood all evening. Let us talk of other things, such as Mr. Sheridan, where is Frederick?" said Mary, which was more than enough to derail the Sheridans into doting on their son, who would be arriving late as he had to check in on his own estate. Shortly thereafter, Mr. Sheridan did appear, and immediately joined Emily' conversation with Lady Wingrave, who had come to inquire after her guests.

"Good evening, Miss Worthing! I see they've started a small area for dancing, would you oblige me?" he said.

"If her ladyship does not mind," said Emily.

"I will talk with you when the dance is finished, do not worry," said Lady Wingrave. Mr. Sheridan led Emily to the arranged dancers.

"I say, I believe this is the first time in our acquaintance we've danced, Miss Worthing. Wingrave has always beaten me to it," said Mr. Sheridan. He was not horrible at dancing, but generally lazy in form.

"You are correct, sir," said Emily, making no comment on Capt. Wingrave. Mr. Sheridan had meant to prod a response out of her, and so continued.

"I would not be surprised if he gave up Reddester to Jonah in the next year," he said.

"Why would he do that?" Emily did not suppose Mr. Sheridan to know many of Capt. Wingrave's motivations, and did not give much of a reaction, which Mr. Sheridan took as disinterest.

"I do not think there is enough to keep him there. No firm attachments."

"I am sad to hear he does not consider his friendships as firm attachments," said Emily. Frustrated with the indirect line, Mr. Sheridan pressed forward.

"I meant to say, no confirmed prospects. I think age may have caught up with him, and he might finally seek a wife. Just the other day I overheard him speaking with an attorney about the best way to ensure his spouse would be entitled to his property at death," said Mr. Sheridan. Emily smiled in girlish glee.

"I wonder why he would be asking without any prospects," she said.

"It is a gentlemanly duty to have everything in order before courting a young lady. I, for instance, had the parlor at Barkrum redecorated to be a room for my lady."

"What if your lady did not appreciate the style in which you decorated it? Should it not be her taste in the room?"

"I couldn't very well ask her, not having a lady yet myself. Tell me, do you like urns, Miss Worthing?" Emily felt the strangeness of the question, and coupled with his vibrant attentions to Miss Morley, thought it out of line.

"I cannot stand the sight of urns, sir. It gives me a headache to think of them," said Emily.

"Oh... Well, what about game that has been stuffed?" A horrid picture of stiff, dead animals atop and beside urns of many shapes and sizes came to Emily unbidden.

"No, sir, no stuffed animals in my house."

"Quite right?" Mr. Sheridan lapsed into thought. They finished the dance, though her partner did not leave as Emily had expected. He followed her back to Lady Wingrave, and quietly listened to their conversation.

"As I was asking before, have you enjoyed your evening?" said Lady Wingrave.

"Oh yes, very much. I've learned so much about my new friends," said Emily.

"Perhaps too much. Maybe you should tell her ladyship something of yourself? Perhaps your pact not to marry, or how your sister has engaged the romantic attention of Mr. Edward Annesley?" said Miss Morley, sliding in.

"I did not think the trials and ramblings of the young and unmarried were interesting to her ladyship," said Emily, "But if they are, I shall be happy to go on about them."

"Edward Annesley?" said Lady Wingrave.

"Yes, he ventured to Tripton not long after your children came there. He's been staying at Reddester with them, and Miss Morley," said Emily. Miss Morley scowled at having been connected with him when it was her object to keep that light on the Worthings.

"Oh, they must have reconciled," said Lady Wingrave.

"They did, and quickly from what I understand. It seems Edward was not at all the source of the problem," said Emily. From his spot, Mr. Sheridan piped up.

"Miss Morley, do you like urns?"

Annoyed and upset with him for dancing with Emily, Miss Morley answered, "No! They are the ugliest things in the world!" Hurt and disillusioned, Mr. Sheridan walked away. Emily and Lady Wingrave, disgusted with Miss Morley, would not speak until the wretched girl scampered away, quite embarrassed. Miss Jones approached them, a touch unsteady with wine.

"Miss Worthing! I've heard you equal our Elijah at the pianoforte, and I would be the judge, if you would humor us with a song," she said.

"I would be honored," said Emily. Miss Jones led her, in a roundabout way, to the side room where an instrument slumbered.

"I haven't played this old thing in over a year, hope it still works," said Miss Jones with the air of a barmaid. Emily giggled and plied the keys. She decided a lively tune would please her hostess the most.

"On a tawny bridge,

Dammed up with sticks,

I lost my hear-r-rt.

On those ruby lips,

I left a kiss,

For we did par-r-rt.

For many days, it kept my head above the clouds,

For many years, it kept my hope without a doubt,

On an old black bridge,

Dammed up with sticks,

I got my hear-r-rt.

On your wrinkled lips,

I got my kiss,

Never to par-r-rt." As Emily sang the chorus twice more to finish, she wondered if the song was not most appropriate for her situation. Would Capt. Wingrave hold them apart until they grew old and cared not for the movings of society? Surprising to her, a crowd cheered for an encore when the song was over. Emily sang until her breath ran out.

"Delightful! We haven't had a true proficient since Elijah went away," said Miss Jones within earshot of Miss Morley. Emily would have felt sorry for the girl if she hadn't done everything in her power to be unpleasant.

"Tell me, Miss Jones, do you drink too much to appear lively, or to forget that you are passing five and twenty unwed?" asked Miss Morley. Bother Mary Wingrave and Mr. Sheridan, to whom Miss Morley had been speaking, nearly spit out their wine. Mortification crept up Miss Morley's back to weigh down her shoulders as her insult offended more than its intended victim.

"Olive, your poor child, hold your tongue," said Miss Jones, gesturing toward Mary's pained face. Miss Morley excused herself and vanished from the party. Emily must have been frightfully shocked for Miss Jones' sighed, "Pay no mind. Her short life has been troubled, what with her father abandoning their family. She took it upon herself to marry well, and lost her sweetness to the cause."

Miss Jones exuded serenity, so much so that Mr.

Sheridan, with stars in his eyes, asked, "Miss Jones, do you like urns?"

"They're splendid," she laughed, much to his pleasure.

With the lips all loosened by spirits, Emily had hoped for more useful information by the end of the party, but Mary stayed close enough to deter any slips of conversation, and Miss Worthing had to leave disappointed.

The next few days saw an improvement in the disposition of all at Landhilton. The Worthing sisters had impressed their closest friends and relations, and so the Wingraves seemed to accept their company with greater grace than they had previously. Lord Wingrave had even taken Genevieve fishing despite protests from the Lady that it was not a female's business to fish. With a bit of Emily's help, they had snuck out with their tackle as she distracted Lady Wingrave by asking her opinion on the new decorative stitches coming out of Dunbarrow.

The day after the fishing escapade, Lady Wingrave seemed to have softened, and suggested they take lunch outside near the garden pond. Lord Wingrave had set aside his work to join them and happily taught Genevieve how to whistle through a reed.

"My goodness, the post is late today," said Lady Wingrave.

"Here comes William with it now. They must have had a lame horse," said Mary. The head servant of Landhilton bowed deeply to his Lady as he explained.

"My apologies, ma'am. The post man tore open one of his bags and had to spend time collecting letters back up again. Yours were untouched, I made sure to ask, my Lady," said William.

"Very good, William, thank you," said Lady Wingrave. He handed letters to his mistress, Miss Wingrave and several to Emily herself.

"I shall take a turn to read them, and be back very soon," promised Emily. They waved her off and set about opening their correspondence. Emily examined her three letters; one from Mrs. Worthing, one from Bridget, and one in an unknown script. Curious, she opened the last one first. A chill set in her stomach and traveled up to her heart as she read.

"Dear Miss Worthing,

When you return to Tripton, I shall be gone. Batteran Phelps, here at the behest of Grander Roberts, requested that I resume my former duties at Fort Jennings. At first, I declined, when my affection for you confused my senses.

Now, having caused undue pain that could have been easily prevented, I see my folly. I will not behave coldly to you in a misguided attempt to destroy your regard for me. Cruelty of that kind is not in my nature, and so, I have taken myself from your acquaintance in the hopes that one day you will forget me.

Best Wishes,

Fortcaptain Elijah Wingrave."

As quickly as she could manage, Emily ripped open the other letters in succession, looking for some sign that this impossibility had not really happened.

"Dearest Emily,

I am all confusion! First, I am told that Mr. Wingrave is actually Captain Wingrave, and that you knew this since nearly the beginning of our acquaintance with him. Then, that he has left for the border without seeing you again. I am severely displeased at being so far out of your confidence, but tell me sister, what has happened?

Love Always,

Bridget."

"Dear Emily,

I apologize for the haste in which this letter was written. Mr. Wingrave has gone from Reddester. I did not want you to return to this news, and expect to see him. I'm so sorry, my darling daughter for the anguish this must cause you, for I know him to be taking up a post on the border which can be no little commitment.

Love,

Mama."

A year could have passed Emily by, and she would not

have noticed. Mr., or Capt. Wingrave was gone from her--he had not pointedly left anyone else--as suddenly as he had arrived. She felt her way to a nearby stone bench and steadied what was left of her nerves on it. He had broken their promise, friends forever. The only man she had ever trusted now crushed that faith with a few lines of stiff prose. Emily preferred the other kind of cruelty to this, at least if he were awful to her, she could be awful in return, but this was silence. He chose silence for himself, but also for her. He'd taken her voice, any say she might have in the matter.

Glancing off the pages which she read and read again, Emily began to hate Landhilton and its secrets. She would have to calm herself before facing the Wingraves again or risk being uncommonly rude to them and demanding answers. With haste, she circumvented their picnic and escaped inside the manor, stopping to succinctly inform William that she was unwell if the Lord and Lady asked for her.

"Do you need a doctor or hot tea, miss?" he asked.

"No, thank you, just rest," said Emily. She shut the bedroom door behind her, folded the letters, and stowed them away in her trunk. Then began the pacing, an outburst of all the frantic energy, and after that the despair. Capt. Wingrave had meant to vanquish her hope. He would not have left without seeing her otherwise. She'd been so blind. Of course it would end this way, did she really think they could grow old together, as friends? Regardless of their good intentions, they had only two paths; an affair, or this, separation. Emily allowed herself to cry, but not to wallow. The destruction of the pitiful future she had clung to drove the pain deeper than any outward show of emotion. Her soul was wounded, the blood of love free-flowing from the frail vessels of logic Emily had allowed when Elijah Wingrave confessed his affection for her.

"The Fates have named us Tragedy," she whispered, staring out the window at anything that moved, from groundskeepers to leaves loosened from their branches. Even as Emily's personal vision crumbled, life went on to a steady rhythm. By the time Genevieve sought out her sister, Emily was composed. Cold and heartbroken, it was the best she could do.

"Em, Mary and Lady Wingrave seemed upset by something, do you know what?" inquired Genevieve.

"Capt. Wingrave has taken up station on the border for an indeterminate amount of time," said Emily as she dressed for dinner. Unbridled shock made no impression on Emily as Genevieve spluttered a denial.

"But! He's... There's not... He loves you!"

"Not all love stories have a happy end. Clean up, you smell of pond water, silly girl," said Emily.

"You do not care?" said Genevieve, derision creasing her brow.

"What is done, is done. I have no sway in this

circumstance. Close your mouth, Gen. I do not wish to speak of it anymore." Genevieve fumed, but obeyed. They understood that neither was angry with the other, but it did not matter.

Dinner at the Wingrave table passed with many stolen glances and discomfited coughs.

"Miss Worthing, you missed out on our picnic. I hope you are well," said Lord Wingrave. Mary and Lady Wingrave tried to signal him, thinking that it would offend Emily to be reminded.

"I have been ill quite a bit recently, my lord, please do not worry on my account," said Emily. Genevieve huffed in bad temper.

"Does something trouble you?" inquired Mary.

"No," Genevieve answered stubbornly. Her dimpled cheeks yet untouched by great anxiety drooped in a frown.

The rest of their visit echoed that night, ending with less than two dozen words spoken by Emily to her Ladyship after the letters arrived. Their softened hearts had once again grown hard and distant. Emily and Genevieve left Landhilton with scarcely a backward gaze. Emily's brooding aura kept Mary quiet for the return journey as well, though all of them had spoken of how much more pleasant it would be without Miss Morley and Mr. Sheridan aboard.

Never had Emily been so relieved to see Charlton on the horizon.

7. OF CHANGE

Charlton House, rather than giving the peace Emily so yearned for, seemed intent on upsetting her with pointed questions. Finally, she shut everyone out of her bedroom after pleading ignorance as to "the meaning of this" for the thousandth time. She had no notion of what her family expected her to tell them. Only Genevieve, witness to the change in Emily, left her alone. The rest of them, never before faced with an Emily who did not care if meals were served on time or whether the wash was put away, boggled at the loss of their junior mother. Mrs. Worthing depended on the instructions Emily left for Velma to manage the house, though they were only meant for the weeks at Landhilton.

Once, when Emily had thought the way to the kitchen

clear, she'd been ambushed by Bridget who made it known that her lack of insight was unpardonable.

"Stop right there. I've been trying to talk to you for over a day now without success. Can you at least tell me if Capt. Wingrave gave you any hints at the future?" pleaded Bridget.

"His future has not changed since coming to Tripton. Is that all?" said Emily.

"I love you, and I'm sorry," said Bridget. Emily sighed.

"Thank you. I know I've not been the best sister."

"You've always been the best sister, but right now you cannot also be our mother, and I think all of us will be better off not expecting you to be." She squeezed Emily's hand and left for the drawing room where Mr. Edward would soon call.

Two days after their return, Emily heard such a crash of the front door as to require all haste in determining the source of trouble. She stumbled down the steps to see Peter embracing Mrs. Worthing, then pulling away. A vase lay in pieces at his feet, broken by someone throwing the door open with too much force.

"Good lord, what is the matter?" cried Emily. Peter scowled and kept his eyes on the floor.

"Miss Wingrave has refused him," said Mrs. Worthing, wincing in pain.

"Oh Peter," said Emily.

"Now we are siblings scorned," said Peter, "Give me peace. I am retiring for the night." Mrs. Worthing and Emily kept their eyes on the ground until the younger sisters rushed to the commotion.

"What is it? Is something the matter?" asked Bridget. Mrs. Worthing explained, much to their overwhelming horror.

"How could she?" whispered Genevieve, tearing up.

"Who are these Wingraves that they break hearts so casually?" Bridget's consternation sent Genevieve and Emily to their rooms, the betrayal too fresh to face. The morning brought no balm of new beginnings. Peter, the last to arrive at breakfast, clenched his jaw and spoke aloud for the first time in hours.

"I will not stay here to face jesting and see her at gatherings. I ride to Dunbarrow in the morning where I will purchase a commission, and go fight the Sypass, do some good, somewhere," said Peter.

Mrs. Worthing beseeched him in alarm, "Peter, you cannot! Do not go off to war on impulse! Think this through!"

"If I stay here it is misery, if I go it is misery, but at least there I will not turn into a listless, privileged son, slighted by a woman who surely played at being in love. I will still have some pride," said Peter. Emily understood, even if their mother did not. She squeezed his hand.

"I wish you well if you must go. I empathize and hope that I might also regain dignity one day," said Emily.

"Emily, you condone this?" gasped Mrs. Worthing. Emily spared her a glance of concern over her health, but did not mask the truth.

"I cannot stop him. No one can if he feels the way I do," said Emily. She nodded at Peter and retreated into herself, allowing the family reaction to play out, waiting to hear what Papa had to say.

"You are a grown man, Peter. If this is what needs to be done for you to feel like one, then I cannot but support you," said Mr. Worthing. All protested but Emily.

"Peter, this is running away," said Bridget.

"I will come back. The story of my failure will be an old yarn by then," said Peter.

"But how do you know you'll come back?" cried Genevieve.

"You have so little faith in your elder brother! I am not mad, or witless. I am attempting to make something positive out of this debacle. It is a risk to go to the border, but so is walking out the front door. My life must have meaning again," said Peter. His sincere plea for their understanding quieted the room, though his mother and youngest sisters did not eat. Bridget stared at Emily, wondering that she said nothing.

"You do not think this is folly?" Bridget asked her.

"We could not forever stay as we are, all of us here at Charlton, in sheltered safety. Eventually, our peace had to be broken," said Emily.

"And the Wingraves have broken it!" said Bridget. A flare of anger welled up in Emily, not opposing her sister but in kindred spirit. She hadn't the energy for bitterness yet, so the thought was dismissed. Genevieve wept into her hand.

"Such is love. Sometimes a homemaker, sometimes a peace-breaker. Let it go, Bridget. You have your happiness," said Emily. Furious, Bridget threw her napkin into the porridge and glared at Emily all the way out of the breakfast room.

"Ashcroft, Bailey, Jakes, Milbourne, Smith, Teetering, and... Worthing?" Captain Wingrave looked up from his list of new arrivals to the line of men before him. Plain as blood on pure white snow, Peter Worthing stood at the end, a crushing blow to the Fortcaptain. His face did not move with the roiling emotions underneath, a practiced mask brought out solely for his station in the military. Captain Wingrave cleared his throat to deliver the welcoming speech.

"This is Fort Jennings. I am her Captain. I am your Captain. Discipline is not an optional characteristic in my officers. No matter your background, you will treat the men under you as if your life is in their hands, because it is. This fort has been held many times through the blood of commoners and nobles alike. There is no money and no social hierarchy at Fort

Jennings, only the rank given to you.

"I have included with your uniforms a manual which I expect you to read and memorize before exiting the new quarters assigned to you, which Swordofficer Barnes will escort you to presently. Swordtenant Worthing, stay behind," said Capt. Wingrave. Swordofficer Barnes led the rest of them out of the office while Peter remained at attention.

Capt. Wingrave's office gave a utilitarian impression. Bookshelves against the walls and a desk in the middle of the room made up the chief furnishings. There were no chairs for visitors, more than likely the Captain would want them to stand in respect. The only luxury, rare among officers, was a diminutive piano in the corner.

Capt. Wingrave faced him with a sigh.

"At ease. Why are you here, Worthing?" he inquired. Peter relaxed and looked his new Captain in the eye.

"Fort Jennings is my assigned post," said Peter.

"Why are you here on the border, Peter? Instead of in Tripton?"

"To serve." Peter's jaw locked in irritation. What did it matter why he was there?

"To escape?" inquired Capt. Wingrave.

"It's a popular destination for those wishing to escape," replied Peter with no polite restraint. Capt. Wingrave gritted his teeth.

"Your personal feelings aside, can you follow my orders impartially?"

"If you have doubts, I would be happy to transfer," said Peter.

"I am sir," said Capt. Wingrave, "I will teach you all there is to know about being an officer, but if you cannot leave your feelings about me at home and address me properly, I will make sure you are not only transferred, but deemed unfit for duty."

"Did you leave your feelings at home, sir?" said Peter.

"That's better. Loathe me, hate me, but respect my command here. You are dismissed. Barnes will be back shortly to collect you," said Capt. Wingrave. Elijah sat down at his desk and perused papers left for him. Peter did not move.

"Was there something else, Swtnt. Worthing?"

"She is destroyed, sir," said Peter. He turned on his heel and marched out. Those four words of torture did more to agonize Elijah than any device of war yet invented. He did not fault Peter for defending Emily, he'd done so many times for Mary, and hearing of Emily's fate only confirmed what he had already suspected from the snippets of news he received. In his mail tray, there was a letter from Reddester, dated five days prior, which he now opened with dread.

"Dear Elijah,

It is done. Our suffering and the suffering we've lent the

Worthings is complete. I refused an offer from Peter two days ago. My heart is broken, and I cannot write much more. I have seen nothing of the Worthings since. Edward is my sole source of information and he only sees the ladies. They are distressed, but refuse to speak of their brother, or Emily, who does not come down from her room, even for mealtimes. I am sorry we ever came to Tripton.

Love,

Mary."

She must not have been informed that Peter had commissioned. Elijah debated sending her the news himself, or waiting until she asked for confirmation. Through his pain, he decided to wait. It would be news in Tripton by now no matter how tight-lipped the Worthing sisters chose to be.

Emily... He had crushed the quality of hers that he admired most—her fiery spirit. If he wrote to her, to beg for her well-being, it would defeat the purpose of his journey to Fort Jennings. Emily could not forget Elijah if he constantly reminded her that he was out there, pining for her. Capt. Wingrave would need to handle Peter delicately to keep his own thoughts unclouded by what he had to leave behind. This, he resolved to.

A knock at the door roused Emily from her reading.

"Who is it?" she said.

"Velma, miss. Mr. Worthing requires your presence in his study," replied the maid. Emily trudged to the door.

"Thank you, Velma." She moved quickly, like a ghost down the stairs and through the library, avoiding Bridget and her mother. Mr. Worthing called her in immediately.

"Come in, my dear. Have a seat," he said. Mr. Worthing set aside a ledger he'd been double-checking. Emily did as requested, feeling more comfortable around her father than the women of the house. He seemed to know when to leave a subject alone much better than her sisters and mother, who wanted or needed to partake in some sort of mourning when it came to the loss of Peter and the Wingraves.

"As of today, my title is official. I am Lord Worthing of Charlton," he said.

"That is good news, Papa. You will always be the noblest of men in my eyes," said Emily. Lord Worthing smiled.

"I want you to understand the ramifications of it, on your end. People will now expect you to give up your idea of never marrying, if you haven't already, in the name of society. Some men may court you, and your sisters, merely to increase their own wealth. We're a quiet people, the Worthings, and we've never drawn much attention to the fortune we've acquired. Make no mistake that we are of equal consequence to even the Annesleys of Dunbarrow," said Lord Worthing. Emily gaped, the meaning behind his words striking a blow.

"But... How is that possible? They are known throughout Endland, and we are a small harvest family," said Emily.

"I wanted you and your siblings to grow up as humbly as we could manage. I feel it has grown your character to appreciate your advantages in the light of what we pay others to do for us on a daily basis. Your mother and I were always of the opinion that arrogance of position has ruined a great many men and women. However, my elevation makes our circumstance much more obvious to the world at large. I cannot disguise us entirely from the vultures of high society. This means, that though our home and practices will not change very much, if you venture to Dunbarrow or any other center of social commerce, do not be surprised if you are treated with deference and made the prey of false friends," said Lord Worthing.

"I am all astonishment, dear Papa. I had always known we were fortunate, but never that we equalled a family like the Annesleys. You've done a marvelous job of raising your children, and I agree that riches often accompany an attitude of importance. I applaud that you've given us the correct kind of importance, that many lives depend on our good choices, instead of that many lives should be grateful for our benevolence," said Emily.

"You take it in stride, that is well. I have worked

diligently to be sure that just such an opinion would come from the mouths of my offspring one day. Now, to difficult business. I will not pry in your affairs, but I do want you to consider that if it should come to pass that you are made an offer of marriage the mantle of responsibility does not cease. I would be most pleased with Capt. Wingrave as a son-in-law. He is wise beyond his years. Should he have left Tripton for good, I beseech you to search out another as wise and as humble, if you are ever inclined to accept."

"Papa, I--"

"I know, you do not wish to speak of it. I am simply making my wishes known to you," said Lord Worthing. Emily gave him a grateful smile.

"Thank you, Papa."

"Such a serious mood has taken over my house, and I will not be the one to stoke more gravity. I have to say, I miss my son, for all his playful tricks, he is the best heir I could have produced. He feels the honor of his station without letting it weigh down his interactions. I do hope Peter does not take a liking to the military. There are too many females of intensity around me now, with nothing to balance it out."

"Lady Worthing summons you to the drawing room, miss."

"Thank you very much, Velma," said Emily. She

dreaded the happy news. Mama would not have summoned her for anything less than Bridget's engagement. Emily could not rise to be jealous, but it did hurt her to think of what might have been with Elijah Wingrave. He could have knelt and asked her to follow him to hell and back; she would have said yes. Yet he did not ask. Capt. Wingrave had chosen his family's mystery, perhaps their honor. Emily mused at the shaky illusion of their honor. If it was tainted by some past event, then it was tainted, no matter who knew of it. The Wingraves' false principle of protecting themselves from those who loved them was not just or good. It was a delay, a delay only.

"Secrets surface like pebbles in the sugar bowl," whispered Emily, "Like gems in the sand..."

She had taken to reading every book in her memory with a love story, comparing her experience to that of the hero or heroine. Tragic endings were no longer satisfying or sensical. What was feeling if it was all for naught? Emily had never felt more human, with her veins splitting farther every day that passed, blood would pour out of her body at the slightest cut.

Emily entered the drawing room, expecting to be beset with joy, but no one appeared any more enthusiastic than they would normally. Mr. Annesley greeted her first.

"There you are, Miss Worthing. I have not seen you in weeks, though I've frequented the company of your family. How are you?" he inquired.

"Tolerable. I've been doing research, in my room. Mama, I was summoned?" said Emily.

"That was my doing," said Mr. Annesley, "I've come to extend an invitation to you and your sisters, from my mother. She wishes to meet you, and begs you to stay at Amberose, in Dunbarrow." Tangible happiness exuded from Bridget, though Emily was less enthused by the idea.

"That is extremely gracious, but I'm afraid only Bridget and Emily are old enough to accept. Genevieve has never been to such a large social sphere, and I would not have her go without her parents," said Lady Worthing.

"It is lucky then, that she is with Ms. Pierce at the moment, for her disappointment will be tremendous," said Bridget, "Emily, you will accept, will you not?" Keeping the panic away from her expression took most of her energy, and it was replaced by nothing, a blank stare.

"Um, excuse me. I am caught off guard by the suddenness of it. I can think of no reason why we should not go," said Emily.

"Excellent. I confess to boasting about your family to my relations in the letters I have sent, and they are all very curious. If it is agreeable, we shall leave in approximately three weeks," said Mr. Annesley. It would have been improper to attempt going back to her room, so Emily mechanically sat at the pianoforte while the other three planned the visit.

"There are many more parties and balls in Dunbarrow, so you may need more clothing than you are used to packing. And don't forget what I've said about the wind, it is stronger in the confines of the city," said Mr. Annesley.

"Ah! I will finally get to hear the wind music," said Bridget.

"Perhaps, if you do not cover your ears from the ache," he said.

Emily shut her door, and breathed in the sweet air of solitude once more. She had a few weeks to steel herself against constant company or risk frayed nerves. Bridget's joy would come first over any melancholy moping of hers.

Later, after Mr. Annesley's invitation, Lady Worthing knocked on Emily's door.

"Come in," called Emily. She set her book aside. Her mother floated in, and rested her back against the doorframe.

"Close the door," sighed Emily.

"Will you talk to me, love?" said Lady Worthing.

"I suppose it is time," said Emily. Lady Worthing sat on the bed and motioned for Emily to join her.

"Will you stay up here forever?"

"No. Didn't I agree to travel to Dunbarrow with Bridget?"

"That is a place with no memories. I meant, are you lost to our family?"

"Of course not, Mama. I will not dramatically perish of a broken heart in my room. The depth of these feelings are incalculable, but it does not follow that my affection for Capt. Wingrave usurped my person so wholly that I would pain this family any longer with my malaise. I cannot guarantee that which you seek, a full return to spirit, but I will make an effort to be present," said Emily.

"That compromise, while not soothing, will have to do. Do you know why he left?"

"We were becoming too close, too linked together. He would not propose, could not, he said. So, he left. I've never felt more abused," said Emily. Lady Worthing closed her eyes.

"My poor children. You ache so. I would not have wished you to experience love this way," said Lady Worthing.

"I can hardly complain after the bliss I've given up to this point. If Capt. Wingrave had not come to Tripton, I would still be merrily unaware that not all love is good, certainly when shrouded," said Emily, "I've been put on my guard."

"That is the point, dearest. I would not have you treat love with suspicion. But... it cannot be helped after a disappointment like this. He is a good man, Emily, I am sure of it. Capt. Wingrave must have had a good reason."

"You'll excuse me if I treat your assertion with derision,

Mama. What reason in the world can there be for abandoning one you love to a lifetime of speculation about a future that could never be? I conclude two possible truths from this question. Either he did not love me as I thought, or Capt. Wingrave is so concerned he might injure me when he changes into a werewolf during the full moon I must be kept at a safe distance. Hazard a guess at which one is plausible?"

"Oh Emily, don't be absurd! Of course he loves you!"

"You are then suggesting that Capt. Wingrave is a lycanthrope and of the highest danger to my person. All is solved, as I would not be torn to shreds on my wedding night for lack of planning around the phases of the moon," said Emily. Lady Worthing laughed despite herself when she saw Emily's teasing grin.

"All of my children have such wit about them, and a propensity to use it against me! It is good to see you smile, love, but I will not dismiss the devotion I saw in him with my own eyes. I hope that you will join us for dinner tonight? Mr. Annesley is staying," said Lady Worthing. Emily grimaced, but resigned her evening to being in real company.

"Milbourne, what is one important thing to remember as an officer on the battlefield?" Capt. Wingrave asked his charges. They had all read his manual from cover to cover, though some points would not be driven home without context. Milbourne thought quickly and carefully.

"An officer should not distinguish himself as such on the battlefield unless it cannot be avoided, sir," answered Swtnt. Milbourne. Peter scoffed from his place at the end of the line.

"Something displeases you, Worthing?" asked Capt. Wingrave.

"I think this contradicts one of your cardinal rules stated at the beginning of the manual, sir," said Peter.

"Which rule would that be?"

"Never ask your men to do what you would not, sir. I am to ask them to paint targets on themselves while I hide in the back and pretend not to be in charge, sir?" inquired Peter.

"The capture or death of an officer is a blow to the men of his unit. Hopefully, if you follow my other advice, no targets need be painted on anyone," said Capt. Wingrave stopping his inspection in front of Peter.

"Yes, sir," said Peter. Capt. Wingrave was not going to allow this thread of disobedience stand. Only the daily buzzing of soldiers in the hall disturbed the dead quiet of that Captain's office.

"You think me a coward, Worthing? That I tell my officers not to distinguish themselves out of fear for personal safety? Are you familiar with the Battle of Chatwood Lowe?" said Capt. Wingrave. The rest of the officers stood in tense observation of the personal battle unfolding between their superior and peer.

"I don't recall…" Capt. Wingrave smiled viciously.

"You don't, because you weren't there. It was not a victory for Endland. Before this battle, officers wore different uniforms from their men. Instead of green with brown pants, we wore green, trimmed with gold, and white pants, now our ceremonial uniform. The Sypass targeted and removed over three-quarters of the officers from their posts that day. I lost friends, and brothers. Afterward, I headed the initiative to change what devastated our forces. What you wear now is of my own design. Do you know why we lost, Worthing?" Peter, badly shaken by this thunderous reproach, wagged his head.

"We lost because without their officers, our men were confused. There was no chain of command, no organization. Not only did three-quarters of the officers die, but half the soldiers. Do you think me a coward?"

"No, sir," said Peter. The light of defiance had not left him, but open incivility had.

"Good. Each Swordofficer has two Swordtenants to look after, you gentlemen will be no different. Your Swordofficer will contact you as I assign you positions. Dismissed," said Capt. Wingrave. Peter waited for a moment, as if to say something, then shook his head and joined the others.

"Peter Worthing," muttered the Captain as he resumed

his seat at the desk. Of all the men who had sought Mary's hand, Peter loved her, adored her like no other could. Elijah tapped an empty quill on a blank sheet of parchment. He read her last letter again.

"Dearest Brother,

I must be the worst of wretches. Peter has been driven from his home, in shame, because of me. I encouraged his affection, and I love him, or I thought I did, but how could I do this to one I love? He has commissioned, brother, and you must tell me if you hear of him. He must be safe.

Love,

Mary."

Elijah wrote out a answer.

"Dear Mary,

Swtnt. Worthing is here, at Fort Jennings. He is now one of my officers, and I will treat him as such. I cannot promise you he will return from battle, but I will do my utmost to educate him." He went on to ask about Reddester and made all possible effort not to mention Emily. Mary already took too much upon herself.

Taking her reanimation seriously, Emily set out for Barham Park to visit Anne, who she'd not seen in ages. Upon arriving, she found Anne walking outside, while Jonah Wingrave applied at the door. Emily nodded a greeting, but refused to make an effort to speak with him. He may have been the only Wingrave left whom Emily would not frown upon, and she wanted things to stay so.

"Dear Emily! You have come! I've been so lonely without you," said Anne, clasping hands and kissing her cheek.

"I'm sorry, old friend. My situation is quite depressing, and I did not want to inflict it on you. How fares Barham Park? Is everyone well?" said Emily. They began a long loop around the property, trading stories of their brothers and sisters. Anne's brothers had been promoted, and Victoria was quite in love. Then came the unhappy moment when Emily had to divulge all that had happened with regards to Capt. Wingrave.

"I could not believe it myself when Mrs. Johnston told me that he had gone. And not a word from him since? No letters of understanding?" said Anne.

"Nothing," Emily sighed, "My one chance to break our pact, and it is hopeless. Barham and Charlton will yet have their old maids." Anne nodded.

"I would not have you marry anyone less progressive. But Emily, I..." Anne trailed off as a horse approached the house.

"Oh lord, it's not Jude Annesley, is it? I do not think my heart could take it," said Emily. A young gentleman trotted his mount right up to them, who Emily recognized as the new neighbor Anne met at the Barham ball.

"Miss Anne! Good day!" said the gentleman. He was not handsome at first, but his countenance made Emily think differently as time went on. Anne blushed on seeing him.

"So lonely?" murmured Emily.

"Mr. Welles, this is Miss Worthing, of Charlton," said Anne. Emily stayed quiet during his visit, observing instead of conversing. Anne had deceived her completely, for Mr. Welles looked on Miss Barham with great affection that was returned in earnest. By the time, the gentleman left, Emily was quite diverted.

"I became good friends with him while you were up near Marchwood. Isn't he charming?" said Anne. Emily laughed just as much at herself as at her friend.

"Very charming. It seems I will be an old maid all by my lonesome," said Emily.

"I could not resist, dear Emily. Mr. Welles has no trouble with my retaining rights to my fortune. And he's as handsome as I've ever wanted. Please do not be angry!" said Anne with genuine concern.

"I would not keep your happiness from you. It is right that you should fall in love with someone who respects you, and that you respect. There is, according to some sources, someone for everyone. Just not me," said Emily.

"I do not believe that! Capt. Wingrave is a fool if he

would ruin your chances over a measly secret."

"I fear it is no measly secret. Let us talk of Mr. Welles instead. Who is his family?" Emily persuaded Anne to change the subject with ease.

The Amberose Mansion impressed even Emily with her deadened enthusiasm, while Bridget could have fainted upon stepping out of the carriage. A massive house in the middle of Dunbarrow did not exist without a significant fortune, of which Edward was the heir, attached to it.

"Em, pinch me," said Bridget, "Ow!"

"Are you hurt? Did you hit your foot?" inquired Mr. Annesley.

"No, no, quite alright. Hunger pain," said Bridget.

"Mama waits for us inside, most likely with refreshments," he said, leading the two of them toward the imposing entrance. Mrs. Annesley did not wait for them inside, she bustled outdoors to greet them in a jovial spirit. It was not so exuberant as to be shocking, but more a natural case of friendliness.

"Edward! It is good to see you," said Mrs. Annesley, kissing both of his cheeks.

"I am happy to be home, Mama. Let me introduce you to our guests, Miss Worthing, and Miss Bridget, of Charlton, daughters of Lord and Lady Worthing."

"How beautiful! And I've heard, quite accomplished. Which of you is the musician?" inquired Mrs. Annesley.

"I am, ma'am. Bridget is our artist," said Emily.

"Fantastic! I will expect a demonstration of your skills while you are here. I am very fond of the arts!" said Mrs. Annesley.

Bridget mumbled to Emily as they were taken inside, "Why does everyone want music?"

"Because it is exactly what you cannot give them," Emily whispered back. They laughed a bit to themselves.

"Are you speaking of Edward? He is something to whisper of, if I do say so myself. A very fine son," said Mrs. Annesley. Mr. Annesley cleared his throat in embarrassment, and looked to the ceiling.

"While that is certainly true, ma'am, Bridget was merely joking that she should paint me at the piano while I play music for her, a mixture of the arts, you might say," said Emily, coming to Mr. Annesley's rescue.

"What a capital idea! Miss Bridget, you are clever to think of it. What a fine time we shall have with you girls in the house," said Mrs. Annesley.

"They are not here purely for entertainment, Mama," said Mr. Annesley.

"Of course not, I shall amuse them in return. Tonight

we have a dinner party! You must all get dressed before the guests arrive."

"Mama, we just arrived, I think our guests may want to take a rest," he said.

"Nonsense! You are all youthful and vibrant. I remember the day I could travel and dance all night, and you won't even have to dance," said Mrs. Annesley.

Their quarters, for the Worthing sisters had been given a whole set of rooms, were quite comfortable, and afforded a view of the street. They dressed, as requested, for the family dinner party.

"I think she likes you, Emily. Maybe Mrs. Annesley can find you someone among the Annesley relations," said Bridget.

"If Mr. Annesley left you tomorrow, would you search out another in two months' time?" said Emily.

"Well... no. I apologize for my callous remark. If you are not ready," said Bridget.

When the dinner party got underway, Emily and Bridget were left to wonder at the strange and sometimes hostile glances they received from several groups of people around the room. They'd become quite uncomfortable when finally a young gentleman approached them.

"Excuse me, are you Miss Worthing? I am Mr. Corwin Annesley, Mr. Corey, if you please, Edward's cousin," he said. Mr. Corey smiled at them like an old friend.

"Yes, I am, and this is my sister, Miss Bridget, pleased to make your acquaintance," said Emily.

"Forgive my relations, but they've heard your father is a newly-titled Lord," said Mr. Corey.

"Is that offensive in Dunbarrow?" inquired Bridget, much amused.

"Of late, yes. The King is ill, and in his stead the court has been issuing titles as favors, regardless of one's property."

"Our father has earned everything we have," said Emily, scowling in offense.

"Please, do not be upset, at least, not with me," he said.

"Forgive my sister, our family cares little for the workings of the court," said Bridget.

"I would not have them think us pretenders nonetheless. Will you correct any wrongful assumptions, should you hear them again?" said Emily.

"Of course, Miss Worthing, if you would favor me with your company, we might correct them together," he said offering his arm to the ladies. Mr. Corey was rather handsome, and wanted to pay them every attention, two factors that did not recommend him to Emily. However, among the Annesley relations, he seemed the only willing friend at the moment. Mr. Annesley stole Bridget shortly thereafter to introduce her to someone he had mentioned in Tripton, and Emily became the social prisoner of Mr. Corey, who took great pleasure in

introducing her around the room as "my particular friend,"
which did not suit her at all either. Emily's favorite guest may
have been Mr. Canton, a quirky, if not addled old man claiming
to have been a royal priest in his former life.

"Is he related to you directly?" Emily inquired of Mr.
Corey as Mr. Canton cackled in the background.

"No, fortunately, he married one of my great aunts,"
said Mr. Corey.

"What a pity. This is the best laugh I've had in weeks,"
said Emily. Mr. Corey gave her a curious frown.

"What could trouble you so?" he asked. Emily flushed
and bit her lip. "You don't have to answer."

"It's alright. I... lost a friend, to a misunderstanding,"
said Emily.

"I'm sorry for you. Friendships are very important, and
I believe should not be lost to misunderstanding. A connection
to another person, if deeply felt, should be treasured over all the
follies of communication," said Mr. Corey.

"That is a sound philosophy. Tell me, Mr. Corey. Are
you often this disposed to speak with strangers?" said Emily. He
smiled, a charming smile for certain, if Emily had been receptive.

"You are not a stranger, Miss Worthing. You are my
particular friend," Mr. Corey stopped in front of an intimidating
group of women about Emily's age, "And these ladies are also
Annesley cousins of the Canton branch. Miss Canton, Miss

Dinah Canton, and Miss Barbara Canton. Cousins, this is Miss
Worthing, visiting here with Mr. Annesley and his mother." The
eldest blinked in haughty disinterest.

"You've been admitted to our society so quickly. Pray
tell, what does your father do?" Her hidden implication being
that Lord Worthing must be a tradesman.

Mr. Corey interrupted the retort Emily almost gave
about tradesmen being more useful than sluggish pretend
princesses who contributed little to anyone besides themselves.

"Lord Worthing is a country gentleman with extensive
lands, isn't that right, Miss Worthing?" She bit her tongue, and
nodded fiercely. Her conversation with her father about the
different social climate of Dunbarrow made perfect sense now.

"Oh, I see," said Miss Canton, yawning into her hand
and dismissing the introduction. Miss Barbara took her sister's
lead, but Miss Dinah looked on Emily with fascination.

"What is it like, to live in the country?" she asked. While
her two sisters edged away, Miss Dinah continued conversing
with Mr. Corey and Emily until he impatiently made excuses to
take his particular friend across the room.

"Oh, well Miss Worthing, I hope you will not consider it
too forward if I call on you?" said Miss Dinah.

"No, that would be welcome," said Emily, though she
wasn't convinced she could truthfully mean it. Miss Dinah took
Emily's every word in, and agreed completely; an unnerving

habit Emily couldn't read. Did Miss Dinah really agree, or did she want to collect Emily as a prize like Mr. Corey had? Emily had never had to think so much about the sincerity of those around her and the headache it caused knit her eyebrows together.

"Where were we? Oh, yes, have you met Edward's younger sister? She's with him now," said Mr. Corey. Emily followed his gesture, and with surprise, saw a woman heavy with child laughing next to Bridget.

"I have not," she said.

"Let us go there. She is most delightful, Mrs. Randall," said Mr. Corey. With all the confidence of a crowing rooster, Mr. Corey strode Emily across the room and joined the conversation. Emily felt quite paraded around, as if he made his possessive intentions clear to the entire room.

"Good evening, Corey! I see you've been entertaining Miss Worthing with our family tree," said Mr. Annesley, "Have you met my sister Mrs. Randall yet, Miss Worthing?"

"I have not, but I am delighted to do so," said Emily.

"Alas I will not be downstairs much longer. I see Mrs. Pratchett, the midwife worrying her hands over my state already, but I hope to see you again before your visit concludes," said Mrs. Randall. As if stricken with the plague, Emily's face went white at this seemingly harmless statement. Mr. Annesley noticed first, and he alone knew why.

"Miss Worthing! Might I have a word with you, about the um... the length of your visit?" She shook her head in wordless denial as the two instances in her life when Mrs. Pratchett had been mentioned connected in Emily's memory.

"Emily? Have you taken ill?" said Bridget, feeling her forehead with the back of one hand.

"No, no..."

"Please, Miss Worthing, to the study. I have a change of dates, and Bridget was unsure if your parents would need you," said Mr. Annesley. He took her arm from Mr. Corey, who was quite shocked at having his dinner partner thieved, and whisked her out of the room before she could break into hysterics. They did not come however. Emily internalized the trauma, most sure she looked as senseless as old Mr. Canton. Mr. Annesley did not take her to the study, opting instead for a nearby parlor with a lit fire.

Emily pronounced each word with fiery care, "Tell me why. Why would Capt. Wingrave be upset at the mention of a midwife?" Mr. Annesley sighed, rubbing his face with both palms.

"I cannot tell you why," he said, "But I urge you to forget ever hearing the name."

"I will guess then. Someone had a child," said Emily, anger rising that he would still try to keep her ignorant with such inexplicable facts shouting him down, "Is that not what a midwife is for?"

"Do not tread here, Miss Worthing," said Mr. Annesley, "I am honor-bound to secrecy."

"Do not treat me as one dumb, and nonsensical. I know your brother was engaged to Miss Wingrave, and that it was broken. Tell me who had a child!" Emily demanded.

"Mary," he said in defeat. The confirmation of her darkest fears was not just another hammerblow, it was an earthquake.

"And the father?" she said. He cringed and stared into the fire. "The mystery is gone then, why you disowned your brother. You should know, we would never think the worse of you for his actions."

"I have done what I can to make amends in his place. Will you keep this to yourself?" said Mr. Annesley.

"I shall. I would not spread such a thing," said Emily, "Please, make my apologies to Mr. Corey and your family, for I need rest after our travels."

"Thank you, and goodnight," he said, bowing out of the room.

Emily did not remember how she found her quarters in the dark hallways, but eventually they were found and made use of to hide the second breaking of her heart. The Wingraves would not allow anyone close enough to find them out, to find that Mary had an illegitimate child. In truth, if it became common knowledge, Miss Wingrave would be forever known as a fallen woman, and the family tainted with the association. Without some mitigating circumstance, their family would have to do the same as the Annesleys, disown her, and then where would Mary be? A penniless woman with no trade skills often fell to the worst work.

Elijah had been protecting his sister, and yet... He must have known that Emily would not hold him accountable for Mary's mistake, just as Bridget would think no less of Mr. Annesley. It led Emily to a cold conclusion--Elijah had not trusted her as she'd trusted him. His love for her was not so great as she and her acquaintances had imagined. This, of all things, wrung tears from her eyes. She had been foolish to believe a man who admitted to deception.

The next day, Mr. Corey came to call, and since Bridget and Mr. Annesley were busy with Mrs. Annesley, it fell to Emily to entertain him. Mr. Corey made it fairly effortless, since he had only come to see her anyway.

"I missed you last night at dinner," he said.

"I apologize for my absence, sir. The hours of travel overwhelmed me," said Emily. They sat in a guest parlor on the ground floor, grand as the rest of the manor.

"I hope you will be recovered by tomorrow evening.

There is a ball at Karina Hall, and Mrs. Annesley will surely
attend, being a good friend to the Sharps, who are throwing it,"
said Mr. Corey.

"I should be."

"Then, I will take this opportunity to ask if you would
reserve the first two dances for your particular friend?" Emily
smiled. Mr. Corey thought himself extremely charming, and
though he was not incorrect, such obvious overtures merely
amused her.

"I would be delighted to. But I must warn my particular
friend that I have not danced in some days. I may be out of
practice," she said.

"That can be no deterrent, Miss Worthing. Your beauty
will astonish all, and conceal any slips you may make until you
regain your footing."

"True, mistakes are more forgivable when one is pleasant
to look at."

"Not at all. They just go unnoticed, nothing to forgive.
You said you play the pianoforte, might I persuade you to tutor
me, during your stay?" said Mr. Corey.

"I am always happy to teach others music."

"Good, then perhaps we shall play together one day. A
duet? What a grand idea, now it must be. Tell me of your
family, Miss Worthing." They spoke at length of her parents and
sisters. When it came to Peter's commission, Mr. Corey scoffed.

"One woman breaks his heart, and he leaves his family for battle? An odd decision," he said.

"What is so odd about it, sir?" inquired Emily.

"Why, Peter is the heir of Charlton is he not? He's a bit too important to go galavanting about with a sword on some quest for dignity. As a gentleman of such rank, with a large inheritance to secure, I cannot believe he would bother with a decades-old border war. That occupation is quite beneath him." Emily had no answer that would not be a short and sweet end to their friendship. Indisposed to lose one of the only people in Dunbarrow who wanted to speak with her, Emily glossed over his rudeness.

"I think Peter will do just fine. Are you in a mood for learning?" She directed him to a drawing room with an instrument, and bestowed her knowledge on an all too willing pupil. Thankful to find he had some training, and that they would not be starting with scales, Emily procured the music for a duet in a nearby cupboard. She knew it, but Mr. Corey still slowed down the difficult passages. He tried many times to brush her hand with his, but Emily always moved away. Continuing to be Mr. Corey's particular friend would have tested her patience normally, but the departure of love from her spirit dulled any irritation into stubborn resistance.

The arrival of Miss Dinah Canton may have been the only thing that could hasten Mr. Corey's departure, though

Emily did not know which she preferred. Mr. Corey took his leave and the two ladies claimed seats in the parlor.

"Miss Worthing, I've been wondering, how did you come to know Mr. Edward?" Other than their being distant cousins, Emily thought it strange for Miss Dinah to refer to Mr. Annesley this way. They'd not spoken at all during the dinner party, but then again, Emily had left early. Bridget came to the room at this moment, carrying her artist's case and a fresh canvas.

"Oh, hello Miss...? I'm sorry, I met so many people last night."

"Miss Dinah Canton. I'm not sure we were introduced, Miss...?"

"Miss Bridget Worthing, pleased to meet you. Mrs. Annesley has requested a painting so I thought to work in here. Shall I disturb you?" asked Bridget. Though Miss Dinah did not seem pleased, Emily shook her head.

"We are just talking. Please, continue." As Bridget set up and began, Emily answered Miss Dinah's question carefully, "We were introduced to him by our neighbor at a party in Tripton."

"Which neighbor?" asked Miss Dinah.

"Mrs. Barham, of Barham Park." Emily didn't know why she avoided mentioning the Wingraves other than the name made her uncomfortable.

"Splendid. I heard though, that you also met his brother, Mr. Jude Annesley?" Miss Dinah fished, but for what, neither Emily nor Bridget could interpret. Bridget quietly pretended to ignore them, hoping that the false privacy would draw out Miss Dinah's purpose.

"I did, though the acquaintance did not last."

"Oh? Why is that?" Genuine surprise threw even Emily off balance. Was Miss Dinah ignorant of his behavior? That could not be; he had been disowned. Everyone in Dunbarrow had to know.

"Um..." Emily cleared her throat, "He made himself unwelcome in Tripton." Miss Dinah thought about this, much longer than Emily would have deemed necessary.

"Oh well, 'tis a sad thing. What is your favorite pastime, Miss Worthing?" And for the rest of her visit, Miss Dinah questioned Emily on all of her favorite things and opinions on this or that. Winded from answering, and exhausted from deciding how much information to give, Emily bid Miss Dinah farewell just before dinner. Despite the shaky start, she did seem truly interested in what Emily had to say. Emily sighed and hoped that Miss Dinah would eventually have no more things to ask about.

"An odd girl," said Bridget on their way to change for dinner. "She's taken a liking to you."

"So she has. I hope she knows I will not be a social

stepping stone worth all the trouble she's gone through."
Bridget laughed, and they forgot all about Dinah Canton in
speculation about Mr. Annesley and when he might propose.

Mr. Corey kept his word about the first two dances at Karina
Hall, and proudly introduced Emily around the room, taking
great pleasure in watching the dismayed faces of other young
gentlemen. One young man did not allow Mr. Corey to claim
Emily without a challenge.

"Miss Worthing, this is Mr. Sharp," said Mr. Corey, "He
is the heir of Mrs. Sharp, whose ball you currently enjoy." Mr.
Sharp appraised Emily as one appreciates fine art.

"Let this day stand in history as the day I first saw one of
the most beautiful women in Endland. It is the greatest honor
to meet you, Miss Worthing," said Mr. Sharp. Emily nearly
laughed at his ridiculous flattery. Just within touching distance,
several beautiful women resided. Her novelty, she assumed,
enhanced her beauty, along with the knowledge that many of
the women present were attached already, or related to the two
gentlemen who waited for her response.

"Thank you, I think your mother has thrown a very fine
ball," said Emily.

"Indeed she has! We should be dancing, Miss Worthing,
if you would consent to be my partner," said Mr. Sharp. With
no engagements, she accepted. Mr. Corey gave a huff of

agitation before Mr. Sharp led her away to the floor.

"Mr. Corey has monopolized your attention all evening, Miss Worthing. One might think from across the room that you have attached yourself to him," said Mr. Sharp.

"Is that a question, or merely an observation, sir?" said Emily. Mr. Sharp gave her a wry smile. Some years over thirty, his manners had the polish of one afforded access to the highest society.

"Both, if you'll oblige me."

"I have no attachments in Dunbarrow."

"And elsewhere, is there an attachment back where you come from, perhaps?" Emily thought, and realized she had been thinking too much of her answers since coming to the Annesleys. Her honesty had taken leave in the wake of feeling so vulnerable.

"No, I have no attachments, and am not likely to make any," said Emily. Her mysterious statement intrigued her dance partner.

"Some would consider that a challenge, Miss Worthing. I would not advertise it. Regardless, you are far too charming for Mr. Corey. You should vary your attentions."

"Oh? Who else should receive my attentions? Perhaps old Mr. Canton, if he is present, or another aging man of fortune, to secure my future? I have no need to travel the high circles of the city, for my motivations are not what is expected or appreciated in such a circumstance."

"You need not choose an aging man to find fortune," said Mr. Sharp, delighted with her candor and wit.

"You are correct. I should draw up a list of the richest young bachelors in Dunbarrow, and present myself to them, a high bidder with a handsome face wins." She and Mr. Sharp chuckled at the dissection of antics so popular in society.

"You are very different from other young ladies," said Mr. Sharp, "I wonder that you have not married."

"I wanted to be, but my prospect had other obligations. I have no inclination to marry now."

"Mr. Corey will be very disappointed. Or at least, discouraged."

"That is all the better, for him." Mr. Sharp led her away after the dance concluded, and so began the battle of suitors. Mr. Corey and Mr. Sharp took turns asking her to dance and bringing her punch.

"Mr. Sharp, I have heard it said that you do not enjoy reading, is this true?" said Mr. Corey.

"It's true that I prefer the company of people to books. I appreciate the real qualities of a complex individual rather than a character designed to demonstrate some folly or virtue," said Mr. Sharp.

"I give you that most people have a depth that cannot be replicated, but a closer examination of follies and virtues can lead

to rich self-discovery. But, of course, I am a voracious reader,"
said Emily. Mr. Corey nodded in satisfaction.

"You see? This is why I prefer live friends. I have learned
so much about you this night, Miss Worthing, that it would fill
twenty volumes. Mr. Corey may prefer a summary of fiction,
but I wish to have the entirety of a worthy person laid before
me," said Mr. Sharp.

Their threesome confused a good portion of the
attendees, unused to seeing two men behave so uncivilly to one
another in order to gain favor. Emily encouraged none of it, and
after several dances in a row, refused to stand up any more. She
escaped into the company of her sister and Mrs. Annesley,
though the latter attempted to convince her that dancing once
more with Mr. Corey would do no harm.

"My apologies Mrs. Annesley, I..." Emily grasped for
something to save herself and her feet.

"She has promised me some conversation and I've not
seen an inch of her," interrupted Miss Dinah, sweeping in from
the side to take Emily's arm. Emily smiled on her with gratitude
as Mrs. Annesley relented. Miss Dinah, as good as any socialite
at disappearing when she did not want to be seen, found a good
corner for them to relax.

"My thanks, Miss Dinah. I don't think I would have
been able to walk tomorrow if you had not stepped in," said
Emily.

"It's no wonder. I've seen hounds run slower on a hunt. Is it not exciting though, to be the talk of the ball?" Miss Dinah looked up at Emily with her too open eyes. Emily felt as if the girl could see right through her, and examine every thought that crossed her mind.

"It's flattering, but I would not wish this every evening." Emily tried to remember where she'd seen that look before, one of calculation and measured reaction. Miss Dinah smiled.

"I admire your humility. And you've made my sister ill with envy. You're a remarkable woman." Miss Dinah laughed, though not at what she said, something silent that Emily did not hear. She supposed Miss Dinah's attitude to be a product of growing up in this environment, where everyone competed against each other, and Emily pitied her.

Mr. Annesley watched Miss Dinah charm Emily with a hard eye before turning back to his friends.

The evening ended with Mr. Corey as the victorious suitor, as Mr. Sharp would be taking to the country for sport after the ball. Disappointed that Mr. Sharp would not be around, for he had made her laugh the most, Emily examined her other feelings about the men and found them unchanged. Neither inspired more than friendship.

8. Sorrow's Door

A solid month of training had done the new officers a great
service. Capt. Wingrave, military cap atop his head, assessed
them. A few of them would not stay past the first contract,
either ill-suited to leading or tiring of the lifestyle already.
Several would advance if they kept their chins up and eyes sharp.
Then there was Peter. In a vexing turn of the tables, Peter
Worthing had the most potential as a candidate for long-term
service as a strategist. Capt. Wingrave would have preferred that
Peter had no aptitude for this life so that he could justify sending
him home to his family, but in every instance the boy proved
himself. Other than his lack of knowledge regarding the battle
of Chatwood Lowe, Peter knew of the most decisive encounters
in the Endland-Sypass War, and could apply the lessons within

them to theoretical situations. For Peter's sake, Elijah hoped that translated into strategic prowess on the battlefield and not a dead officer, caught thinking too long.

"Today, you go out on your first mission. There will be real blood and real death. You are to do everything your Swordofficers order to the letter. Any deviation and your safety is forfeit. Is that understood?"

"Yes, sir!" barked the men.

"You will march in two hours. Swtnt. Worthing, I would speak with you. The rest, dismissed!"

"Yes, Capt. Wingrave, sir?" said Swtnt. Worthing.

"At ease. Look me in the eye when I say this, Peter. If you've come here to die, it is easily done," he said. Shocked at such a statement after weeks of Capt. Wingrave refusing to acknowledge they had a connection at all, Peter gaped in disbelief.

"We men do stupid things for love. My sister would have you live," Capt. Wingrave continued.

"With respect, Captain, I do not wish to hear of your sister," said Peter. They nodded at each other, and parted ways, Peter to battle, and Elijah to worry.

Emily checked her calendar. They'd been in Dunbarrow nearly three weeks. Homesickness had caught up with her. Bridget nor

Emily fit in well with the city, most definitely because they made no attempt to further their position. Mr. Annesley kept careful watch on how Bridget fared among the high born residents of Dunbarrow. She was not disliked, but also not considered a formidable connection. Emily detested the neglect perpetrated by some of the Annesleys because they did not understand Bridget's true station. Lord Worthing had warned them of false friends, but it seemed news of their actual wealth had not traveled far as of yet. The sisters were treated as country folk, though their consequence exceeded almost any three ladies put together. Emily regretted it only because it seemed to affect Mr. Annesley's opinion of Bridget as a future spouse. He knew the truth, and Emily could only account for the change by concluding that he valued the impression that others had over Bridget's substantial inheritance. It gravely disappointed Emily to see him put distance between them.

Mr. Corey had advanced his evident plan of securing Emily's hand, only too happy to wait for the Worthings' identity to spread, and seemed to think it only a matter of time before she swooned in his presence. She did like him. He was pleasant to converse with, and never left her guessing at his meaning. A bouquet of flowers from the gentleman had arrived on her birthday, not too presumptuous, but romantic. Bridget did not press the issue, knowing Emily's state of mind. The problem with Mr. Corey may have been that he hid nothing, not even that his feelings for her were of light weight, regardless if they would grow as he spent more time in her company.

Miss Dinah had also continued her substantial attentions, and Emily began to expect to see her everyday. No rival to Anne's friendship, Miss Dinah, while asking everything under the sun of Emily, offered little of herself unless Emily expressed blatant curiosity, and even then the details were sparse. Miss Dinah had grown up in Dunbarrow, her parents died at a young age, and the Canton sisters lived with their aging aunt and uncle. Old Mr. Canton, the self-proclaimed reincarnation of a high priest, accompanied them to parties while Mrs. Canton called it all foolishness.

"Miss Worthing, I was hoping I could persuade you to a walk today," said Miss Dinah when Emily made her way downstairs.

"Oh? Where should you like to go?" inquired Emily. Bridget admired her finished painting in the corner, a fantastic landscape of no name. While her eyes caressed the paint, Mr. Annesley observed her; his troubled gaze more than upsetting to Emily.

"First, I thought you might like to see the harbor, then on to the music shop I mentioned before," said Miss Dinah. Mr. Annesley's attention focused back on their ever-present guest.

"It's a bit windy for the harbor today, isn't it?" he asked. Miss Dinah laughed and waved her hand at him.

"Is that a joke, Mr. Edward? It is always windy in Dunbarrow, you have said so yourself."

"I may indeed wish to stretch my legs. Allow me to fetch my things," said Emily. When all was set for the ladies' walk, Mr. Annesley waved goodbye from the front step of Amberose, biting his lip in anxiety. Mrs. Annesley had taken Bridget to find a frame for her painting, and so Emily had left alone with Miss Dinah.

"Corbin," he called.

"Yes sir?" said the butler from the next room.

"Is Henry in today?" asked Mr. Annesley.

"Aye, sir. He had some news to report and waits in his room for your summons."

"No time for summoning. I'll be going straightaway."

"Oh..." sighed Emily when she saw the ships for the first time. Gulls soared on the promised breeze, and the seawater flashed in the summer sun.

"Come, let us get a good look," said Miss Dinah, leading Emily onto the docks. They'd already walked a good distance across the city to get to the harbor; the slick boards of the dock did not invite closer examination.

"Are you certain we should go down there?" said Emily. Already several men blinked in astonishment at seeing two high born ladies without an escort in such a rough setting.

"No worries, Miss Worthing, I come down here often."

"I apologize, Miss Dinah, but I really do not feel comfortable. We would get in the way of the men's work." Emily looked between the street level, where the foot traffic of the city, including women and children, went about their business, and the dock itself right on the water, a healthy four or five yard drop down. Only the crew of the ships milled about where Miss Dinah pulled her, insisting Emily go down the steps.

"Are you frightened of pirates, Miss Worthing?" she laughed, "Or should I call you Miss Emily? It rings like church bells." The cold fire of recognition slid down Emily's bare nerves, melting her spine like wax.

"What did you say?" said Emily.

"I asked if I could call you Miss Emily. We are good friends, are we not? Come on, Miss Emily, let us see the ships!" Dinah Canton pulled harder on Emily's arm, succeeding in making Emily stumble down a few steps.

"You are going to make me fall! Miss Dinah, I insist upon going back to Amberose. You are behaving very strangely," said Emily. Dinah pulled her lips into a pout, but they relaxed, and her eyes glazed over as she looked behind Emily. Dreading to see what she might find there, Emily twisted. Jude Annesley grinned down at her from the top of steps, hands on his hips.

"Miss Emily. So good to see you," he said. Emily turned

back to Miss Dinah, but she was so engrossed in the appearance
of Mr. Jude she paid no mind to Emily. Feeling the danger,
Emily forced herself out of it.

"I will be leaving," she warned.

"Yes, Miss Emily, to Tadoros. Our ship is ready to sail."

A little faster, a little farther, Mr. Annesley repeated to himself.
He cursed, and cursed again as the horse recovered from a
stumble on the cobblestone. Finally the docks came into view.
He needed to see only one thing, Miss Emily Worthing still
ashore, and see her he did, but so close to being gone from them
forever, that Edward shouted in quite an ungentlemanly way.
The two conspirators saw him, but he came upon them so
quickly they could not force Miss Emily any further.

"Jude! I'd have your head if you weren't my blood," said
Mr. Annesley, dismounting and stationing his body between
Emily and his forsaken brother.

"It is good then that you still care, dear brother,"
laughed Jude, "I'll be away now, if you could step aside. I've a
few lads who don't mind taking a few swipes at you Edward, just
leave my new traveling companion, and go home," said Jude.
On his signal, a gang of seven men, crusty with salt and equally
as unconcerned with morals as Jude, started up the dock steps
toward Emily. Miss Dinah silently stepped around Emily and
watched from behind Jude as the tension mounted. Mr.

Annesley had only a moment to note that Miss Worthing remained in good health, though shocked beyond pale; her skin becoming a map of veins and muscles. He hadn't seen her like this since she returned from Landhilton, and yet she did not scream or faint, merely gazed upon her would-be captors with a hardness unexpected in a lady. She warned them, in her own way, that she would not go quietly, that they had perhaps chosen wrongly when deciding a mere woman would be no trouble. Emily would lose of course, in a battle of strength, but no one in the area would be able to doubt that she needed aid. It halted their steps enough for Mr. Annesley to make his proclamation.

"I have men on their way," Edward announced, voice loud with warning, "If you leave now, you can avoid what they'll do to you. Kidnap Miss Worthing, and they will run you down in the open sea and take no prisoners. Avoid them, and they will race you to Tadoros where the Annesleys are very welcome, and you'll spend the rest of your life in a Tadi jail. Jude cannot be paying you enough to go through the hell I wish upon you."

Mr. Annesley watched the fight leave their eyes, and as one they abandoned Jude, scrambling to get their ship out of the harbor. Jude looked on Edward with hate that turned into viciousness.

"Oh, Edward. Only with Miss Emily as a prize could I have been persuaded to leave Endland forever. All at once I was going to hurt every one of my detractors, every single person

who has contributed to my state of poverty and exile from
society. Now I will have to stay here, and go about my
business," said Jude.

"Take me with you!" Miss Dinah tugged on his coat,
her too-open eyes wide with hope.

"Why would I do that? Stealing you away would not be
one tenth as amusing." Jude shook her off and disappeared into
the city. Emily unconsciously grabbed Mr. Annesley's arm until
she could breathe normally.

"Miss Emily? Miss Emily? I am deeply sorry," he said.
She did not speak, not when his men arrived, or when he
ordered a carriage, or when he scolded Miss Dinah until her ears
were raw.

"He said he loved me, but he wanted her," said Dinah,
glowering at Emily before tears rushed down her cheeks, "And I
could not refuse to help. Not if it would make him happy."

"Your mistake is in thinking a man like Jude can be
happy," murmured Edward. They deposited Miss Dinah at her
home, with a stern warning that she was to stay in until Mr.
Annesley returned to explain. Then, Emily and Mr. Annesley
rode around the city of Dunbarrow in silence, not returning to
Amberose just yet.

Emily gratefully accepted the extended carriage ride. Jude's
nightmarish scheme had been thwarted, but how near she had

come to being his captive brought her to the brink of inward hysterics several times, much to her shame.

"How could I have let this happen?" she said, "Why didn't I realize?"

"It is my fault. I should have told you that Miss Dinah has always tried to put herself in Jude's company. Most in our family dismiss it as girlish fancy, but I knew they'd met in secret before, not that he could be interested in the second daughter of a minor family. He applied to her for news, and it seems this time, for information about you. I would understand if you wish to leave Dunbarrow," said Mr. Annesley. In truth, Emily did want to leave. Dunbarrow could keep its games and plots. She'd met so few people of value that she despaired for Bridget settling here. Yet, Bridget loved Mr. Edward, and Emily could not ruin her chances, even if the man himself needed persuading.

"No, sir. We will stay until our intended departure. Give me a few more moments and I will be well enough to return to Amberose. Let us not speak loudly of this to anyone unless necessary," decided Emily. Mr. Annesley turned from the window to look at her. Resolve plainly visible, he nodded.

"I've never met a woman so unaffected after encountering Jude, especially not if they had almost been kidnapped," he said.

"Pardon me, I am wholly affected, but it is over, and I trust that you are now on your guard," said Emily. A glint of cold anger passed through his eyes as he thought of all he would do to drive Jude from Dunbarrow.

"I am. This was scandalous and depraved, moreso than I've ever seen from him. It has ensured that I will never underestimate his behavior again." Emily breathed deep and long.

"Then all is well. Miss Dinah took ill and I called for you to escort me home."

Emily did not speak much to Bridget about the event, treating it as a routine outing while they were in public, and only informed her of the true particulars after the lights had gone out that night.

"Emily! I cannot believe you did not tell me at once!" shrieked Bridget.

"Shh! Shh! We aren't to speak of it openly. Mr. Annesley prefers you not to know."

"Is that why he left so soon after returning?"

"He told me later that he went back to the Cantons. They want no part of Jude's disgrace and have said they will send Dinah away to a relative that is far more strict," said Emily. She clucked her tongue.

"Do you want to go home?" Bridget whispered.

"No, love. I will recover just as well here. Pray, do not tell Mama and Papa about this. I don't want to worry them without cause." Bridget rolled around in the bed in a frightful temper.

"That man! How could he and Edward be brothers?"

"I know you may not want to hear it, but if Mrs.
Annesley had paid more attention to her sons than her rank,
Jude's outcome might have been different." Bridget huffed and
lay still.

A week passed, and though Emily had avoided any trouble by
staying in, late that Tuesday evening trouble came anyway. The
arrival of an express letter interrupted Emily in her quarters.
Bridget and Mr. Annesley listened to Mrs. Annesley in the
parlor; she analyzed a dinner they'd had at a rival's house. Idly,
Emily hoped Mrs. Annesley would continue do all the social
gymnastics if the couple married, so that Bridget would be left in
peace.

"Excuse me, Miss, the head servant sent me with this.
It's just arrived and is marked for haste," said a maid from the
hall. Emily thanked her kindly, and with a speeding heart looked
upon the envelope. Express mail did not come for her unless it
was an emergency. It was from Charlton.

"Oh dear," gasped Emily. She could barely stand to
open it, a thousand worries screaming loud in her head.
Whispering prayers and wishes all the while, Emily slid a finger
under the seal and unfolded the paper.

"Emily,

I won't prolong this, it pains me to write. Your mother and I received a letter from Batteran Phelps. Peter is missing in action, and presumed dead. We still hold out hope, though we know there is not much to be had. We ask for your return so that we may all be together.

Deepest Love,

Papa."

"Bridget!" Emily screamed, unconsciously drawing it out in agony, "Bridget!" The echoes of it rang throughout Amberose, leaving no one in the house unaware that something terrible had happened. Bridget wrenched the door open, half expecting an intruder to be in the house, and seeing only her sister with a piece of paper, immediately fell to dread, with Mr. Annesley not far behind her. He fielded questions in the hall while Bridget went to Emily and shook her until a rational response could be had.

"Emily, Emily! What has happened?"

"Peter is gone!" Mr. Annesley turned at this last scream with utter incredulity on his face.

"But... Elijah wrote to me... Peter was... doing well," he said. Emily could only nod as she and Bridget collapsed together on the floor, harsh sobs indistinguishable from sister to sister. When the rest of the house had been assured that no one present was dying, Mr. Annesley closed the door and handled anyone who came near, allowing Emily and Bridget a moment of privacy. The need to pack their trunks, to proceed home, halted the weeping. The Annesleys were extremely sad to see them go under such circumstances, and Mr. Annesley accompanied them, taking no objections.

When they descended from the travel carriage, Mary Wingrave happened to be walking to the dress shop and waved with a smile to her three friends. Emily unashamedly directed some of her anger and hatred toward Mary in a terrible gaze, fit for the eyes of the devil. Mary stopped, thinking Emily to still be upset over the proposal when Mrs. Johnston, who had a good view of the scene, rushed outside to whisper in Miss Wingrave's ear the news that everyone else knew. A spasm of horror in Miss Wingrave took Emily by surprise as Mary clasped her hand over her mouth, and ran away in tears. Emily sniffed in hollow satisfaction. Every irrational and hurt part of her hoped Mary felt the full force of Peter's death. Emily shook her head.

"Peter made his choice," she mumbled.

Lord and Lady Worthing, despite their claim to hope, despaired beyond anything Emily had yet witnessed, and Genevieve cried constantly. As a family, they sat in the parents' bedroom and did not leave all night, talking and leaning on each other in the darkest of times.

Charlton became a tomb of sorrow and disappointment. Mr. Annesley, Bridget, and Genevieve banded together, while the rest of the house took up solitary occupations. After a week without any more communications from the border, the fading hopes of the Worthings vanished. The solid truth of Peter's death beat a bitter stake into their hearts, one more strike would do the family in forever. Mr. Annesley retreated to Dunbarrow, to give them privacy.

First, Emily took to walking, wanting solace in nature. However, blind with grief, the lessons the natural world held were lost on her, and she could not be bothered to go outside after several fruitless days of retrospection. She could not stand to see anyone, their tears and sadness added to her own, and so Emily retreated to her room again. Then, the real manifestation of mourning began in the form of incurable illness.

"Was it not you who said that to die broken-hearted in your room was dramatic?" said Lady Worthing. She stared hard into her daughter's face, unwilling to lose two children.

"I am not attempting to die, Mama," said Emily, "Though you all suspect me, I'm not willfully weakening myself."

"The doctor is baffled, at least," said Lady Worthing. Emily sighed.

"I'm not well enough to despair. If you will to accuse me of anything, make it apathy." Emily turned over, sallow cheek smushed into her pillow. It was not a fever or cold that ailed her, but an unstoppable wasting of spirits. She did not care to eat, she fell when walking, and had lost most weight that could be spared in the month since they'd lost Peter. Emily did not read or embroider to pass time; she remembered, cementing every thought of her brother before time could fade them. To this she added cruelty to her daily regimen by allowing herself to imagine a double wedding, Peter and Mary, and herself to Elijah, over and over and over. A thousand weddings later and Emily moved on to daily life at Reddester, how she would arrange the house to her liking, visiting her family often, and then, perhaps, a child of her own. She looked forward to the conjurations of her mind much more than the bleak nothingness practicality would force her to acknowledge. In truth, she did not wish to get well, and did not take any actions to do so, but it could not be admitted aloud.

"Apathy is enough to ruin nations, let alone one heart like yours, so used to the strong coursing of opinion through it. Every day I lay in bed I wished to get up and join my family, so many things I missed, and now Peter is... Do not ruin your health," said Lady Worthing. Emily cringed, guilt meshing with her negativity.

Days, nights, meals, visits. The doctor gave in.

"I can cure the body, but not the mind or heart. I'd wear myself out trying," he'd told her parents.

"No more!" shouted Lady Worthing at her bedside, an afternoon six weeks since they'd come back from Dunbarrow.

"What?" said Emily from her bed, confused that something so real had startled her. With all her regained strength, Lady Worthing did a thing so uncharacteristic of her station that the servants would speak of it for years with unbridled respect. She threw Emily's covers away from her, grabbed her ankles, and hauled her clear from the bed.

"Mama!" Emily yelled before hitting her head on the floor.

"I am so angry! I AM the mother of this house, and I will not allow you to behave this way!" Lady Worthing continued shouting as she dragged Emily into the hall. "Peter would never want this! I will not allow it!"

Lord Worthing, and the younger sisters came to see what was the matter, along with every available maid. Emily, rubbing at the knot on her head, thanked the Four Virtuous that her bedclothes were modest and sensible, though holding them below her hips took the other arm allowing no power to struggle. No one dared stop Lady Worthing, the fire bursting from her spirit the strongest since her last bout of illness. This was the fierce truth of Lady Worthing, were she not held back by her body.

"Mama," Emily gasped. Her mother took her straight down the stairs, minding no bumps or bruises. When they reached the bottom, Elizabeth Worthing took hold of the back of her daughter's neck and marched her outside, down the front walk, panting with effort.

"Look at the sun, feel it on your face. Does it not remind you of him?" Lady Worthing sniffled and let go, collapsing to her knees. Emily could not stand without help, and cut her leg on the stones, no extra layers protecting the sharp bones of her shin. As ordered, she turned her face up to the sun. Emily balled up her clammy fists, and allowed hot tears to roll and fall. Both men she had lost felt like this warmth, an incomparable glowing happiness.

"Mama... Mama." Emily reached out a hand. Lady Worthing wiped her tears and took it.

"That's my girl. Reach for me, and I will help." Lord Worthing hugged his two daughters, and not one handkerchief among the witnesses stayed dry. They all thought that maybe Charlton could be healed, if it could not be whole.

Just once in her adult life, Mary Wingrave wanted everything to be well. In no way did she shirk responsibility for Peter's death.

"I'm am a cursed creature," she breathed. Every mistake, every misstep stabbed at her temples. The window shutters swung back and forth, calling to Mary. What did she have left? The tribulation she had begun fifteen years ago was as awful as she ever wanted to witness. With parents who befriended no

one for fear of betrayal, a brother giving his life so that they
might escape the ruinous fate Mary had assigned them all, and
Peter now a casualty of war, driven to service in much the same
way as Elijah, she concluded that her presence brought only
disaster.

"Would they be relieved?" she wondered. Mary grasped
the sill and bent her head, stopping to rest her forehead on it,
tears leaking onto the wood.

Emily Worthing appeared unbidden in her mind, that
last stare she'd bestowed before Mary heard the news.

"Why couldn't I be more like her?" Agony strangled her
throat. Emily would never have believed a man like Jude had
good intentions. She would never have misled Peter, a true
gentleman, into a courtship with no satisfying conclusion.
Emily's strength humbled Mary, struck her to the bone. Pure
shame lifted her head.

With nary a pause, Mary stepped on the chair.

"Excuse me, your ladyship, a letter has arrived for Miss Emily,"
said Velma.

"Thank you, V. Read it. The script is unfamiliar to me,"
said Lady Worthing. Emily pinned a lazy bun, for she had not
the strength yet to hold her arms above her head for very long.
Yesterday she would have welcomed a quiet death, to pass into

her dreams. Had her mother not taken drastic action, that reality would have come to pass. But today, Emily had a letter from a mystery writer, and she took some happiness in this small surprise.

"Who would be writing me?" she wondered. Her fingers, spindly and frail upon examination, now that Emily used her real eyes to see, unstuck the wax.

"Dearest Emily,

Peter is alive, as a prisoner of war, and I am negotiating his release. It may take time, but I will do whatever is required to procure his safety. As his commanding officer, I offer an apology for what has occurred. I wish your family good health.

Capt. Wingrave."

Emily shrieked and flung herself into her mother's arms, bowling the Lady off her feet.

"He's alive! He's alive!" Emily tried to stand and help Lady Worthing up, but her condition forced dizziness.

"Peter?" said Lady Worthing, trying to hold Emily straight.

"Yes! Call Papa! Call my sisters! He's alive!"

"Roland!" Lady Worthing shouted, quite surprising everyone who thought her outburst to be over. She hustled to the railing above the stairs, leaving Emily to pant with the effort of being so happy and out of bed. Lord Worthing rushed from his study, assuming someone had been hurt.

"Yes, my dear? What is it?" The news of his son had taken its toll on Lord Worthing as well, his haggard face drawn up in alarm.

"Our son lives! Emily has had a letter," said Lady Worthing, "Bridget is about the grounds with Genevieve and Ms. Pierce, you must tell them." He obeyed at once, striding outdoors without his coat. Lady Worthing returned to Emily and helped her to sit.

"Who wrote you? What does it say?" said Lady Worthing. Emily read her the body, skipping the greeting which puzzled her. 'Dearest Emily,' when the rest of the letter was so formal and curt? Was it possible that he loved her? Her feelings had run away with the assumption that he could not have felt as deeply as she had, but then discovering from Edward exactly what the secret was had tangled it up in mystery again.

The Worthings celebrated that night with Emily's first large meal since returning to Charlton. They danced and played and anxiously whispered. Then, the wait began. Every day that ended without a letter burdened them like a prison sentence. Emily's health returned and with it a renewed sense of her feelings. She was at once angry with, and grateful to Elijah Wingrave. Very angry, and very grateful. And still very much in love. All the Mr. Coreys in Dunbarrow could ask for her hand and Emily would still choose Capt. Wingrave every time. She cherished the only two words he'd given her in months, ashamed to be so excited about a pittance.

Mary's breath was lost in the high wind and the world began to spin in hypnotic color. She cried. For herself, her child, Peter, the Worthings, her mother and father, her brothers. At the last, she may have even shed a tear of pity for Jude.

"Peter," she said. He, Elijah, and Emily swam in her head.

The maid Katherine knocked on the door, and entered, thinking that Miss Wingrave had gone out, to see Mary perched on the window ledge looking down. Mary went limp as she saw the terror in Katherine's face, causing her to fall back into the room.

"Miss? Miss!" Katherine rushed over to her mistress and patted her cheeks. "What were you about Miss Mary? Tell me you weren't thinking of leaving us early."

"I... I... Sorry," muttered Mary. Katherine, even at her age, sprung to the door and assured another servant that all was well before shutting and locking it. She put Mary in bed, and frowned down at her.

"Sorry is for accidents, ma'am. Listen to this old woman. There is no point in life at which you are lost until you surrender." Mary wept.

"Katherine, you remember, don't you? What is was like at Landhilton before?" Mary's throat was raw as if she'd been screaming. Katherine pursed her lips.

"Excuse me for plain-speaking, Miss Mary, but I was good friends with Mrs. Pratchett. I am the only servant in this house who knows what happened here, and I can tell you one thing. You're not to blame. Your parents blame themselves, and your brothers blame that man. It's a wise thing to own your guilt, milady, but impossible to own the guilt of others. You've been tearing yourself asunder thinking you made this house tremble, and I am here to tell you, life would be much worse without Miss Mary Wingrave," said the old woman. Mary blanched at this impromptu lecture, but Katherine was not finished.

"And another thing. That boy that died, the one that made you an offer. He was right to do so. He was also right to do something useful after being refused. Remember him with honor, and don't shackle him with your death. Do you think he'd feel alright, sitting up in the Afterlife, watching you jump out a window?"

Morbid curiosity got the better of Mary, and she asked, "Katherine, how many children do you have?"

"Thirteen, counting my sister's orphans."

"They have a good mother," said Mary. Katherine smiled on her mistress.

"Are we at an understanding, Miss Mary? Will I worry if I leave the room?" Mary took a deep breath and nodded. "There now. I've a letter from Mr. Elijah, maybe it will cheer you."

Mary took the letter. She waited as Katherine brushed dust off her dress.

"Thank you, Katherine. I needed what you said."

"Absolutely, Miss. Ring if you need me, I mean it," said Katherine, slowly leaving the room.

"I am weak," said Mary to herself, "to try and escape this pain." Even though she'd had word from Edward that Emily fared no better, Mary still hated that she lacked the fortitude so present in Miss Worthing. Even Katherine outpaced her pitiful constancy.

"Elijah..." she whispered, tracing his script. Without much thought as to what he could have written, she tore it open.

"Mary,

Peter lives. I cannot write much more as I have much to do to guarantee that statement. I hope this can ease your deepest despair, at least.

Love,

Elijah."

"Katherine, your monthly wages have just increased," said Mary, hugging the parchment to her chest.

SEVEN DAYS PRIOR

In the end, Elijah could not bring himself to write Mary about the loss. In part because he didn't know how to deliver the blow, and because he didn't believe it himself. Capt. Wingrave had inspected every body that came back from the front line that day. He'd written a personal letter to the Jakes family when he recognized their son. Peter was nowhere to be found. Elijah knew very well that it meant little; there were places he could have fallen where no one would find him, especially if the wildlife had their way. The Captain shook his head.

Five weeks had passed, and not a letter had arrived from Mary. She could not have escaped the crushing news, so she was either angry with him, or so despondent she couldn't pick up a quill. Edward had written him several times to ask for absolute confirmation of Peter's fate, and Elijah disappointed him every time. One particular line haunted Capt. Wingrave.

"Bridget will survive, being of a positive temperament, and Genevieve is too young to be forever scarred, but Emily, coming to this event in poor spirits, has fallen ill and may not possess enough resilient fiber to recover despite the innate strength I have witnessed in her myself."

"Captain! Captain! An emissary has crossed the battlefield with a communication, sir," called Swofr. Barnes from the other side of Elijah's personal quarters door. In only trousers and his undershirt, Capt. Wingrave threw the door open.

"What does it say?" he said.

"I do not know, sir, it is addressed to you," said Swofr. Barnes. Capt. Wingrave took the scroll and unwound it. Choppily translated in spots, Elijah made it out.

"Fortcaptain Elijah Wingrave of Fort Jenning,

I am your equal to the Sypass. I have prisoner I wish to trade, has spirit. Took this many days to beat name from mouth. Peter Worthing. My demands are list down. He is alive--'I learned from Chatwood Lowe, sir,' is his message. Send response.

Col. Jyrander."

Elijah spilled ink on two parchment pieces as his quill flew across the page.

Blood around him. Peter couldn't see it, not well, with his swollen eyes. He smelled it whenever he took too long to inhale; the scent clogged his lungs. Living with pain, being beaten daily while asked ill-worded questions; it was the worst time of his life excluding the moment after Mary stiffly apologized for any misunderstanding they might have had and denied him her hand. His cell door opened, and Peter braced for another round of punches and kicks. Harsh laughter bit into his ears. The rhythmic, and sometimes guttural, speech of the Sypass flowed from the broad man who had beaten him. A translator stood nearby. When he finished speaking, the broad man smiled.

"Col. Jyrander wants your understanding that Captain

Wingrave has your message. Talks are going for your release. You are a good prison dweller for Endland. Useless to us. Col. Jyrander honors your name," said the translator. Peter gasped. He'd been sure of dying in this horrible place.

"Thank you," he said, tears stinging the infected cuts on his face. Col. Jyrander said more.

"Thank your Captain. Without trade, you would stay," said the translator. They left him with ale and bread, which he consumed with fervor. Peter would see light and home again, and that gave him cause to strengthen his body.

His men stood at attention like bowstrings as Capt. Wingrave met Col. Jyrander at the border. The Colonel looked the Fortcaptain over with an amused grimace before he spoke into the dead quiet of the plains they'd chosen to make the exchange.

The Endland translator began, "I have long wanted to see you in person, Captain Wingrave. They call you a courageous leader. Your youth makes me appear foolish." Elijah kept his face stony though a smirk lay underneath.

"I do what is needed. Where is my soldier?" Col. Jyrander inclined his head; a particularly large man carried Peter under one arm and dropped him in front of his Captain. Peter groaned and cursed. Elijah's eyes flashed.

"We agreed he would be in good condition," he said. Col. Jyrander smiled, and replied.

"Col. Jyrander says alive is good," said the translator. The Sypass hooked their horse to the cart of goods and materials, Peter's price, and backed away from the line of Endlanders. Though he wanted to, Elijah made no more reply to the enemy commander.

"Get the stretcher," ordered Capt. Wingrave. He knelt down and turned Peter onto his back. His injuries were severe and needed immediate disinfection. Looking into his swollen face, Elijah registered his own feelings of friendship toward Peter. He had enjoyed their mental chess game and teaching Swtnt. Worthing, an astute pupil. "Worthing?"

"Sir," Peter wheezed, opening one eye to a squint.

"Did you know that Endland does not permit negotiating with the country's goods for prisoners of war?"

"No, sir. How...?"

"That entire cart was from my personal stores." Peter cringed.

"I will take my punishment, sir," said Swtnt. Worthing. Capt. Wingrave breathed out, so relieved he smiled.

"It won't be as horrible as some. You've done me a great service by continuing to live."

"Aye, sir. Does... she know?" Peter let his eyelid shut, though the discomfort plainly showed.

"She's ecstatic. I permit you to retain hope," said Capt. Wingrave.

"Thank you, sir." Peter passed out as soon as his head lay on the stretcher. Though Peter Worthing would never know it, the Captain stayed with him until he could be assured that his charge would wake again.

A fortnight crawled by, then another, and finally an express came for Lord Worthing. After assuring the ladies that Peter had been rescued, he took to his study to examine the letter. He came back to the drawing room after a full half hour's absence.

"What else, Papa? What else do you know?" said Emily. She held one of Bridget's hands and one of Genevieve's while Lady Worthing gripped the back of a chair.

"He is most definitely alive. Capt. Wingrave has invited me to visit him, in a hospital near Fort Jennings, and to report back to you all, but I am essential to Charlton just now, as the harvest is days away," said Lord Worthing.

"I will go," said Emily and Bridget together.

"Can I come with you?" said Genevieve.

"No, I will go," said Lady Worthing. Lord Worthing looked at the four of them and nodded.

"Emily and Bridget will go. Genevieve, you stay, and you my lady, will also stay. If you are to travel to Dunbarrow for the winter, this trip would be too much," he said.

Lady Worthing protested, "Emily has also been unwell."

"Even so, I am in better health now. You have not yet

left Tripton, Mama, and this journey will be difficult, in more ways than one, " said Emily. Lady Worthing relented, proud of Emily's renewed spirit.

"I'll be sending Aloysius with you, Emily. It is a long way for two women by themselves," said Lord Worthing.

"As you wish, Papa. We will leave as soon as may be," she said.

The family celebrated even more that night, until the sisters insisted on packing their trunks, which took the rest of their time before exhaustion forced sleep.

Denton, the gutted community on the Endland side of Fort Jennings, had been stripped of all but essential war services. There were ten men for every one woman, and Aloysius turned away more than one wandering eye. They secured a room at the local inn, and got direction from the innkeeper to the correct hospital. Bainheart Hospital, a repurposed manor on the outskirts of Denton, had been a fine estate in its day, before the war had damaged the surrounding property. Being so close to the border, Denton itself was a shabby excuse for a village, having changed hands many times over the last few decades. Emily and Bridget thanked their father for suggesting they pack clothes that would not stand out as a marker for thieves. As lawful as the inner fort might have been, Denton had no constables.

Bainheart brought tears to Emily, not only for the sad state of the house, but for the recovering patients taking advantage of the grounds outside. In several instances, pieces of flesh were missing; the easiest way to prevent infection from spreading when medical help was unavailable. In others, the patients seemed so traumatized that they simply stared at the horizon. Once more glad for her extensive education, Emily thought that she might be sick if she had never heard of such conditions before. Bridget kept her eyes fixed on the ground.

"Let us find Peter," said Emily. A kind nurse pointed them to Peter's room, though Emily motioned for Bridget to wait outside with Aloysius at first. Peter looked as if he'd been kicked in the face by an errant horse. Bandages covered one eye and bruises shaded the rest of his skin. Traveling three-quarters of the way across Endland was nothing to seeing her brother in such a state. Emily floated in, so light with the surrealism of the moment.

"Peter? Are you awake?" she said. He twisted his head to see her with his open eye.

"Emily? Is it really you?" he said. Peter propped himself up on his pillows and reached for her. She gladly, but gently embraced him and wept. Not so much of a hardened soldier, Peter cried as well, very aware of the rarity of his situation.

"I came in Papa's place so that he would not miss the

harvest. I could not direct the farmers if something went awry, "
she laughed when they parted.

"It is just as well. I would not want my parents to see me
this way," he said.

"They will get a fair enough description. Bridget, please
come," said Emily.

"Did you make her wait outside?" inquired Peter.

"I wanted to be sure that... it would not cause
nightmares," said Emily.

"That is a legitimate concern," he sighed, "Where is my
Bridget? My rascal in arms?" Bridget rushed in, and gasped.

"You look awful!" she said. Bridget embraced him with
much less care, eliciting several groans and wounded chuckles.

"If I had any pride left, you might have killed it right
then, sweet Bridget," said Peter.

"If I had any care for your pride instead of your body
just now, I might not have said it," said Bridget. The girls settled
on each side of his bed.

"What happened? I've had the sparsest of information
about all this," said Emily. She rubbed his hand between her
two palms. Peter let out a loud sigh.

"I called attention to myself on the battlefield to provide
a distraction for our troops. We were losing ground that would
have seriously hampered a major supply line, so I began acting
above my rank to entice the Sypass to target me. Instead of

killing me, they captured me for ransom," said Peter. His one
eye, though puffed and red, looked with guilt on his bedsheets.

"You... sacrificed yourself? Are you mad?" cried Emily.
He closed his eye and swallowed.

"I am so sorry. Given the chance, I would do it again,
but it was still foolish."

"Pray, don't tell Mama or she'll do the job for the
Sypass," said Bridget. Emily left the bed and paced around the
room, highly agitated. Peter smiled.

"I haven't had a proper lecture in that tone since I left
home. Here, it's all measured disapproval in the form of Capt.
Wingrave," he said.

"And that's another thing. In all your letters, you never
mentioned he was your commanding officer," she said.

"I did not want to cause you pain by associating my time
here with him. I'm afraid it's unavoidable now." He adjusted
his blankets revealing a cast on his left leg.

"Was it broken?" Emily inquired.

"Twice. Capt. Wingrave ordered whatever was mended
be broken again because the Sypass hadn't cared to set it for me,"
said Peter, "Though I think it was a bit of punishment for his
losing a fifty-year-old bottle of brandy in the deal." Emily
laughed despite herself, as did Peter and Bridget, a joyous sound
none thought they would hear again. They talked until Peter
began to tire.

"Before you go, Capt. Wingrave left this for Papa, when he visited. I suppose you should have it instead," said Peter, pointing to a letter on the stand beside his bed. Emily took it, and gave Peter a kiss on the forehead before departing. She read it on the way to the inn.

"To Lord Worthing,

I would be honored if you called on me during your visit. Merely tell the guard at Fort Jennings that you wish to see me, and that you are Swtnt. Worthing's relation. I would wish the opportunity to make my apologies in person.

Capt. Wingrave."

Emily gave the letter a wicked smile, and informed Aloysius of a new stop in their schedule for the day.

"You mean to go to the fort?" said Bridget.

"I do. You will stay at the inn. Do not go anywhere until we get back," said Emily.

From the outside, Fort Jennings made as much an impression as a mountain up close. Solid walls, reaching far into the ground, went up above the tallest tree in the area. Though many trees had been cleared near the fort, the road they'd traveled was still cut through the forest, ever encroaching on the man made paths.

"It's a castle, or a keep," said Emily who had not envisioned it to be so grand.

"Aye, milady, Endland's Rock Bastion. Never been taken by the enemy, even when the town was overrun," said Aloysius, "'Scuse me, milady, but are you certain you should go in there?" Worse than Denton, Emily could see no women whatsoever enjoying the last of the year's good weather. She supposed the reason for this to be that the Fort would lose its nurses to child-bearing, and so the women kept to the hospitals, far away from the soldiers. Nervously, Emily took note of the appreciation she garnered, and gathering no hostility, she put on a courageous show of comfort.

"I am happy you are with me, Aloysius. Let us be on our errand," said Emily. A guard at the open front gate, astonished at their approach, welcomed her.

"Good day, Miss. For what reason do you visit Fort Jennings today?"

"Good day... First Soldier. I've come at the behest of Fortcaptain Wingrave. Where might I find him?" she replied. The poor First Soldier had been shocked on many levels; Emily's purposeful speech, not timid at all, her recognition of his insignia, and that she had been summoned by the very Captain who had trained him. He had standing orders to prevent nonessential women from entering Fort Jennings, but he would be punished if he delayed one of the Captain's appointments. His obvious confusion drove Emily to produce Capt. Wingrave's letter.

"Here, I come on behalf of my brother, Swtnt. Worthing. My father is required in business just now, so I will function as the relation. Do you know where I might find the Captain?" she repeated. A passing officer caught the guard's eye and, in his panic, he shifted the responsibility.

"Barnes, sir! Your assistance, if you please," said the guard. He explained what Emily wanted, and the man nodded.

"This letter is from the Captain, I'll show you the way, Miss Worthing, follow me," said Swofr. Barnes.

"Thanks Swoffy!" said the guard as he saluted his farewell. Barnes grumbled a bit at being the funnel for all trouble in Fort Jennings being that he was Capt. Wingrave's second. Emily reddened, though luckily Barnes did not see it. Her blushing caught many other eyes along the great halls, until the Swordofficer heard whispers of a "fine lady" from all around him, enough to wake him from his inner reflection.

"That's enough you lads, she didn't come here to be gawked at. Are we not assigning you enough duties?" he warned them.

"Give us a break Swoffy, we haven't seen a tender heart since we left home!" one soldier jeered, safe in numbers. Aloysius rose to his full height and prepared to tongue lash the offender, when Emily stopped him.

"Hands offend, not eyes. I am not bothered," she said.

"And gracious, too. Marry me, fine lady?" jested

another.

"I'll find you later, Holmes. Please, Miss Worthing, this way," said Swofr. Barnes, gesturing down a close hall where the admirers could not follow. They complained, but relented. "My apologies, I didn't know we had forgotten our manners. I'll inform the Captain of their crude behavior."

"Please, I meant what I said. If I can remind them, even a little, of someone they have waiting for them, it is no trouble," said Emily. Swofr. Barnes gave her a puzzled look as he stopped at a large wooden door carved from oak.

Swofr. Barnes knocked twice on the Captain's door.

"Come in," called Capt. Wingrave.

"Sir, Swtnt. Worthing's relation to see you, sir," said the Swordofficer from just inside the door.

"Send him in," said Capt. Wingrave, rising from his desk.

"Er, yes... sir," said Swofr. Barnes, saluting. He vanished through the door, and Capt. Wingrave looked down to make one last note.

"Captain," said a voice out of memory. His head whipped up to see none other than she, followed by a manservant.

"Emily?" Stunned, the Captain forgot all propriety.

"Excuse us, Aloysius, I will call if I need you," she said.

"Yes, miss," he said and closed the door behind him.

"What are you doing here?" Capt. Wingrave inquired with a touch of anger.

"I came to see Peter, and your letter to my father requested that he call on you, so as his proxy, here I am," said Emily. Elijah was very handsome in uniform, his green coat immaculate and trousers without a wrinkle.

"You should not have come," he said. His throat caught with bliss at seeing her.

"Oh, I think that I should. You and I have matters that need discussing." Emily's former fire sparked in her countenance. "May I sit?" She waved at the piano bench.

"No. You may leave," he said, marching around his desk to face her.

"You're being very rude. I have come all this way, and not to be ordered around like one of your officers."

"I am but moments from giving up the very reason I came here," he begged, already lost in the bend of her mouth and eyes that held him accountable for every moment of his absence.

"Why did you come here? To hide? Was it for my own good, or yours?" she asked.

"For everyone, to not disgrace my family by leaving them open to exposure, to not disgrace you by asking that you love me outside the confines of an honorable marriage. I came here to protect you, and you would sabotage me by coming into a fort full of men like you were just walking down to Sunday breakfast.

You've lost none of your boldness," he said.

"My boldness has only been enhanced by a brutal reminder of mortality, mourning my brother, and then having him rise from the dead. I don't want to live my life a martyr to your family's deception. Tell me why I cannot know the secret. Tell me why you don't trust me," said Emily.

"It is not my decision. It may be a secret I keep, but I do not own it. It is not mine to tell."

"So you will never let anyone closer than I am now? You would be a slave to this forever?" Capt. Wingrave's jaw flexed several times before he could answer. Emily saw his dark temper welling to the surface.

"I will fetch the chaplain this instant and marry you, if it would make you happy," he said. Phantoms of their many imagined weddings blurred Emily's vision, erased by the callousness of his offer.

"How dare you impose upon me while half of you still lingers in shadow."

"I come with shadow! If it is outside the bounds of your acceptance--"

"Why did you bother promising me honesty then?" said Emily.

"I tried to give you what I could. I will protect my family's secret for as long as is needed."

"Don't you mean your sister's secret?" said Emily. Elijah

turned a hard eye on her.

"My sister?"

"She owns the secret, does she not?"

"What do you know, Emily?" Suspicion drove him dangerously close to her, within reach.

"Does it matter? The issue is not whether I know, it's whether you trust me."

"Answer the question," he growled. When she did not, Elijah stepped toward her, until Emily raised a hand, which he then caught and used to pull her into him. He kissed her with dizzying passion. Almost immediately, Elijah released her and moved back behind his desk, facing the wall.

"Forgive my impertinence," he said, low and quiet.

"I know about the engagement, " said Emily as he turned to look at her, "I know it was broken. And that... there was a child." All of the color drained from his face, but a quizzical squint drew his brow down.

"Is that all?" he asked.

"Is that all? Can there be more?" said Emily. He gave a short bark of humorless laughter.

"And you still don't understand the breadth," he whispered.

"Tell me, what else can there be?" In pained desperation, Elijah approached her again.

"Can that be enough? Can you let one detail slip past?

So I might tell you I live for you? I would cut my soul open and allow you to examine its essence, if you leave the last of the secret alone. I would marry you, and we could live, side by side, with no reproach. You know enough to satisfy. Can I at last tell you how much I love--"

"No! I will not consent if there is anything else. I will not enter into a union in which my husband would hide things from me," said Emily. Tears flowed down her face. Elijah blotted them with the back of his hand.

"I would give you everything I have," he whispered.

"Why should I believe you? You promised to be honest with me, and yet secrets have tied up your tongue," said Emily.

"Please...don't look at me that way. If you knew how I long to tell you everything... Can you forgive me for the sake of happiness? Will you wed me with the understanding that you know all that makes up my character?"

"What kind of a marriage would this be that it must start with forgiveness for the unimaginable pain you have caused me? Your secrets nearly destroyed everything that I love, and your selfish flight to hide behind the shield of duty lends me no security in your promises," said Emily. Elijah's hope and expression went limp.

"If you truly believe nothing I say, it is of no use." Emily scoffed at his offense.

"Mary aside, you still kept secrets, Captain."

"Have you ever held a dying man in your arms? Would you want to remember his last whispered reference to your rank every time someone addressed you? Whatever has convinced you of malice on my part, I have nothing more to communicate to you except my apologies to your parents that Swtnt. Worthing went through such an ordeal. He has made his Captain, and his country proud. Good day, Miss Worthing."

"Dismissed like an errand boy? A person you just asked to be your equal?"

"No, no, Emily Worthing has no equal in this room, for I have sinned. Add disrespect of a superior to my lofty pile of charges."

"These are the last words you would speak to me?"

"You've cast aside my feelings as if I haven't suffered every day since leaving Reddester. My civility ran out at the first farewell. Leave, and never think of me again," he said.

Though her body moved, Emily's heart was stationery, stuck to the spot where she lost it.

Emily and Bridget stayed near Fort Jennings until Peter could get out of bed regularly. One by one his bandages were removed, and at last he was given a patch for his eye which would take the longest to mend. Luckily, he had not lost his sight. Emily knocked on his door the day he was to be released.

"Come in," called Peter. She pushed the door wide.

"Peter, I--" Her voice failed her when Peter's visitor stood from his seat.

"Good day to you both. Worthing, I'll see you at the fort," said Capt. Wingrave.

"Aye, sir," said Peter. Emily swallowed when Elijah passed by her with nary a glance.

"Still angry with him, are you?" said Peter when the man had gone. She'd said nothing of what happened the day she visited Fort Jennings.

With a skeptical brow raised, Emily said, "Should I not be?"

"He saved my life, you know. Batteran Phelps does not usually permit negotiating for prisoners, and did so because Capt. Wingrave expressly wished it."

"He has my thanks for that."

"I don't think we have the whole story, Emily. From what I know of him since coming here, Capt. Wingrave is the most honorable of men," said Peter. Emily balked in betrayal.

"No, we don't have the full story. That in itself taints his honor," she replied, "When will they release you for home?" Peter shook his head and stood. His pant leg had been hitched above his cast, but otherwise he was fully dressed in uniform.

"I'm not going home yet," he said.

"You can't go into battle like that," said Emily.

"No, and I've been given permission to break my contract, but I'll be staying here through the winter. Capt. Wingrave has offered me a position as his second now that Swofr. Barnes has promoted to Lineleader. I will be home in the spring." Peter picked up a cane from the bedside table. Affronted by his answer, Emily whirled and began walking out.

"Emily, wait, where are you going?"

"This visit has been most unsatisfactory with the exception of seeing you well. I must travel home and tell our parents that after mourning your death, they must wait to see you so that you may be at the convenience of Capt. Wingrave. Between your two kinds of stupidity, I hope you fall very much in love," she said, slamming the door behind her.

"Emily?" called Bridget as her sister stormed out the front where she'd been conversing with one of the nurses.

"I will wait for you in the carriage. Peter is out of bed," said Emily, not bothering to turn.

9. Friends of Dunbarrow

Emily met with Peter once more that night to bid him a short farewell. Bridget did not think very much of his decision to stay at Fort Jennings either, but forgave him more readily.

"What if he dies?" said Bridget during their carriage ride home.

"Flaws and poor judgement are not erased by death. Passing on does not make one saintly, contrary to the glorification that always goes on at funerals. If Peter dies, he will die knowing that I love him and by his own choice in staying here when he needs a cane to walk," said Emily.

"It has nothing to do with his choosing to be Capt. Wingrave's second?" said Bridget.

"That is merely salt in the wound," replied Emily. She

scowled at the mention of Elijah Wingrave. He and Mary had behaved in a way that deserved ridicule, inviting and encouraging affection where they knew there could be no attachments. Shame did deal Emily a few blows upon examination of her behavior. She had been dismissive of Capt. Wingrave's feelings, as she was accused. Living with the doubt of his affection had made it effortless to suppose it was fantasy all along, but if Capt. Wingrave expected her to behave rationally after a false proposal like that, he may have overestimated her composure. She only hoped that after Peter decided to return home, Capt. Wingrave would never be mentioned again.

After the busy days of the harvest, a sort of peace came back to the Worthings, though Emily discovered that enforced peace was not at all calming. When Anne and Victoria left Tripton to visit Landhilton with Jonah Wingrave, Emily felt the loss of company, but also that Reddester Hall was completely empty as Mary had left shortly after news of Peter's capture. Anne wrote to Emily and expressed the same dulling of spirits that came with the Wingrave family, and hope that it would be over soon because Mr. Welles waited for her.

Emily took to her old habits; reading in the drawing room, teaching Genevieve music, spending her pocket money at the bookseller. She began to feel much more like her old self, though now with an undertone of jaded bitterness. Her ability to trust had been damaged, and time did not mend it with much

success. Capt. Wingrave had been like the sunshine on a closed
bloom, coaxing it open only to sink behind the clouds and leave
it in darkness. Cold and vulnerable, Emily closed her feelings
away much tighter than before, vowing that no promise of
sunshine would tempt her.

Even Bridget could not cheer up the house, having been
separated from Mr. Annesley for several weeks. She had been
certain he would return to Tripton before the Worthings took a
house in Dunbarrow that winter, for that was months away, but
he did not. None of them, it seemed, could persevere past the
enormous fear that had been struck into their hearts. Even
knowing Peter was alive, the whole family now comprehended
what it would be like to mourn one of their members. The
specter of grief hung over the parents, and the sisters.

At last, Lord Worthing was pried from his farms, and
duties that amounted to little more than fussing during the cold
weather, and they made haste to Dunbarrow, for Bridget's sake.
The Worthings took a manor by the name of Daylily House. It
was not so grand as the permanent home of the Annesleys, but
for a winter home, its significance shone. Mrs. Annesley called
on them immediately, both wanting to gain advantage over
other socialites, and to satisfy her curiosity.

"Miss Worthing, Miss Bridget! So good to see you
again," she greeted them in the drawing room.

"Absolutely, Mrs. Annesley, we are honored by your

visit," said Emily.

"Excuse Edward for not joining me today, he's been away for several weeks now but I expect him back any day now," said Mrs. Annesley.

"We should be glad to see him," said Bridget. Emily tried to assess how her sister felt and still pay their guest every attention.

"Ma'am, this is my father, and mother, Lord and Lady Worthing. And my youngest sister, Miss Genevieve," said Emily.

"My, what a pretty young lady! Taking after your sisters?" chuckled Mrs. Annesley. Genevieve could only blush and giggle in response. "Well, you are all just in time for my ball. It is but twelve days away, I feared you would miss it if you delayed any longer."

"My apologies, it took more effort than usual to close up business this autumn," said Lord Worthing.

"He means it took more effort to get him away from business when there is nothing to do," said Lady Worthing.

"Quite right! I understand the Worthings to be a productive family, and it seems they come by it honestly," said Mrs. Annesley. Their guest did not stay too long, so immersed was Mrs. Annesley in the details of her ball that everything needed her attention. Bridget brightened after hearing that Mr. Annesley had not only been busy, but would return to Dunbarrow soon. And return he did, though not without some confusion on Bridget's part.

"He has not yet visited, though the ball is tomorrow, and he has been here five days," she mumbled to Emily that night.

"Perhaps Mrs. Annesley has taken him over for ball preparations?" Emily thought it rather suspect herself, but that was not to be talked of. Bridget needed support or she would enter the ball looking wretched.

"What could a man have to say about it? They have enough servants, and he cares so little for those particulars. At least that is what he told me," said Bridget.

"Let us hear what he has to say for himself before we put words in his mouth or motivations in his mind," said Emily.

Gazing up at Amberose again had an odd nostalgic quality, though Emily had never seen it in its full splendor. In the dark, lit by the warm orange glow of tinted lanterns in the windows, Amberose was the stuff of fairytales. Genevieve had been most unhappy to stay with Ms. Pierce at Daylily, but Lady Worthing would not be budged on the matter. She insisted that Genevieve was yet too young, and would brook no arguments.

"You'll have to paint Genevieve a picture of this," said Emily to Bridget.

"Aye. For all of us to remember," said Bridget. Emily kept a firm hand on her sister's arm as they were ushered inside, comforting her as Mr. Annesley came within sight. He and Mrs. Annesley stood on a circular dais at one side of the ball room, to differentiate the host and hostess.

"I cannot go over," said Bridget.

"What? Why?" inquired Emily.

"Something has changed, I can see it, in his face. He did not come to Tripton, he did not come to visit on purpose. He was sending me a signal," said Bridget.

"That is ridiculous!" was all Emily could say.

"No, it's right there, in his expression. An unhappy hardness that is not my Edward," said Bridget. She looked down in pain as Emily took stock of Mr. Annesley. To her, he appeared bored, and, truthfully, exactly as Bridget had said. He caught sight of them, lingering near the entryway, and his eyes widened. He collapsed his surprise into forced boredom and looked away.

"That is inexplicably odd. What would change him so?" said Emily, more to herself.

Bridget shook her head, "I do not know, but I am not wanted here. Excuse me while I attend Mama." Dissatisfied with this turn of events, Emily wove in and out of the guests, on her way to the dais under the guise of greeting Mrs. Annesley.

"You look lovely, dear sister," said an all-too-familiar voice from behind her.

"Peter?" she said, whirling. There he stood in a freshly-pressed uniform, with no cane to aid him.

"Have I been forgiven yet?"

"Why are you here?" she said, embracing him with enthusiasm.

"As Capt. Wingrave's second, I go where he goes, so here I am," said Peter.

"Do you say that simply to upset me?" said Emily.

"Do not be cross. I could not be here without him. As a lowly Swordtenant I hardly rate leave. Besides, he was invited, being one of Mr. Annesley's oldest friends. You're lucky we could not arrive before this afternoon or we may have visited," said Peter.

"He is really here?" inquired Emily. At once, she felt ill.

"Yes, Emily, haven't I already said so? He's over there, speaking with Mrs. Annesley now," said Peter. Emily breathed out as she realized she almost walked straight up to him. He was, in fact, next to Mrs. Annesley, slightly hidden by a plant overhanging the marble railing.

"Oh, I think this might be enough to convince Bridget to go home early with me," muttered Emily.

"Miss Emily! How wonderful it is to see you!" Mr. Corey strode up to her with all familiarity still intact and kissed her hand. "I was about to visit your family in Tripton before I heard you would all be coming here for the winter."

"Hello, Mr. Corey. Peter, this is Mr. Corey, we met

during our last visit to Dunbarrow. Mr. Corey, my brother, Swtnt. Worthing," said Emily. Suspicion soured Peter's bliss upon seeing Mr. Corey's manner toward Emily.

"Charmed," said Peter. Capt. Wingrave had moved toward Peter after greeting the Annesleys, until he saw Emily, and then decided to keep walking on past them. Peter reached out as he passed and tapped his shoulder, enough to stop his progression.

"Worthing, are you in need of something?" inquired Elijah with a raised brow.

"I thought you would like to compliment my sister on the stunning arrangement of her... hair," said Peter. Capt. Wingrave took stock of the small circle and, while confused, nodded.

"Yes, it's a fine artistry you managed with your curls," said Capt. Wingrave.

"Thank you, sir," said Emily. He gave Peter a hard look.

"I've just met Mr. Corey, who happens to know Emily well since last summer. Are you acquainted?" said Peter. Mr. Corey smiled easily at Capt. Wingrave.

"No, I've not had the pleasure," said Capt. Wingrave.

"Oh, well then, Mr. Corey, this is Capt. Wingrave, a particular friend of ours from Tripton," said Peter, "He and Emily play the best duets."

"Really Peter, we have not played in months and are not

likely to anytime soon," said Emily.

"Indeed, Miss Emily and I were learning a duet before she had to leave so suddenly," said Mr. Corey, "Perhaps we shall play it tonight? Do you remember it, Miss Emily?"

The light of comprehension in Capt. Wingrave's eyes made Emily feel as if she were about to be in the middle of a dog fight.

"I already knew it. I was teaching you, remember Mr. Corey?"

"Yes, of course. I've been practicing in anticipation of your return. I hope that you'll spend a great deal of time here in Dunbarrow now that you are in society here," he said.

"I hope that she does not, for our family would miss her in Tripton," said Peter.

"But, Miss Emily is too grown to have that much attachment to her home. Indeed, some may think it is only a matter of time," said Mr. Corey. Emily could feel the heat leaving her skin as the three men stared each other down like statues that had grown eyes.

"Excuse me, I was on my way to greet our hostess," said Emily.

"Allow me to escort you," said Capt. Wingrave. Mr. Corey narrowed his eyes, but Emily took the Captain's arm. Peter and Mr. Corey parted in their wake.

"Such interesting friends you've made," said Capt.

Wingrave.

"Mr. Corey is very attentive," said Emily.

"To you, or your status?"

"What an assumption! Apparently my myriad charms are only worthwhile to you."

"Nonsense, but I very much doubt that a man like Mr. Corey can appreciate them to their fullest."

"You speak very harshly for one whose last words were to tell me never to think of him again," said Emily.

"I am still keeping my word to you. And it matters not what I said, you take pleasure in doing the opposite, therefore you must have been thinking of me profusely." Emily's mouth dropped open.

"I have spent my thoughts much more wisely than that, on those who can and have attached themselves to me," she said.

"It is not by my doing that we are not attached. Or do I need to ride off to battle and let the Sypass beat me senseless to prove my despair?"

"Do not shirk responsibility for this, it is by your actions, and those you choose to condone."

"As you wish, Miss Worthing," said Capt. Wingrave as he delivered her to Mrs. Annesley, then vanished into the crowd. Emily politely chattered with her, and completely forgot to speak with Mr. Annesley.

Mr. Edward Annesley did not speak to Bridget until it would have been absolutely impolite to ignore her. Her wounded countenance and weak smiles cut Emily to the bone as he addressed her.

"And Miss Bridget, how are you?" he said after paying his respects to Lord and Lady Worthing.

"I am well, sir, thank you," she said. With none of her usual vigor, Bridget made a pathetic impression.

"Good, good. We here in Dunbarrow have been enjoying mild weather," said Mr. Annesley.

"What a pity. Not as much wind music," said Bridget. He gave a forced beat of laughter.

"Most people do not believe in wind music. I hope you enjoy the evening," he said, taking his leave. He met Emily's eyes as he left, and whatever he saw there startled him. She could only imagine it to be an uncontrollable fury, breaching her practiced visage.

"Bridget," she said, going to comfort her sister.

"It is alright, Emily. I told you before, I want someone who will look at me with love forever, not just for a time," said Bridget. Dread swirled in the notes as musicians warmed up to play. Emily whispered to herself that nothing hugely terrible could ensue if she begged forgiveness to stay with her sister. No one could possibly argue that Bridget looked well.

"Emily, dear sister, let's have a dance," said Peter as he snuck up behind them.

"I... I need to stay with Bridget," said Emily. Her excuse made no impression on him.

"Bridget has Mama, and I want to speak with you. Come," said Peter. Of all the people in her life, Peter ignored her scowling the most.

"I will be fine for a bit without you, Emily. Do not spoil the ball over me," said Bridget.

"Fine, let us get this over with," said Emily. She glared and Peter smirked as they began the dance within sight of Capt. Wingrave, a slow, flowing performance.

"I do not like your friend," said Peter. He did not bother with a gentle lead into the conversation, just like him.

"Oh? Which friend? For I have many," said Emily with no little snark implied.

"He is not the equal of certain other people," said Peter, turning aside her play at sarcastic insensibility.

"Certain other people should not be as high in your estimation as they are."

"As high, and more. Being his second, I've seen all I need to know of Capt. Wingrave. He is beside my father in wisdom, and just as honorable." Emily squinted at him.

"Should I take Mary Wingrave into my confidence and profess her to be a shining example of women then? You are

journeying toward traitorous remarks, sir," said Emily. Peter
sighed.

"I know it must seem that way. Again, I pose to you
that we don't know the whole story, and that perhaps the
Wingraves have a just reason for their behavior," said Peter.

"You don't know," Emily muttered. Peter cocked his
head.

"You do. What is it?"

"It seems our family is just as guilty of keeping secrets.
Regardless, you are advising me to hurt a friend to please one
who is not even that to me. The wisdom of that rings hollow."

"I am advising you not to overlook how much in love
one is, while the other relishes in your convenience. You will not
tell me, what you know?" The room spun despite the slow
tempo, and Emily nearly stumbled.

"Let us not speak of love. It cannot be satisfied, and may
as well not exist. It would bring us all less pain. Do not apply to
me for answers. Ask your Captain," said Emily. Peter colored.

"I know my Captain, and that he thinks of you. Do not
slight him in a childish fit of revenge," said Peter. The earnest
manner of his request kept Emily from storming away mid-
dance, and sealed her lips against angry retorts.

"I loathe that you like him," she said. Peter laughed at
her petulant pout.

"He has a host of good qualities, and is, I daresay, quite

handsome in his green coat." Emily blushed and laughed.

"As you are, brother. I almost never got to see it. Take care to come back to Tripton wearing it and Mary may accept you yet if she ever returns to Reddester." Peter gave a half-hearted smile.

"If that was all it would take. Besides, I would not ask again after being refused."

"Then by your standards, Capt. Wingrave is lost to me," said Emily. Peter turned a sharp eye on her.

"You refused him?"

"I think so. I cannot be certain he was really asking."

"You should not have done so," said Peter.

"You were not there, having the conversation we'd just had. Don't badger me, Peter." He gave an annoyed huff. The dance ended and they walked toward Lady Worthing.

"If you--" Peter started.

"Miss Worthing! I have not seen you in ages!" cried Mr. Sharp, intercepting them. Were it not for his genuine smile, Emily might have groaned at the appearance of him.

"Hello, Mr. Sharp, allow me to introduce my brother, Swtnt. Worthing." The men nodded, Mr. Sharp more jovial than Peter who suspected exactly the truth.

"How have you been in these weeks? I had a fine hunt, but could do with another dance, if you'd consent to it and your brother is agreeable," said Mr. Sharp.

"I have been very well, and Peter is agreeable, thank you," said Emily, switching partners. She did not give Peter time to object because she could see that he wanted to. Mr. Sharp's happy manners soon made her ignore the lecture Peter had delivered. Emily had no obligation to slight others in favor of Capt. Wingrave after all that had happened. She wasn't accepting their proposals, just dancing and talking.

"I heard that you left Dunbarrow earlier than planned. Mr. Corey was heartbroken for a few minutes until another party was had," said Mr. Sharp, "I'm sorry for the confusion you must have gone through, thinking your brother dead."

"I would have taken confusion over despair. We thought he was gone for an entire month. It was the worst time of my life, but it is over now. You said you had a fine hunt?" said Emily. Speaking to Mr. Sharp of her troubles felt out of place within his casual banter.

"Oh yes, didn't actually kill many things, I'm not a good shot, but being outdoors with my friends is reason enough to go," said Mr. Sharp, "I only wish the servants at the lodge we hunt were more respectful. You know, I had to ask three times for them to serve my breakfast in my room before they understood it should be served that way every day? And they never got my boots really clean, still scuffs around the soles." All of the good humor Mr. Sharp inspired deflated at this entitled speech. She frowned, but tried to salvage the discussion.

"How were the servants to know, unless you expressly wished it, that your breakfast should be delivered to your room?" she inquired. Mr. Sharp laughed, though now it had a different tone to it than she'd noticed before, an unbecoming, and cavalier haughtiness.

"After the first day of my requesting the correct behavior, I expect them to get it right the second day. But that is droll, let us talk of the ball," and so he did, with little encouragement from Emily. Had she not noticed that Mr. Sharp's carefree spirit came from want of responsibility? With a shake of her head, Emily chided herself for being so absent-minded during her first stay at Amberose.

Mr. Sharp released her from his company only for Mr. Corey to claim her for a dance. He spoke of many things, disparaged the military service of heirs, flattered her figure in her gown, among other superficial statements. Peter's opposition to their friendship did not at all please him. Emily fell to one line of thought that intrigued her, and so acted upon it.

"I am so happy you are come back to Dunbarrow, and wish that you had never gone. I was desperately lonely," said Mr. Corey.

"You said, Mr. Corey, that you thought of visiting Tripton, but didn't because we would be wintering here. It was months away though, and I wonder that you had the patience to be without my company since you so enjoyed our time together," she said. His mouth worked open and closed for several seconds before he smiled politely.

"I had business," he said, "It could not be delayed, or I would have visited you anywhere."

"Oh, I see. That is understandable," she said. Emily could not admit disappointment, for her feelings had not been caught up in the schemes of the Dunbarrow gentlemen, but she did feel pity for them. Perhaps they were self-aware, and acted knowingly in such a way, or perhaps not, and Mr. Corey, and Mr. Sharp had made designs on the wrong woman. She pondered them by herself in the courtyard after escaping the next invitation to dance. Emily leaned against a tall hedge on the outskirts of the lit ballroom, close enough to hear, but not within sight. With no peace of mind to be had, Emily sucked in a breath and rejoined the party, thinking she could finally beg an unwillingness to dance. She returned to her mother, not realizing who Lady Worthing spoke to until it was too late.

"Oh, Emily, I was talking with Capt. Wingrave of Peter's capture. Forgive me for morbidity," said Lady Worthing.

"If I were his mother, I'd want to know as well. Excuse me, I'll go get a beverage," said Emily.

"Once you have refreshed yourself, I hope to have the pleasure of dancing with you again, Miss Worthing," said Capt. Wingrave. He smiled, knowing he tested her patience.

"Thank you, I'll be happy to dance, again," said Emily.

She drank her punch in front of him with agonizingly slow progress. He continued smiling, an infuriating gesture of serenity.

Emily glanced about the room, and started at seeing the Cantons in attendance. Fortunately for her nerves, Dinah was not with them. Shrugging it off, Emily sipped again.

When at last she had finished, Capt. Wingrave raised his eyebrows in satisfaction.

"Shall we?" he said. Emily nodded. They did not speak for several steps.

"How has your day been, Miss Worthing?" he inquired.

"With the exception of seeing Peter, rather disheartening," said Emily.

"I am sorry to hear that, but how is it possible that you can be disheartened with your friends around you?"

"It's a lesson I've been learning these last few months, that friends can be disappointing."

"Friends, family, humans. You're putting your trust in the wrong race if you wish to be constantly transparent and in lock step with your fellows. I, for example, have had the great agony of a promise being broken to me this very day, but I am not in ill spirits," said Capt. Wingrave.

"Dare I ask what promise has been broken?"

"You don't remember? Made by yourself, you promised me that I could have every dance."

"Before, when I thought you cared enough for me to stay my friend, I made that promise."

"There were no conditions attached, unless you are positing that there are certain circumstances under which a promise can be broken." Emily glared at Elijah's smug grin. She wanted to say something that would hurt him, that would cause him the pain she had felt, but none of the venomous words would be spoken.

"In making friends here, I took your advice. Was it not you who criticized my lack of knowledge? I have been studying the masculine sex as suggested, and I still find them wanting. It is by your design really, that I made an effort to know Mr. Corey, and Mr. Sharp," said Emily, "It would be rude to befriend them, and then refuse to dance." Capt. Wingrave scoffed.

"You would search out men of character among the high ranking gentlemen of Dunbarrow?"

"Should I instead venture onto the battlefield and seek a husband there? I've been to the country, and the city, and none of my examples of manhood fit your idea of experiencing men." Capt. Wingrave laughed.

"If you are naturally drawn to men like Mr. Corey it is no wonder why your examples don't fit my ideas." Anger tinted Emily's cheeks.

"Do your ideas include men that keep secrets?" said Emily.

"My ideas include men who act justly, with attention to their duties that spring from love."

"Some love. Not all." The bitterness drew Capt. Wingrave up short.

"I am a damned man, Miss Worthing, destined to choose who I hurt, instead of whether I shall. Would you choose your lover over your mother and father? Your brother and sisters? Would you gratify your own happiness at the cost of theirs?" said Capt. Wingrave.

"You've been duped then, Capt. Wingrave, into thinking that your family has been made at all happy by the deception you so valiantly uphold. They may still be in good standing in society, but they are miserable. I would give up my station and live as a milkmaid before I let it hold me captive," said Emily. She walked away from the dance, mid-step, followed closely by the Captain. There were whispers, but with a polite nod from Capt. Wingrave, they were dispelled. Emily plotted a course for the cool air of the courtyard, hoping it was just as empty. With the exception of a few inebriated guests, it still was.

"You can make that choice for yourself, but what about your family? What about the servants and services they employ? We are noble by birth, and while that comes with privilege, it comes with responsibility. We are not single entities, making decisions for only ourselves. Would you also turn your mother, Bridget, and Genevieve into hardworking milkmaids?" said

Capt. Wingrave.

"That is not my circumstance," muttered Emily.

"No, but it is mine. If you cannot or will not see the love behind my choices, then you are not as I thought you were," he said.

"At least you've had the opportunity to accurately make out my character. If it displeases you at last, then I can only bid you good day, sir." Emily kept her eyes locked with his.

"You have never displeased me," he said, "Just as I am not displeased with the rain for causing a flood. The rain is beautiful, and necessary, just as you are."

"Stop this! Everything you say is confusing. Why did you falsely propose to me if you wouldn't choose a lover over your family?"

"Had my offer been accepted, I would have, in a way, chosen you over them. I would have said farewell to them, and disassociated myself from the house of Wingrave, so that they could live without fear of my choice, and I could live with the greatest part of my happiness. It would not be the impeccable connection I can offer a lady as the heir to Landhilton, but I had hoped you cared enough for me that it would not matter." His eyes offered her his hand again, even if he did not speak the words.

"You would ask me to sentence you to a life without your family? Do you think I am selfish enough to accept something so against your best interests?" said Emily.

"It is as I expected then, a hopeless business. Allow me to return you to your family," said Capt. Wingrave. Emily accepted his escort, feeling as if every step were her last in his company. Elijah was silent for a long time after that, leading Emily back to her mother where Mr. Corey waited.

"Miss Emily? May I ask permission to visit you in the morning? It is of great import," said Mr. Corey. Capt. Wingrave stiffly stood, waiting for her answer.

"If it is important, I can spare a moment in the morning," said Emily. Mr. Corey nodded his thanks and took leave. Emily took Capt. Wingrave a few steps away to say goodbye.

"It has been... an enlightening evening, sir. I wish you well," she said.

"Do not accept his proposal out of spite," he said, "You'll come to regret it." Emily gazed at him in shocked hurt.

"I would not compromise my entire future that way. If I accepted, it would be out of sound judgement."

"No sound judgement could lead you to him."

"This is hardly any of your concern," mumbled Emily.

"It is, as his rival. Why do you think he chose to ask for a meeting in front of me?"

"You cannot rival someone when you're not in competition," said Emily. Capt. Wingrave smiled again.

"You may only take me out of the competition when you no longer think of me, and I've already explained that you were thinking of me profusely."

"Yes I was, thinking of how much you hurt me, over and over again. You come with shadow, and I will not live in it."

"That is not at all how I would have you remember me," he said, raising her hand to his lips. Elijah circled around her, and bent close to her ear. "I knew when I saw you at Fort Jennings that despite trying to end this, I would never stop offering myself up to you. I will always be waiting for you to choose me." Emily could not turn for a full ten seconds, and by then Capt. Wingrave was gone. She could find him nowhere at the ball, or in the manor. His disappearance made her so unhappy that Emily cried herself to sleep that night.

"Mr. Corey to see you, ma'am," said the maid. Lady Worthing, Emily, and Bridget stood to welcome their visitor. He made no hesitation in stating his purpose.

"Good day, Lady Worthing, I was hoping to be granted a private audience with Miss Emily this morning." Lady Worthing nodded, barely letting her surprise into the look she gave Bridget.

"Bridget and I will see to tonight's table setting," said Lady Worthing. Bridget flinched, knowing what Mr. Corey sought in juxtaposition with her own troubles, and thinking of table settings, which did not interest her in the least.

"Yes, Mama," said Bridget. They exited with rushed decorum only to mill about in an adjacent sitting room to wait for news. Emily smiled at Mr. Corey, a polite, but unexcited show of civility. He slowly stepped toward her.

"Miss Emily, I have not had the pleasure of meeting many women with your qualities. In addition to superb breeding, you are accomplished, beautiful, and possess great humility. As an Annesley, I feel the responsibility upon myself and Edward to choose spouses of sense as well as station." Mr. Corey paused to walk around the room, though whether he prolonged his purpose intentionally, Emily did not know. Something about how he included Edward Annesley in his speech struck her. Spouses of sense? Was that something impressed upon the Annesley heirs? She kept the thought for later examination.

"Upon recognizing your superiority over all other women, I endeavored to secure your affection, and to convey mine," Mr. Corey said as he stopped his stroll in front of her and took one of her hands. "I feel that one day, I will love you as greatly as any hero in a tale. So, it is my prerogative here today, to inform you of my intent to make you an offer."

Emily waited, for any sort of continuation, but Mr. Corey spoke no further, and obviously thought he had said something of importance.

"I confess, Mr. Corey, to a bit of confusion as to how I should reply. You are telling me that you will propose?"

"Yes," he said with pride.

"I thank you, then, for the information," she said.

"You are most welcome. I did not want to leave you with any doubts," said Mr. Corey.

"Peter!" came a muffled cry from the hall. The door was summarily thrown open and Peter came into the room with no ceremony or acknowledgement that he had just interrupted a private conversation.

"Good morning sister! Isn't it a bit early for guests?" said Peter.

"You may be correct sir, I shall be on my way. Miss Worthing," said Mr. Corey, smiling and giving Emily a wink. When he had gone, Emily turned to her brother.

"That was abominably rude. I'm sure Mama told you that Mr. Corey asked specifically to speak with me, alone," Emily chided him.

"I could not let that reach a conclusion. He may have been so pitiful that you were induced to accept him."

"Well, it had concluded," Emily huffed, and left for the other sitting room where her mother, and Capt. Wingrave waited. Bridget had not obsessed over the outcome then.

"Do you mean to tell me he proposed?" said Peter,

following her into the room.

"Peter," she hissed.

"So, that was a smile of success?" Peter asked with incredulity, causing alarm all around.

"Really, Peter! Have you gotten so coarse over your military service that you'd discuss such things out in the open?" said Emily. Lady Worthing was so caught up that she said nothing, waiting only for the final word from her daughter, while Capt. Wingrave's shadowy temper took over his face.

"Fine," he said, dragging her back into the hallway, "Now answer the question."

"What has gotten into you? This is none of your business," said Emily.

"If you accepted him, I may disown you," said Peter.

"What a horrible thing that would be, to have you never speak to me again, of your Captain and your notions!"

"Little sister... Do not forget who knows you best. I could, if prevailed upon, recite many instances during your childhood that you would wish to keep secret, and perhaps Mama would join me in mirth. I'm sure the Captain would be most diverted," said Peter. Emily worked her mouth like a fish, opening and closing with no sound.

"And to think that I missed you, cruel boy! He did not propose, I could not accept him," said Emily.

"I stopped him in time? Marvelous!" Unaffected by her

stab at his imprisonment, Peter grinned.

"No, he had not intended to."

"Then why the audience?"

"That is outside the bounds of what you requested with your threats," said Emily.

"And you will not accept him, should he ask?" inquired Peter. Emily glared at him and returned to her mother. Lady Worthing and Capt. Wingrave made a wonderfully awkward picture, sitting in discomfort across the room from each other. The whole morning had been so comical already, that Emily laughed when she saw them, so stiff in their seats.

"Emily, get a hold of yourself! This is no time for laughing," said Lady Worthing. Peter joined his sister in a jovial release of tension. Emily wrested her mouth into a lopsided smile, only bursting with chuckles every few moments instead.

"Did Mr. Corey conclude his business here?" inquired Lady Worthing when Emily and Peter finally sat.

"Oh yes, he was quite satisfied when he left," said Emily. Peter recognized this as teasing Elijah, and scowled at her.

"That is well," said Lady Worthing, "Did he also visit your father?"

"You know Papa is not at home," said Emily, giving away nothing.

"Oh," said Lady Worthing.

"I doubt that he would. Mr. Corey has no business with

Papa," said Peter. Capt. Wingrave looked at Emily in annoyed amusement and shook his head. She pretended not to see, instead leveling her gaze at Peter.

"How long shall we have the pleasure of officers in our house? Is Fort Jennings taking care of itself?" she said. Capt. Wingrave's infuriating, serene smile did not wear on Emily as it usually would. Like one who had been underwater too long, she desired to breath the air free of the sadness surrounding their impossible romance.

"The winter months tend to take more life than the fighting if both sides persist, so other than current border keeping, we are in stasis. We are in Dunbarrow on assignment," said Peter.

"A secret assignment," said Capt. Wingrave, with no little emphasis on the secret. Emily colored in rage. How dare he treat it like a joke!

"Good, it will keep you busy. Excuse me, Mama, I think I should tend to Bridget," said Emily. She rose, and with a hateful look at the Captain, exited their company.

10. The Long Cold

"He did not propose?" inquired Bridget.

"No! He told me that he would propose, sometime in the future. Apparently, he wanted to erase my doubts," laughed Emily.

"What rubbish," said Bridget, joining in.

"Oh, and that he would love me, eventually," Emily continued.

"Is that right? Excuse me while I swoon!" Bridget draped herself over the corner of the bed.

"I am glad he did not propose, actually. Perhaps, in putting it off, he will never get back around to it, and I will not need to come up with an adequate refusal for his adequate affection," said Emily, "But he did say other things that I wanted to speak with you about."

"Oh?" said Bridget, lapsing back into poor spirits upon hearing Emily's tone.

"He said that responsibility had been impressed upon he and Edward, that they were told to choose spouses of sense. Does that sound familiar?" Emily sat on the bed next to her sister as Bridget became rigid under the subject.

"No, it does not. Mr. Annesley spoke of the wonders of Dunbarrow often during our time together, but not so much of his family."

"I cannot explain his sudden distance, unless something happened whilst we were absent, that would affect his feelings." A knock on the door sounded.

"Mr. Annesley come to visit, misses." Bridget and Emily straightened themselves in astonishment.

"Why on earth would he visit after treatment like that?" said Emily. They made haste to the sitting room, where their mother, the Captain, and Peter spoke with Mr. Annesley.

"Good day, ladies," said Mr. Annesley, bowing, "I've come to ask Miss Emily to walk with me downtown." Confusion rang in the mind of everyone, like the thinnest of glass cups played by a musician. It broke when Emily answered.

"A walk sounds... pleasant, thank you. Allow me to dress for it." Mr. Annesley nodded and resumed speaking to Lady Worthing, though she'd been overwhelmed with the mixing of signals that day she hardly paid attention. Emily took Bridget with her, more of a rescue, so that she wouldn't have to sit with Mr. Annesley while Emily prepared.

"What is the meaning of this?" whispered Bridget as Emily collected her bonnet, gloves and jacket.

"I have no idea. This morning has been one of the most awkward in my history."

"Why did you accept his invitation?"

"I'm curious to hear what he has to say. To go to all this trouble to invite me solely, I should think it important," said Emily. Bridget said nothing. "You wait here, and I will tell you all about it when I get home. I promise."

Capt. Wingrave did not appreciate Mr. Annesley's asking Emily for a walk, and it was made plain in his every feature as they left. She sighed at the rather odd state of the day, unprecedented emotions spilling over, turning sensible people into petty creatures, herself included.

"What does a lady sigh for?" said Mr. Annesley.

"Many reasons, sir. Just now I wondered at the purpose of this exercise," said Emily. Even with the fine weather, a slight breeze still stole around corners now and again as they meandered toward the shop district.

"I feel that you and I are connected in an amiable, and realistic way. I merely wish to nurture that connection," said

Mr. Annesley. True shock furrowed her brow.

"Would it not be better if my sister had come?" she inquired. He pursed his lips.

"Allow me to clear the air, so that there is no mistake. Your sister and I had a very agreeable friendship, but certain events over the last weeks have made me realize that she is too whimsical, too fragile to be considered for what would be a challenging, lifelong commitment. If I were to choose a spouse from the Worthings, and join the considerable consequence of our families, I would want a woman beside me that I could depend upon, one that I could be honest with. As much as I thought I felt for Miss Bridget, I've come to the conclusion that her free-spirited character would not blossom under those conditions. You, though, Miss Emily, have proven yourself quite resilient under duress," said Mr. Annesley.

"Please excuse me for the honesty you seem to admire, but you do not love me, and I cannot injure my sister that way," said Emily.

"You see? Even you fear that she could not handle the loss of a suitor, a man who has made her no promises. You know about Jude, have faced his sacrilegious nature, and as much as you might assure me that Miss Bridget would think no less of me for his actions, I am not so certain."

"A suitor? That is not how she views you, as just a suitor," said Emily.

"Yes, she views things very differently from the rest of the world," said Mr. Annesley. He became agitated with her arguments, but she would not let her sister be dismissed.

"That used to charm you, what has changed?" inquired Emily. He looked around to be sure of no eavesdropping, then spoke.

"I left Dunbarrow once again to clean up one of Jude's messes. He leaves debts and women wherever he goes, and as much as we may have disowned him, I am still in charge of controlling the damage he does to our family name. While I was gone, it came to me that I could not tell Miss Bridget what troubled me. When your family came to Dunbarrow, and I saw you last night, standing strong next to your sister who wilted under nothing more than her assumptions about my behavior, I could not help but admit that you would be a better addition to the Annesleys."

"I would not be so daft as to ignore that you feel something for Elijah Wingrave, as I do for Miss Bridget, and I would not ask for your hand before gaining your affection, and likewise I will be courting you like this, to inspire the respect and love a wife deserves," said Mr. Annesley.

"I am sorry, Mr. Annesley, this seems very much like betrayal to me," said Emily.

"It might, at first, which is why I would not ask you to marry me today. Today, I ask for your continued friendship. Is that agreeable?" said Mr. Annesley.

"I cannot refuse friendship, but I must warn you that I am against anything further than that, and will not be held responsible for any disappointment it may cause," said Emily.

"I think we are already disappointed, are we not? That the Wingraves hold their secrets, and that Bridget has developed so carefree. I have never been disappointed in you, Miss Emily," he said.

"But, I know that I am still in ignorance, that you did not, in fact, tell me every piece of the secret. Is this not true?" said Emily. The logical points Mr. Annesley drew vexed Emily to no end. He made sense of everything but her feelings, for Capt. Wingrave, and her sister. Neither would ever forgive her for turning a blind eye to love and marrying for practicality, even if the alternative was a life with no spouse.

"That is true. I admit to lying by omission, and I apologize. Unfortunately, I would not tell anyone the rest of it, except my trusted wife. This future, I have in mind for you, and I'm glad to continue this friendship with our eyes open." Their walk was relatively short after that, as Mr. Annesley seemed to sense that she needed time and distance to absorb all he had said. He bid her farewell at the door. She rushed past the open sitting room where her father greeted Peter and Capt. Wingrave, straight up to her and Bridget's room. Bridget seemed to anticipate the look Emily had.

"Did he propose?" she inquired. Emily looked on Bridget with surprise. How had she guessed his intention so completely? Emily collected herself and remembering her promise, told the truth, though she struggled to rip it from her own throat.

"No. He told me he intends to. That he might eventually love me," said Emily.

"That sounds so different, coming from him," said Bridget. She collapsed in tears.

"I am so sorry, I—"

"No, I know. You have never attempted to engage him. This is all Mr. Annesley's repentance for his brother. He feels he must be a perfect son, according to the ideals of society, and I do not care enough about pretension or status to fill that need. You so naturally blend, level-headed, responsible Emily. I know him, I know him, I know the real him so well!" Sobbing strangled Bridget's voice, and Emily, gathering her sister up in her arms, cried along with her.

"This has been the worst day of my life notwithstanding when we thought Peter was lost. I would never act to harm you this way," said Emily, "But he loves you. I know he does."

"What is feeling if it is all for naught?" Bridget mumbled, "Didn't you used to say that after Capt. Wingrave left?"

"An offhand remark has made a great impact, and I hate

that it was Miss Morley who first brought the idea to my attention," said Emily.

"She may have had the right of it, and we were wrong," said Bridget.

"I cannot believe that, just yet. I told her then that no emotion was for naught if we are to remain of human soul. I would not take back any feeling I have had with regards to Elijah Wingrave, no matter how doomed we seem to be, because when I feel love for him, I am alive, I am human. My blood spills over my veins, and warms every corner of me. You will be strong for me Bridget, you will not give up," said Emily.

"That is the first passionate speech I've heard you make about him. It cheers me that even after what you two have been through, you still love him. I'll aspire to this. Help me up," said Bridget. She cleaned her face, and smoothed her hair, gave Emily a smile, and gestured that her older sister should lead the way downstairs.

Capt. Wingrave and Peter had gone for an appointment by the time Emily and Bridget appeared. Lady Worthing would not be consoled until she knew all that her daughters knew. She listened patiently, but had no advice to offer, only assurances that their current state of misery could not last forever. Several days later, the Worthings were to attend a concert in a small hall patronized by the Annesleys. Emily would have sooner stayed at Daylily House, but Bridget begged her not to be impolite to Mr. Annesley.

"His actions come from a good place, he is scared, scared to misstep as his brother has. I have faith that he will think differently of me in time, and until then I would have you be kind to him, as a friend," said Bridget. Emily exhaled and rubbed her temples.

"If you wish it, but do know if he proposes to me, I don't care what duty he feels, I will refuse," said Emily.

"He is too careful. Mr. Annesley would not propose unless he were sure of your answer."

"Then I am safe forever. Can I please stay here?"

"No! He is mine, and I will endeavor to show him that. You could help me best by going, and being yourself. Do not take offense, but he fell in love with me, despite your many attractions, there must be something I have," said Bridget. Emily agreed to Bridget's premise, but not necessarily the execution.

They arrived early to the event, adding to Emily's misery. The hall had been decorated in rich colors and crystal, and finely arranged for the wealthy guests it attracted. The double doors to the seating area had been propped open, allowing freedom of movement between it and the refreshments, where most of the gathered listeners waited.

"Miss Worthing!" said a woman near here, which Emily

recognized as the rosy-cheeked Miss Jones.

"Miss Jones! Are you in Dunbarrow for the winter as well?" inquired Emily.

"I am here with Miss Wingrave. I'm not sure we'll be staying all winter, but for a few days at least," said Miss Jones.

"Well, I am glad to see you. It is so hard to make friends here, where the ladies are all concerned with garnering influence."

"Oh, I know. I don't come to town except with relatives anymore, otherwise it's quite boring. And Mary recently gave up her usual travel partner." Miss Jones gave her a knowing look.

"Miss Morley? Has she found a husband at last?"

Miss Jones laughed, "Quite the opposite really. She was so sure of Mr. Sheridan that when he refused to pay her any more attention, you know her horrid behavior, she became withdrawn, and would only rant about him. I'm afraid Miss Morley has been shunned from polite society, as long as she remains an antithesis to it. Mr. Sheridan, on the other hand, has found another lady to court." She blushed and they laughed for quite some time about it, until Miss Jones spotted someone in the crowd.

"Elijah! Dear cousin, is that you?" she said, waving to a passing gentleman.

"Why, Miss Jill! I did not think to see you in

Dunbarrow this season," replied Capt. Wingrave as he joined them. His eyes delighted in the tightening of Emily's mouth.

"Did not Mary tell you we were coming?" asked Miss Jones.

"Mary? She is here?" said Capt. Wingrave.

"Oh, yes, here she comes now," said Miss Jones, gesturing with her chin. Mary Wingrave did approach, though Emily had never seen her in such a state. Gone were the smiles, and bright eyes, to be replaced with a tight-lipped frown just for her brother.

"Excuse me, Jill, Miss Worthing, I need to speak with Elijah for a moment," said Miss Wingrave. He challenged her for a moment, frowning back, until at last her glare moved him. Miss Jones was quiet, thankfully, as she and Emily discreetly watched what would happen. Mary's lips moved, quickly and violently. There could be no mistake that what she said to him was not pleasant. They could not see Capt. Wingrave's face, but his body did not move, as if he were only listening to be courteous.

"Emily, have you seen Capt. Wingrave? I can usually find him wherever you are," said Peter. Emily blushed, and Miss Jones smiled with glee at more confirmation of the gossip.

"I don't know what you mean, but he is over there, with his sister," said Emily. Peter drained of color, seeing Mary so agitated, and so close. As Miss Wingrave listened to Elijah's reply, her eyes met Peter's, and the irritation fell away to complete shock. Capt. Wingrave turned to see what had caused the change, and noting his second, shook his head. He finished whatever he'd been saying and bowed, leaving Mary where she stood. After a moment, she walked away, extremely angry. Capt. Wingrave returned to them. Peter looked at the ground, too preoccupied to continue talking.

"I apologize, a matter of business," said Capt. Wingrave.

"I had better tend to her, gentlemen, Miss Worthing," said Miss Jones as she went in search of Miss Wingrave.

"Excuse me, as well. I wish to sit near our parents. I will hold a seat for you, sir," said Peter. Emily nodded.

"Your sister does not look at all pleased with you," she said.

Capt. Wingrave sighed, "I told her I would be in Dunbarrow, and of course, she knew your family would be here as well. She came to scold me for persisting in our acquaintance. Alas, I may have forgotten to tell her that Peter accompanied me."

"What a horrible slip of the mind. You know she hasn't seen him since he... was captured, don't you?" asked Emily.

"It is as I planned. How has your day been, Miss Worthing?"

"I find it odd that you keep asking me that question," said Emily.

"I told you, I am interested in the every day Miss Worthing, as well as one dressed in finery." Emily sighed.

"In truth, I have been worrying about Bridget," said Emily.

"And why should you worry about her?" Mr. Annesley interrupted the conversation.

"Miss Emily, if you are not otherwise seated, I would wish you to sit with my mother and I," he said.

"Thank you very much, Mr. Annesley, but I've already promised to sit with my sisters. They want my musical background at hand for their enjoyment. Perhaps next time," said Emily.

"Very well, Miss Emily. I will see you at intermission," said Mr. Annesley, and he departed, not at all offended. Capt. Wingrave stared after him in great surprise. Emily could not meet his eyes when he turned back to her for an explanation.

"That is why you worry about Bridget. Edward is making a mistake," he said.

"It's very logical, on his part," she said.

"When logic overruns feeling, we shall become closed off, shall we not?" He echoed her words to perfection.

"Is that any worse than bleeding forever, when love erases logic?" said Emily.

"One is honest. You may not think very much of my principles, but I do choose honesty. The concert is about to

begin, shall I escort you to your sisters?" Emily shook her head
to clear the teardrops forming in her eyes.

"Tell me the rest of the secret, if you choose honesty, and
I will marry you tomorrow," she whispered, leaning far too close
to his face. Emily's plea stunned Captain Wingrave into silence.
At last, she nodded.

"Some love, some honesty. Excuse me, Captain," she
said, walking herself into the concert hall.

Bitterness and flashes of heat ruined Emily's enjoyment of the
music, as Elijah Wingrave took his seat in the row behind hers,
next to Peter. At first, the Captain could not take his eyes from
Emily. Peter nudged him, noticing the inattention, and Capt.
Wingrave split the difference by turning towards the musicians
while stealing glances at her. Emily spent the whole of the
performance waiting for it to end, trying desperately to focus on
the sound and arrangement. At intermission, she did not move,
staying in her seat while the rest of her family stretched their legs.
Mr. Annesley realized that she was not yet comfortable with his
preference in public, and sought to make her at ease.

"Are you tired, Miss Emily?" he inquired after
commandeering the seat next to her. Thankfully, Peter had
forced Elijah to accompany him in order to avoid Mary, and
there were no witnesses close enough to hear their conversation.

"A little, I suppose. It's been a rather trying week," said Emily.

"I'm sorry to hear that. Hopefully, your fortunes will improve in the near future," said Mr. Annesley.

"With all due respect, Mr. Annesley, I doubt it. Your own actions have caused a great deal of the trouble." He thought over her words.

"You told Miss Bridget then, of my plans?"

"I didn't have to. She guessed your motives straight away," said Emily.

"I'm glad we all understand each other then. After the winter, your parents will return to their country estate. Where shall you go? Amberose is always open to you, should you wish to stay in Dunbarrow," said Mr. Annesley.

"I'm sure I shall go back to Charlton as well. I find the city full of life, but also full of pretension. I think I prefer people stretched out over land rather than crowded into small spaces."

"Small spaces offer more intimacy," countered Mr. Annesley.

"And less privacy," said Emily, cutting off any romantic ideas. Bridget chose to come back to her seat then, though not alone. She had entered the company of Mr. Sharp, and, with both of them having jovial personalities, carried on with him like two birds in a tree, laughing and talking, back and forth. Mr. Annesley was taken aback by her gleeful mood, and that she ignored him as if he were a straw man in a field. Emily grinned to herself. Though Mr. Sharp was not a good candidate for a husband, and did not seem to seek permanent attachments regardless, he did know how to entertain those around him. With Bridget's quick wit and willingness to laugh, they were the picture of happiness.

"Strong enough," said Emily under her breath to Mr. Annesley.

"Oh Emily, Mr. Sharp just told me a marvelous story of when he traveled to Tadoros, you must hear it," said Bridget. Mr. Annesley took his leave, though he did keep looking back at Bridget as he left. Emily allowed Mr. Sharp to tell his story, listened to the rest of the concert, and went home with the satisfaction of Mr. Annesley seeing the consequences of his ill-advised redistribution of affection.

Despite the shaking of his faith that he did the best thing for everyone, Mr. Annesley persisted with his idea of courting Emily, often visiting and asking her for walks. They did become good friends during that time, but still without deeper feelings. Capt. Wingrave and Peter left for Fort Jennings a fortnight after the concert, without any resolution for Emily. Or rather not the resolution she preferred. Elijah did not speak to her personally again before their business concluded. Emily supposed she should take it as a sign, that neither of them would concede. Lady Worthing had often told her that happiness in marriage was based on compromise and trust, which made Emily laugh when applied to herself and Capt. Wingrave.

The sisters, Genevieve as well, took to enjoying the city instead of playing social games. They visited every manner of landmark and museum, bookseller and library.

To Emily's surprise, Mr. Corey did not call on her again, and expressly avoided her at parties. She wondered if Mr. Annesley had taken the liberty of declaring her out of bounds since he was the heir of the main family. Bridget suffered more by the day when Mr. Annesley did not give up his unsolicited pursuit, as did he when she refused to be sad in his presence.

Towards the end of the season, when it became time for the Worthings to think of leaving, Mr. Annesley came to Daylily.

"Good day, Lady Worthing. May I request the privilege of a private audience with Miss Emily?" he inquired. Bridget fled the room with as much courtesy as she could manage.

"Certainly, Mr. Annesley. I will go see how Genevieve fairs with her lessons," said Lady Worthing, not at all excited as a mother should be at the cusp of a proposal. Mr. Annesley smiled a bit. Not being nervous or in love, Emily could look straight at him without trouble. Any sensible person chiefly concerned with the truth would have interpreted this look as a preemptive refusal, but Mr. Annesley was far from in his senses, so affected he was by his circumstances and pain.

"I am sorry for everything that has happened to cause you pain. I have seen enough of you in the last three months to know that my decision will bear the expected fruit. I will endeavor to make you happy, and share everything I have with you. Let us make the best of our bitter circumstances, let us promise to each other that the grief we have experienced is over. Miss Emily Worthing, will you marry me?" Mr. Annesley sat beside her during his speech, yet another warning to Emily. He did not say he loved her, did not kneel before her as if he might perish at her refusal. He offered her a business arrangement between good friends.

"Mr. Annesley, you must know I cannot accept. I thank you very much for the care and attention that you have bestowed upon me, but my priorities have not changed. I would hurt my sister beyond repair should I walk down the aisle with the man she loves. I would hurt myself by ignoring my feelings, as unfulfilled as they may remain," said Emily. Mr. Annesley's face hardened at the mention of Bridget.

"I have explained to you that your sister would not survive leading the Annesley family, and I will speak no more of her. I came here for your hand. Our marriage may cause a few pains at first, but when everything settles, I feel we can both be content with our lives."

"I disagree and I wonder at your handling of this situation. Do you think that marrying me will erase the strife from our lives? And as to being content, I'd rather stay true to myself than wallow in tepid acceptance. I do not love you, and I will not believe that you love me. You won't even allow the lie to pass your lips."

"I love you, in a way. It's not the dizzying, irrational affection I may have felt otherwise, but it is a stout admiration," said Mr. Annesley.

"I love you as a sibling, too, but no further. I apologize for the failure of your plan. If emotions could be controlled, it would have made sense, at least," said Emily. Mr. Annesley revolved from mortification to thoughtful agitation.

"Why do you insist that she loves me? I've seen her with Mr. Sharp, and everyone is quite convinced he'll finally take a wife," said Mr. Annesley.

"Mr. Sharp has the happy ability to make anyone laugh, no matter how badly they're feeling. My sister is strong and dignified. She would not let you see her suffer." Mr. Annesley rose and peered out the window. He stood there for several moments; Emily felt forgotten. At last, he turned back to her.

"Thank you, Miss Emily, for your time. Your company has been most enlightening," he said.

"Goodbye, Mr. Annesley," she said. After he had gone, it was but a minute before Lady Worthing descended on the room.

"Bridget is in a state upstairs. Did he make you an offer?" said Lady Worthing.

"He did, and was refused. I am ready to go home."

"We all are," sighed Lady Worthing.

ii. Winter into Spring

Spring beckoned, and Charlton welcomed the return of its family. Lord and Lady Worthing became concerned with the desolation of their daughters, for though Genevieve had not been crossed in love, her temperament reflected the attitudes of her sisters. One night, after they had retired to their room, Lady Worthing fretted.

"I miss our girls, Roland. I miss their smiles. It's all changed since the Wingraves came to Reddester," said Elizabeth.

"It's a little late now to think of the negative consequences of their coming. I fear it was inevitable for our children, of bright and true emotion, to experience the pitfalls of reality, though I did not expect it to come from that corner," replied Roland.

"I still can't fathom what Mr. Annesley was about, romancing one sister while proposing to the other. I am glad that Emily and Bridget stood together though, instead of allowing it to pull them apart, glad that Emily has put herself forward as a symbol of our family's connection to one another in my absence. Look at me, getting misty," said Elizabeth, dabbing at her eyes.

"Time is on our side, Eliza. Spring is coming, a chance to start anew," said Roland before snuffing out the light.

When at last the trees grew buds and the morning frost became dew, the Worthings received a letter from Peter stating that he had been released from his active contract and would be returning home within days.

"Oh, here he comes! Is that... the Wingrave carriage?" said Lady Worthing.

"It is! That carriage was forever frozen in my memory, along with Emily's face when the mud soaked her petticoat," said Bridget. Emily was too close to running away to feel humor.

"It's just the carriage, not the man," she told herself. Capt. Wingrave had left her again, and this time there would be no sound reason for his reappearance. He clearly favored Peter, and had a carriage sent for him. The carriage came to a halt, and the door opened. Peter stepped down, the only traveler. Staving off crushed, ridiculous hopes, Emily smiled at her brother. She allowed everyone else to greet him ahead of her, so that she could gather her wits.

"That was a fine carriage you arrived in, Peter, black as night. Did Capt. Wingrave allow you to use it once you journeyed to Tripton?" inquired Bridget after their greeting.

"No, Capt. Wingrave ordered it for us at Fort Jennings. We stopped at Reddester first to allow the Captain off, and then I was driven here," said Peter. Thought and meaning raced around and around, but Emily did not dare ask questions. With every sidelong glance she received, Emily's irritation blossomed further.

"Hello dear brother," she said when Peter stopped in front of her.

"Hello, Emily. Did you hear my news? Capt. Wingrave and I will be working closely together on developing an official school for Endland's officers. It will be founded near here, on the Dunbarrow side."

"That sounds perfect for you, Peter. Congratulations," said Emily.

"It might take years to establish properly so I hope you don't tire of seeing me, or certain other people," he said, leaning close to her at the end as the family walked indoors.

"If I do, I will be sure to inform you," she replied.

The following day after breakfast, Peter disappeared, presumably to begin work with Capt. Wingrave. Emily had not yet come to terms with Capt. Wingrave daring to show his face in Tripton again. He'd left her alone twice, to wallow in self-doubt and regret. Assuming he did stay at Reddester for the duration Peter mentioned, Emily would see him, and often. As she carried a trio of books to the library, she planned on how to avoid the eventuality until her mind was quiet. Emily walked through the door to the great book room, not bothering to look up until she heard voices. Startled, she dropped the volumes.

"Oh, Emily. Papa gave us leave to use the library for work," said Peter. Emily blinked at seeing the Fortcaptain as he rose from his chair.

"Excuse me," she said, leaving the books on the floor, a capital offense, and rushing out. The nerve of the man, coming to her home, and unsettling the effort Emily had made in setting herself to rights. She was through the front doors and on the lawn before she heard footsteps behind her.

"Miss Worthing, it is good to see you," said Capt. Wingrave.

"Is it?" said Emily in a frightful temper as she turned to face him. The months of resigning herself had built her courage back up to its original forcefulness.

"Yes, most definitely," he said. Capt. Wingrave took her in like a man seeing the sunrise for the first time. Emily walked again, toward a natural meadow at the back of the property.

"How could you come here? How could you put yourself in my presence again?"

"I wish always to be near, should you change your mind." Capt. Wingrave sped up to keep pace with her.

"I have not. You may go," said Emily.

"Now who is being rude? You cannot order me about, Miss Worthing," laughed the Captain.

"I am not in a mood for jokes or mocking, sir." He nodded.

"I love you. You've never allowed me to express it fully, so I have done so now. I am so happy to see you." Emily stopped again, and compromised every principle she held dear.

"I am engaged," she said. It was a boldfaced lie, but he did not know that. It was almost true, however. Emily had thrown herself into the idea of being alone, of not being miserable without him. She had committed to it. That he would come back and hope for their relationship to grow challenged her resolve.

He went white, and reached up to feel the beating of his heart, as if to be sure there was a pulse.

"To whom?" Emily had never witnessed more violent wretchedness in a person. His expression was beyond tears of pain, and recognizing such a look had come from herself, Emily hung her head in guilt for causing it, but continued trudging toward the meadow.

"Myself," she said.

"Emily Worthing," he growled, "You will be my undoing."

"Lies don't feel like paradise, do they, Capt. Wingrave?" He followed her still, keeping a distance.

"My family is not speaking to me because I have come here. Mary is frantic that Peter will find out," he said.

"Maybe she should be the one to tell him then. Why does she worry? She refused him," said Emily.

"Do you seriously think she wants to offer him details of her disgrace? She is so ashamed that even if Peter knew, I wonder if she would accept him. Mary wants the best for him, and to her, that does not entail a fallen woman."

"Then you are both blessed with the same flaw of disallowing others to decide what is best for themselves."

"Is that right?"

"Yes, it is. You left Tripton without telling me, without saying goodbye. I had nothing, but to accept your decision."

"It was a choice I was not ready to make. My parents will not disown me, but they will not communicate any further while I insist on associating with your family. Can't you understand that they were hurt? They trusted the Annesleys with their only daughter and she came back to them, unmarried and with child, heartbroken. On top of that heartbreak came another, to give away that child. My sister hates that I am a sworn brother to Peter. She hates that I am here. It is not just fear, but jealousy. I had to make the choice to disconnect myself from them. I can live in their disapproval, but I cannot bear the thought of watching you join with someone else."

"I very much doubt that I will marry, Capt. Wingrave," said Emily.

"That is enough, for now," he said. He left her at the edge of the meadow, bright spring flowers just beginning to lend peeks of their colors.

After a week of banishment from the library during the day, Emily complained at her brother after dinner.

"Why don't you work at Reddester? I would like to be able to fetch a book without waiting until evening," said Emily.

"I would take your suggestion to heart, but I'm afraid it's a selfish reason that keeps us here. The Captain's sister is returning to Reddester within a few days. Besides, there is no call for you to avoid Capt. Wingrave," said Peter.

"In the same breath you contradict yourself. What happened to logical Peter? Why should Capt. Wingrave come here so you can avoid Mary, and you will not do the same for him?"

"He does not wish to avoid you. The opposite, really."

"Then why are you not on my side? I wish to avoid

him," said Emily.

"I'm hoping one of us can be happy in love." Emily had scolded Peter to no avail. He did not relent to her suggestion. Miss Wingrave did return to Reddester, raising many eyebrows of suspicion. Not two days after that, a public assembly was held in Tripton, much to Emily's dismay. What she feared did not come to pass though, something of greater fear took its place. Instead of Capt. Wingrave asking for every dance, he asked for none, standing up with other ladies all evening. Peter followed suit, not sparing even a glance for Mary. From across the room, Emily could tell she felt the statement he made. As the two gentlemen impressed their partners, Emily snuck over to Mary, now without Miss Morley's company to aid her. Before Mary could dispense with pleasantries, Emily held up a hand.

"Miss Mary, for I feel we are familiar enough for such titles, I want to apologize for the manner in which I acted toward you right after Peter's capture. Let us not trifle with the secrets of the past, what is known and unknown, for I think we are both well informed." Emily offered Mary her arm and, blushing bright red with the forward admission Emily gave, Mary took it.

"You would still befriend me, Miss Emily? Knowing what you do?"

"I believe a woman of nine and twenty has much more sense than one of fifteen. You have learned, have you not, the value of discretion?" said Emily. Her objective in taking Mary into her confidence was achieved, curiosity piqued on the dance floor, and suddenly Capt. Wingrave and Peter did not pay as much attention to their steps.

"I have, ten times over," said Mary.

"I have no quarrel with you then." Mary smiled, and allowed her practiced caution to fall slightly. "Our brothers have seen to a fit punishment by ignoring us completely. What shall we do to them?"

"I cannot fault Peter. I abused him."

"You miss the point. We shall talk of many things, and enjoy ourselves despite them," said Emily. Mary nodded, though she did not know what to talk of. At last, she seized a tolerable subject that did not hinge on the men in their acquaintance.

"Was Dunbarrow to your liking?" she inquired.

"I cannot say I would wish to live there, but it was pleasant enough for a visit. I have not been in the greatest of spirits, so that may have affected my opinion," said Emily.

"I am sorry, Miss Emily. I know I am at the heart of your troubles. Before you consent to my friendship, I want you to know that I came here to persuade Elijah to leave."

"Did you also ask him to leave for the border?" Emily bit her tongue, "I'm sorry, that was impertinent."

"I must appear to be a duplicitous person. I

acknowledge that your family in particular has seen an unflattering part of me. No, I did not ask him to go to the border, merely that he check how he encouraged your affection. I didn't know he would translate that into resuming his duties, away from everyone," said Mary. Her sincerity could not be doubted, though Emily treated Mary's statements with caution.

"Yet this time, you are wanting him to leave. Why is that?"

"This time he is set, and he will stay here, throw off our family. I have been working to keep us together for so many years after... I just want him to come home, before he ruins anything."

"Why do you think his being here will bring ruin?" asked Emily. Mary sighed.

"It's nothing against you, but I know he will tell you everything if he stays. You are persistent and principled, it will eventually break his resolve."

"I wish I could apologize for that, but I cannot. It is enough for you and I to know we are on opposite sides."

"Oh, no! I don't want to be... I cannot stand that I am your opposite. Please, let us be passing friends, not enemies. Not too close, but never out of mind."

"As you wish, Miss Mary," said Emily. The dance concluded and the desired reaction transpired. Capt. Wingrave, for Peter would still not approach Mary, only watch from a distance, joined their conversation.

"Mary, Miss Worthing, I see you have found each other's company quite to your liking," said Capt. Wingrave.

"I am surprised you noticed, you merry gentlemen seemed to be having a marvelous time," said Mary. So it was true, thought Emily, that Mary was not pleased with the Captain carrying on with Peter. The two of them had more in common than Emily realized. The both of them fiercely protected their families, had impossible feelings, and an incorrigible brother.

"If Miss Worthing would oblige me, I might continue having a marvelous time," said Capt. Wingrave. Emily smiled at the peace offering, but had no intention of accepting.

"Do not trouble yourself, Captain, Miss Mary and I will be quite content," she replied. Mary raised her eyebrows at the refusal, then watched her brother's face. His irritated frown at Emily's unconcern both unsettled and fascinated Mary, yet had no effect on the target. He stepped closer to Emily.

"May I speak with you privately?" he asked.

Emily sighed, "As you wish, Captain. Miss Mary, I shall return to finish our conversation, if you don't mind." He escorted her to the balcony, a rather romantic setting for the expressions they leveled at each other.

"Do you seek to punish me?" asked Capt. Wingrave without pause.

"Odd that you would ask, for I thought the same," said

Emily.

"You should decide what it is that you're after. Which would you have me do, court you, or leave you alone? Either way, it would please me if you do not encourage Mary's friendship if it's not genuinely meant."

"I have never been so insulted by one who supposedly judges me as a suitable life partner. When have I ever set out to use a person for my own malicious gain? And you have no right to demand that I choose anything. You have left me and returned more times than I can recall now. I am entirely unconcerned with pleasing you, so I will be rejoining the party, whether or not you mind," said Emily who turned to do exactly that. He moved much faster than she guessed and blocked her way.

"Emily, please, I did not mean... I am more than protective of my sister, and it overtook me. I apologize," said Capt. Wingrave, "But on the same hand, I also do not want you speaking to her for another reason."

"I will accept your apology if you tell me what that is," said Emily, crossing her arms to fend off the spring chill.

"She has come here to pry me away from you Worthings. I do not want her to rally you to the cause."

"Wouldn't it be better if she succeeded?" breathed Emily as she looked into his eyes and forgot about the cold altogether. Grief hung between them, engulfing the happy row of the party.

"Can you really think that? Was I the only one who shied from the horror of never seeing you again? Have I been mistaken?"

"No," said Emily, swallowing the lump in her throat, "But seeing you, every day, it is nigh unbearable. I cannot and will not encourage you, by dancing, or giving you my favor. What I want, and what is right lie down different paths."

"You are stronger than I," he said, advancing and leaning in too close. Emily couldn't move, dared not breathe for fear of crying. "Tell me to leave your side forever. I would go."

Emily shook and the tears could not be blinked away.

"I cannot," she said.

"Not one thing, not Mary's objections, nor yours, matter more to me than that." Capt. Wingrave turned away from her toward the light of the hall. She grasped the opportunity to clean her face, and allow the cold air to calm herself.

"Allow me to escort you back to my sister, when you are ready," he said. Emily accepted his arm, though she did not speak until she and Mary were alone.

"He has said something to you," observed the eldest Wingrave.

"He has said many things to me. It's been an occupation of mine, discovering which to believe," said Emily as they resumed their circuit of the room.

"Elijah does not lie, but that does not mean he is always right," said Mary. The two ladies quite frustrated everyone by refusing to dance, instead amusing themselves with cards that someone had produced.

Later, after the Worthings arrived back at Charlton, Peter cornered his sister.

"You are a treacherous maiden," he accused her.

"I warned you that if you continued on with Capt. Wingrave as a close friend that I would take revenge. Mary is a sweet woman, though misguided." Emily hung her bonnet and faced him.

"The entire town of Tripton knows that I proposed to her. I will not be taken in again. Your being friends with her makes me appear foolish."

"As does your friendship with Capt. Wingrave! I say, you are losing your mind, Peter. Do you not remember that I was abandoned and the whole town knew of it? Don't bring societal opinion into this, it does you no credit. We can both do each other favors by not mentioning the Wingraves, don't you agree?" He fumed, but gave in.

"Agreed." Emily nodded in lackluster triumph.

As the horse and rider came closer, Elijah's frightful temper peaked. He waited on the front landing for the rider to ascend the steps.

"How much nerve you must have to face me again, Annesley," said the Captain.

"I came to offer my sincere apologies," said Mr. Annesley, stopping in front of Capt. Wingrave.

"You may leave us, thank you," said Elijah to the stablehands before speaking to Edward, "How could you possibly be sincere? First, you tell Emily the better part of the thing we have so carefully concealed, and then you propose to her knowing that she is the object of my happiness. We were friends once, don't you remember? Before Jude the Ruiner? The intervening years must have taken its toll on your mind for you to think I would ever accept an apology for such actions."

"I did not mean to tell Emily. She came across Mrs. Pratchett in Dunbarrow, found out she was a midwife, and deduced it all on her own. I suppose I can be blamed for indirectly giving her knowledge that led to this conclusion. I am sorry for that. As for the proposal, it was misguided, but a genuine attempt to salvage what I could. Miss Emily helped me to see that I did not love her, and that she could not love me as long as you are alive. I have come again to Tripton to repent, but this time for myself. I have many apologies to make, with little hope that they will all be accepted. But I also come with a warning," said Mr. Annesley. Capt. Wingrave waited, but Mr. Annesley hesitated in giving the purported warning.

"What is it? What's happened?"

"Jude came to Dunbarrow to ask for more money, blackmailing us much like he has Mary, but... this time I've had reports that his behavior is increasingly erratic, nonsensical," Mr. Annesley let out a breath of air, "He's formed a bit of a fascination with Emily, even muttering about her and Mary when he dared to call on me at Amberose. Standing up to him has made her a rankled obsession. Emily's refusal to be charmed haunts him. And..." Capt. Wingrave stood back, eyes wide with fear.

"And...?"

"Once again I apologize. I should have told you what happened during Emily's first visit to Dunbarrow. I could rationalize that I didn't think you'd want to hear it, but in truth I was afraid of what you would do," said Mr. Annesley.

"Spit it out man, enough of your stalling!"

"He tried to kidnap her with the help of my cousin Dinah. They got Emily all the way to the docks before I intervened, hoping to get her on a ship to Tadoros." Edward Annesley had never before feared for his life quite like he did when Elijah Wingrave grabbed his collar and yanked him off his feet, though Elijah was several inches the shorter.

"And you rode like the Devil from Dunbarrow to tell me...?"

"He's coming. Jude found out in town that both Emily

and Mary are back in Tripton. I had a man follow him to be sure. Their magnetism is drawing him here. I don't know when he will arrive. His course seemed to be in this direction, but it wasn't straight," said Mr. Annesley. Capt. Wingrave let out a curse that he wouldn't even utter in Jonah's presence and set Edward to rights, though his collar was permanently rumpled.

"This problem goes away when he arrives, do you understand?" said Elijah. Mr. Annesley nodded, accepting the verdict.

"I have recognized that I cannot change him, and that Jude delights in causing misery. I do not know when he came upon this pastime, but I admit that he is warped beyond repair."

"And you will tell Mary yourself," said Elijah, turning on his heel and marching into Reddester. They found Mary in the drawing room and startled her greatly by arguing at high volume all the way down the hall.

"That's not possible Wingrave, not without alerting everyone at Charlton," said Mr. Annesley.

"Then Peter, at least, must know," said Capt. Wingrave.

"What is the meaning of this? Edward? Are you mad?" asked Mary.

"If only I were the most far gone of my family," said Mr. Annesley as he expressed his purpose in coming to Reddester, with several offhand remarks by a pacing Elijah. Mary listened with the utmost attention.

"Oh, no. If he hurts Emily... Elijah we should leave. You have to know that he'll target whomever we befriend," started Mary, before Edward held up a hand.

"It's too late, Mary. He's crazed, fallen into the true terror of his illogical and destructive ways. It's Emily he wants now."

"Could we persuade Emily to visit Landhilton with us then?" said Mary.

"She would want to know why, and if she knew the reason, she wouldn't leave," said Elijah, more quietly than anything else. Mary gritted her teeth. She'd resolved to imitate Emily's strength until she could muster some of her own. She would not wilt under the fear of Jude.

"You're right. Very well, we stay here. Keep close to the Worthings, Elijah, invite Emily to dinner as often as you think will be accepted when the time draws near. I will prepare myself for the worst." The two men nodded their agreement, acknowledging that she was the only one who should make the decision. Capt. Wingrave sent Mr. Annesley with the butler to find a suitable room.

"Sister, are you certain?" Elijah asked of her when Edward had gone.

"We have run. Now we stand, and I will accept my fate. You have been the best brother, and I can ask you no longer to go against what you deem right and true. This is the end.

Promise me, though, that if Peter shuns me, you will say that I loved him above all things?"

"In truth, I can hardly guess what that trickster is thinking half the time, but I do not fear for you. In his eyes, you are the life he came close to having. But I promise, if the ocean turns red and the sky evergreen, I will tell him." Mary hugged Elijah and kissed his cheek.

"I swear, Capt. Wingrave must be working Peter to the bone these days. He's here when the sun rises, and leaves well after dinner. Ouch!" yelped Bridget when Emily pulled her corset. "That is unnecessary! I am not going out today!"

"You should always look your best, my dear," mumbled Emily. She and her two sisters dressed for the day, Bridget still in her undergarments, while Genevieve and Emily waited for their hair to be done. After being secured, Bridget took an opportunity of Emily's inattention to shove her onto the bed. Emily shrieked as she bounced once and fell to the floor.

"Bridget Worthing! Of all the...!" said Emily as she got up and started shaking her sister. Bridget and Genevieve laughed so hard that Emily could not resist and joined in, tugging at Bridget's braid and ears until she apologized. Even more astonishing, the door was flung open, Peter and Capt. Wingrave ready to do battle on the other side. Bridget quickly slid behind

Emily to hide, looking over the elder's shoulder, still giggling with abandon.

"What are you doing, barging into a ladies' room?" asked Emily. Capt. Wingrave blushed and looked elsewhere, while Peter sternly reprimanded his sisters.

"We thought you were in trouble, but apparently screaming is standard for you silly women," said Peter. Emily handed Bridget a blanket to cover herself, then approached Peter.

"Silly women? I beg your pardon, but what were you expecting? An intruder to have gotten past all the servants this busy morning? We appreciate your efforts, gentlemen, but we don't appear silly here, you do," said Emily. Capt. Wingrave looked down at her, blushed again seeing her hair undone and sweeping across her shoulders, and pursed his lips.

"Take care that you only raise alarm when it's needed," was all he could say.

"You'll know when Emily needs help. I still remember how she screamed when we got the letter about Peter... Oh! I'm sorry, Emily," said Bridget, realizing her error. The remembered pain washed away the color from Emily's face.

"Thank you, Bridget. If you men are done peeping, could you please leave?" said Emily. Peter frowned down at his sister, then unexpectedly embraced her, crushing the air from her lungs.

"Oh really," said Emily, "Have all my siblings forgotten their propriety today? We are not in any danger, so get yourselves back to work." Peter released her, and bowed, grinning a bit.

"We would do anything to protect you, even invade your dressing room," said Peter, "Isn't that right, Captain?"

"You've a crude sense of humor, Worthing. Let us leave these ladies in peace." When they'd gone, the three sisters laughed all the more at Capt. Wingrave's blushing.

The next few days passed with Emily convinced that Capt. Wingrave became more anxious around her. Peter even invited her to sit in on their work and advise them.

"What on earth do I know about schools or the military? I would be of no use," said Emily.

"You've run this house. You know about the supplies it takes to feed and care for everyone. We can design the training program, but it will take a master manager to get us started on the living infrastructure," said Peter.

"For that you will have to hire people anyway, you may as well do so and get their opinions now," said Emily.

"We don't have time for that right now. Will you do me this favor or not?" Peter scowled at her obstinance.

"Fine, I will be in after breakfast," said Emily. With

grudging steps, she went to the library, the last to finish her meal. Capt. Wingrave and Peter leaned over plans, diagrams, and papers of all sorts.

"There you are, Em. Would you like to see the plans?" asked Peter.

"I suppose," she sighed.

"I thought you'd be more enthusiastic. We are building a legacy here. And I will get to work close by Charlton," said Peter.

"I am very excited for you, Peter, but I do not see how I can contribute. I know how to manage a domestic household of no little means."

"I've heard from the shopkeepers that all the orders from Charlton are sensible and not more extravagant than would be expected. I asked for your help, to be transparent. You are a very clever person, and I think you can adjust your ideas to our needs with no trouble," said Capt. Wingrave. Emily narrowed her eyes at him, sensing a grain of falsehood.

"Did you not manage Fort Jennings? Shouldn't this be your specialty?" inquired Emily of the Captain.

"I delegated a lot of our resource management so that I could focus on training and personnel," he explained swiftly.

"Oh, then why not send for those delegates?" Capt. Wingrave smirked, knowing she asked the correct questions.

"It is spring, and the war is back on. Those delegates are

otherwise engaged."

"Really, Emily. You're being cantankerous," said Peter.

"Where are the plans?" she sighed. Emily spent most of
the afternoon avoiding eye contact with Capt. Wingrave. She
made suggestions and told them what she knew, surprising them
both with her extensive logic.

"Mama was ill for two years. More than one crucial
servant had days off, during which I had to figure out how
things would work, especially with Papa gone during the day.
You didn't really expect to get anything useful from me, did
you?" inquired Emily.

"It's not that, it's just as you said. We weren't sure how
much would translate to a large school," said Peter. Still
suspicious, Emily made no reply.

"I will need more help tonight, but I fear I have
trespassed too many times at your dinner table, so at the behest
of Mary who would also like to see you, Emily, I am inviting you
both to dine at Reddester this evening," said Capt. Wingrave.
Being in his company had already unsettled Emily enough for
one day.

"Peter may go, but I shall stay. All of this work has made
me eager for retirement," said Emily.

"Excuse us," said Peter, leading Emily out of the room,
"You wouldn't make me go by myself? Not to Reddester?"

"Come, Peter, I have been at your convenience all day,

despite my feelings. You would ask for more?" said Emily.

"Just today, Em. I cannot refuse to dine with him, but I do not want to be in her company with no one on my side."

"So now I'm on your side? I thought you and the Captain were content as brothers? You've agitated your own blood for him."

"I have not insisted you marry him against your objections, I've merely provided the opportunity for you to have a change of heart," argued Peter.

"I do not want your opportunity. I will go, but only because I am truly loyal to my actual siblings," said Emily.

"Be careful, Emily, of the word actual, it permits no room for the gray areas," said Peter, mystifying her completely.

"What does that mean?"

"Nevermind. I will tell Capt. Wingrave, you may change or ply your feminine arts or what have you."

12. Shooting in the Dark

Mary warmly greeted Peter and Emily and led them into the dining room, already set for the meal. Emily met Capt. Wingrave's stare first, then she noticed their other guest.

"Mr. Annesley? I did not know you had come to Tripton," said Emily.

"Aye, Miss Emily. It is a short visit, bringing news to Wingrave here," replied Mr. Annesley.

"Oh? I should like to hear news of Dunbarrow over dinner," said Emily. The two gentlemen looked away from her in discomfort.

"You are beautiful tonight, Miss Worthing," said Capt. Wingrave.

"Thank you, Captain. I was able to dress in peace," said

Emily. Mary gave her brother a puzzled frown.

"Peace or chaos, you always look lovely," he said, clearing his throat.

"Indeed, in chaos Miss Emily blossoms," said Mr. Annesley, earning him a glare from his host.

"I hope to hear a duet tonight," said Peter, "It as been a dreadful long time since I've heard one."

"I may have forgotten how to play a duet," said Emily, "I've practiced none of them since last summer."

"I would be happy to hear you play anything," said Mary.

"Anything I can do, to please my hostess," said Emily. They sat to dinner, and ate in relative silence. The Wingraves and Mr. Annesley seemed preoccupied by something. After dinner, instead of taking Peter to the study, Capt. Wingrave and he joined them in the sitting room.

"I thought we came so that you could work while I visited with Mary," said Emily.

"I decided it would be best to enjoy our company instead of working. We've been productive and consistent, allowing a bit of respite," said Capt. Wingrave.

"I see. So Mr. Annesley, what news did you have of Dunbarrow?" asked Emily. A servant's cries from the hall cut off his reply. The party as a whole jumped to their feet, ready to help him.

"Master! Master, I couldn't stop him!" cried the butler, as the door nearly came off its hinges, and Jude Annesley strode into the room. He took in the surprise with relish, happily counting Emily among the faces.

"What a gathering," he said.

"Jude Annesley, it is my duty to inform you that you're trespassing, and I will take action if you do not leave immediately," said Capt. Wingrave.

"No, I'm afraid you won't, because if you lay a hand on me, I will tell your guests here what I know, give them a little history lesson," said Jude.

"No. No..." said Mary, struggling to stay calm.

"State what you want, so you can be gone," said Mr. Annesley.

"You should know, dear Edward. I need money to go on living, and since you refused to provide it to me, I had to come here. With the additional pleasure of seeing Miss Emily Worthing again. She is ravishing, as always," said Jude. He walked forward, meeting all eyes in turn.

"You are a cad without honor," said Emily. Her response rattled him momentarily.

"Honor means nothing. It's but lines in the sand, drawn by a few insufferable men for the rest of us to follow. Men who never enjoyed themselves like I would with Miss Emily," said Jude. Capt. Wingrave's darkness rose to the surface at such talk.

"I hope to kill you one day, Jude. I tried once already, and you were lucky others saved you," he said.

"Perhaps eventually, you'll get your wish, but for now... Mary? If you would be so kind as to write a cheque, I'll be on my way," said Jude. Mary looked at the ground, tears dropping to the rug.

"Mary?" said Peter. She met his eyes, the questions and the confusion. She would have to pay Jude in front of him, engage in underhanded business right before Peter. The shame of all the instances she had handed Jude a cheque fell on her. Peter wanted her to be a better woman than that, thought her to be superior to satisfying a snake like Jude. Proving him wrong was too much to bear.

"No," she whispered.

"What?" said Jude, furrows of anger crossing his forehead.

"I won't pay you," said Mary.

"Then I shall start at the beginning, and you can tell me to stop, with money of course," said Jude, "Do the lovely Worthings know that we were engaged to be married?" Silence met his question as the five of them exchanged glances.

"I do," said Emily, in the quiet.

"Oh, and what else does Miss Emily know?"

"I..." said Emily, looking at Peter and Mary.

"Emily knows that you manipulated me into believing

that it was acceptable to lay with my betrothed before the wedding. When I refused to continue with that behavior, you began mistreating me, and when I told you that I..." Mary stopped, tears soaking her gloves as she wiped her cheeks, "That I was with child a week before our wedding, you broke the engagement. You didn't tell your family why, you simply sent me away. Edward only found out last year, and came to Tripton to offer me amends by settling a small fortune on the child." Emily watched Peter more carefully than she ever had. His face went through several stages of shock, and ended with righteous anger focused directly at Jude Annesley.

"You've been practicing for the day when you'd have to admit it, haven't you?" said Jude with a cruel grin.

"I have been practicing since I met Peter Worthing, hoping that one day I would have the courage to tell him," said Mary. Her eyes were fixed downward, her confession without hope.

"How charming. And now the rest of it, Mary. Tell them the rest," said Jude.

"That's enough. You've already humiliated her for fourteen years," said Capt. Wingrave.

"No, I'm not leaving without a cheque or a complete removal of Mary's illusions. The rest, Mary!" ordered Jude.

"I will pay you," insisted Capt. Wingrave. Jude chuckled.

"That is something, that you would pay the man you hate the most. It's delightful, actually. All these years you've been coming to Mary's defense, and here is the ultimate triumph," said Jude.

"No, Elijah. No more. I cannot let this go on," said Mary.

"But..."

"No, brother. It's time," said Mary, "My child was placed with another family, and I thought never to see her again, but when Elijah came back from the border and wanted to take a house, I asked him to settle in Tripton, so that I might know her. She is very well taken care of, and is called by the name I picked out for her—Genevieve."

Emily would have fainted if she were that kind of person, but as such she could only stare. Peter did not seem as surprised as she. Into the sea of turmoil that Jude drank like expensive brandy, Emily spoke.

"Did you know?"

"I knew that Genevieve was adopted, not her lineage," said Peter.

"Amazing, have I crushed two birds with one stone? One fallen Mary, and one broken Emily," said Jude. Emily could not look at Capt. Wingrave for she now understood why he protected her from this last piece of the puzzle. It would not be the ruin of her family because she loved Genevieve any less. If it did permanent damage, it would be because her parents and brother had kept a secret from her, one that she felt need not be kept, exactly as Elijah Wingrave had done.

"Broken? What a foolish man you are," hissed Emily, "As if your sick ways could shatter me. I'm no more broken than you are respectable." Her brazen speech drew ire from Jude and admiration from Mary, too used to being under his boot heel. The cool relief of knowing quieted the embers of fury within Emily for the time being. She met Jude with cold truth and it took away his words, all the words he used to take power over others.

Peter could stand it no longer, and went to comfort Mary. He bent over so that their faces were level, but did not touch her without permission.

"Mary Wingrave, is this why you refused me?" he whispered. Still, she could not look at him.

"Yes. I am not what you should have," she said.

"But you are what I desire," said Peter.

"Still? After hearing all this?"

"Absolutely. The love I offer you is not contingent upon a mistake that you have atoned for."

"How do you know I've atoned for it? I had to give up my daughter," said Mary, tortured face finally rising to see his.

"Because you've just told the truth when you could have continued hiding, and without your daughter, I would be short one lovely sister. Please, accept my hand," said Peter. He held his hand out to her, beckoning an answer to his question. With a smile that would have melted pure winter's ice, Mary took it.

Every moment, Jude lost some of his enjoyment in tormenting Mary. Until he started laughing, Emily hoped he would leave empty-handed.

"Well, isn't that fine. Without a cheque, my dear Mary, I'll just have to go to town and begin spreading the news. Farewell all," said Jude. Mary frowned again, accepting the inevitable outcome, yet guilt-ridden over the affect on everyone she loved.

"Jude Annesley, I challenge you to a duel. Pistols, before light fades from the sky," said Capt. Wingrave, "To the death."

Enticed by the drama and chance to kill, Jude shouted, "I accept!"

Despite Peter and Mr. Annesley's objections that they should be the ones to duel with Jude, Capt. Wingrave would not retract his challenge.

"It was my sister that was wronged, before you engaged her, or you knew of it. I have been carrying this burden the longest, and were I the eldest I would have dispatched it fourteen years ago. You will not dissuade me from this," he said. Peter shoved Emily into the room where Capt. Wingrave prepared his gun, separate from Jude to avoid "misfiring," and told her to convince him.

"I'm so sorry," she said, her own tears welling up. He stopped and examined her face.

"What do you have to be sorry for?"

"I should have accepted you, last winter. Please don't do this," said Emily.

"Would you allow me to ask you now, before I risk the beating heart that has been yours since the first?"

"Not if you are going through with this duel," she said. He laughed at her.

"Does it matter if I die, whether or not we are engaged?"

"No, I suppose not, but I wonder how you can treat it with so little concern," she said. Capt. Wingrave gave her a small smile.

"I am a good shot," he said, "And I've been taking aim at Jude Annesley since I was thirteen."

"He could kill you purely by luck. I don't know if I'd survive," said Emily.

"Why is that, Miss Worthing? Is there something you want to tell me?"

"You know very well why," she said, heat burning her face.

"I seem to have forgotten, remind me."

"If you want to know, you'll have to come ask me

tomorrow," said Emily gruffly as she walked away. He caught her, and kissed her again, long and slow this time, caressing her neck.

"That is the best incentive you could have offered me," said Capt. Wingrave.

"Please, please, stay," she said, kissing him again and drawing him closer than was excusable. He pulled her away and held her there in front of him, both breathing heavily.

"Your persuasions are of the most alluring kind. You give me what I have wanted all these months, just when victory over the demon of my family presents itself. No, I cannot bend to you now. I must finish this, so we can all live in peace," said Capt. Wingrave. He let go, and went on preparing his pistol.

"You never do as I ask!" said Emily. It struck him through the heart to hear those words, but before he could turn, she was gone.

"Isn't she right, Elijah," he muttered to himself.

Cleaned and loaded, Peter took both pistols. Capt. Wingrave faced Jude in front of everyone.

"Standard rules. Ten paces, turn, and fire. If either of us breaks the rules by turning early, he will be shot by the other's second," said Elijah.

"I have no second," said Jude.

"Then don't turn early," said Capt. Wingrave, "I won't forfeit my second because no one will vouch for you." Jude bared his teeth in contempt and spit at the Captain's feet.

"Agreed. I've waited a long time to get revenge for the beating you gave me."

"You're going to wait forever," said Capt. Wingrave.

"Outside, gentlemen, " said Peter.

"Annesley, take the ladies to the back of the house, please," said the Captain. Emily and Mary shook their heads in betrayal.

"Are you out of your senses, brother?" said Mary.

"I don't want you to see this."

"I'm sure I don't care. We will keep a distance, but Emily and I deserve to know immediately," said Mary. Capt. Wingrave frowned, but relented. Emily remained silent, fear and anger gripping her words. Elijah felt the resentment radiating from her. It drove him to promise her in his head that he would spend the rest of his life making amends.

The men took their places, Peter in the center with the loaded pistols, and Capt. Wingrave staring down Jude Annesley. Mr. Annesley kept careful watch on the ladies, keeping them on the front step while the duel took place on the lawn. Emily couldn't hear what they said, but she understood that it was about to begin. Peter handed them their weapons and backed away twenty paces, his own pistol ready to shoot if Jude cheated. Capt. Wingrave and Jude faced away and began walking as Peter counted aloud. That, Emily could hear, one, two, three... Time went by so quickly, it seemed nothing at all between that day when Capt. Wingrave had ruined her dress to this day, when one man would die.

"Ten!" shouted Peter. Emily did not see much, for her eyes closed by reflex when she jumped at the sound of gunfire. The patch of cloth that flew from Capt. Wingrave's uniform burned into her vision before reflex took over.

"Was that just one shot? What happened? Wingrave didn't fire!" said Mr. Annesley, rushing to the lawn. Mary dragged Emily behind her. Emily could not look, could not bear to see. She clamped her hands over her eyes, and hid behind Peter as they all waited to the side.

"I won't miss," said the beloved voice. Emily unclenched her hands to see him. Capt. Wingrave still stood, bleeding from the shoulder. A bead of perspiration fell from his jaw, his eyes focused on his target. Emily swallowed against the closing of her throat, overjoyed that he still stood.

"What do you mean?" asked Jude, real fear drenching the air about him.

"I am granting you this one chance for asylum. You will be escorted to a boat, you will get on this boat, and you will never return to Endland. Do you understand that I've won the right to kill you? Do you understand that I will if I ever see you again or hear of you contacting my friends and relations?" Jude shook all over, unarmed before the man with the most reason to end him.

"I understand," he whimpered.

"Your days of power are over," said Capt. Wingrave, "Daniel, please begin." A manservant nodded, and with two others, shepherded Jude into the stables.

Dark realization overflowed Emily, her happiness quickly becoming a murky memory.

"You let him shoot at you?" said Emily over the ensuing excited chatter.

"I did. It was the only way to grant him mercy, and save my family," said the Captain.

"Peter, take me home," said Emily, whirling to her brother. Hot anger welled up in her chest.

"But..."

"Now! If you ever loved me as your sister, take me home," Emily demanded. When he looked between her and the Captain, Emily shoved past him and marched toward Charlton.

"Emily, it will be dark soon!" called Peter.

"I will escort her," said Mr. Annesley. He called for his horse, and caught up with her easily.

"Excuse me, Miss Emily, but it will be much faster if you would ride with me." Emily accepted after thinking to refuse in her spiteful mood.

"Thank you, Mr. Annesley. You are always dependable."

"We admire that in each other. Tell me, why are you so upset?"

"I have always done whatever I could for those I love, but I've been taken for granted. No one seeks to please me because I am always there, ready to sacrifice for others. Capt. Wingrave went forward with the duel, and let Jude shoot to protect everyone. Everyone except me, who would be hurt the most by his loss. I am weary of being his least priority," said Emily.

"I do not think that you are. In truth, I think he did all of this for you. You would not accept a marriage that held him away from his family, correct?" she nodded, "Then all is solved. The Wingraves can now be your happy in-laws. Elijah could have dueled Jude last spring, but he did not. He allowed Mary to pay him. This time was different, both because Mary would finally refuse, and because Elijah wants you so badly. You are remarkable, " said Mr. Annesley.

"Remarkable?" asked Emily.

"Indeed. You did this, you saved the Wingraves. And me. I am free. Free from Jude at last. Is it forward of me to inquire after your sister?"

"She is resigned, but not melancholy. Her spark is dimmed, but not out. Would it be too forward of me to suggest a mountainous apology?"

"No, I know. Earning her trust is my chief objective

until it is achieved, or she marries," said Mr. Annesley. Lord
Worthing and Bridget waited outside when they heard the horse
on the road, but neither expected its burden.

"Emily? Mr. Annesley? Where is Peter?" inquired Lord
Worthing.

"I apologize for calling unannounced, Lord Worthing. I
would like to request an audience with you and the lady of the
house, to inform you of certain events that transpired this
evening that will undoubtedly affect your family," said Mr.
Annesley.

"I think Bridget should be privy to this audience as
well," said Emily, "It will be hard enough now that she is the last
to know. I am retiring to my room, and I would not disturb me
for three kingdoms."

Bridget faired tolerably well, for while Emily did not wish to
speak with anyone, she listened to the aftermath of Mr.
Annesley's audience. Peter returned an hour or two after Emily.
One person she did not hear was Genevieve. Emily, upon
perusing her practiced memory, discovered every instance in
which she had failed to see the truth. Mary's obvious curiosity
about Genevieve and her upbringing had not caused anyone
alarm, nor Mr. Annesley's doting. When the Wingraves had
objected to Emily and Genevieve's presence something should

have triggered Emily's suspicion, but she'd been so engrossed in ideas of love that sense eluded her. Many times Emily cried thinking of when her parents must have concealed the truth from her, and Mr. Annesley telling her just enough to repulse the subject. A mire of vices, that is what Emily concluded.

Up before the cock crowed, Emily would not hide, nor let anyone else hide from the terrible hypocrisy uncovered the night before. She marched down to breakfast when it was served, spoke to and looked at no one, just waited. Bridget chewed her porridge with morose disinterest, much depressed by the mood. Lord and Lady Worthing stared at each other from their seats at the end of the table, while Peter happily pretended to ignore Emily's weighted presence. At last, Genevieve, wringing her napkin to threads, spoke, just as Emily had expected.

"Emily?"

"Yes, Genevieve?"

"Are you very angry with me?"

"That is a difficult question, my dear. It is strenuous to discern who I am angry with just now," said Emily.

"Emily, allow me to explain," said Lady Worthing.

"By all means, if you have an adequate explanation I should love to hear it, for I've become too weary of reasoning why my family, who held their honesty above all other virtues, should have hidden so much from me." Lord Worthing puffed up in his seat, ready to defend his wife.

"Roland, no. Emily is right," said Lady Worthing, "We accepted our role in this subterfuge when we let Genevieve decide how much to reveal. Let me tell you where it began, from our end. I had been ill for some months when I received a letter through one of our servants here. It was from a relative of hers near Marchwood. Mrs. Pratchett, without speaking of any names, inquired if we would be open to adopting a child. She let it be known that the baby was illegitimate, though of high birth. Our servant had suggested inquiring at our house because a pregnancy could have easily caused me to be bedridden, and most people knew that.

"I had just begun to recover, though as you know, it would not be the last time illness forced me to prolonged rest, so I accepted their offer. Your father and I wanted more children, you see, but my condition was such that the risk was too great. I convinced Peter, who was old enough at the time to realize I had not been with child, to pretend the tiny baby delivered to me by carriage was his own sister regardless of origin. You and Bridget easily forgot the details in the excitement of a new baby, and our scheme was complete.

"By then, I knew Genevieve's mother was Mary Wingrave, and I told her so at the age of ten. I did not think it would ever be relevant other than to Genevieve's peace of mind, and I allowed her to choose whether or not anyone else should know. Unfortunately, I could not have predicted that Mary would risk our secret to see Genevieve, though as a mother I certainly understand." Emily wavered between rational and irrational responses to Lady Worthing's tale. She wanted most of all to laugh, to understand, and forget. Her mother had handled a delicate circumstance to the best of her knowledge. If only it hadn't caused Emily such tremendous heartbreak, it might have been a trifling matter.

"I kept it secret because I love being your sister so much, and I didn't want anything to change. It was selfish, please forgive me," said Genevieve.

"You are the easiest to forgive in all this. You are very young, and someday you will understand what it means to be kept ignorant. Then, I will get a complete apology," said Emily.

"I have disappointed you," said Genevieve beginning to cry.

"Only in that you did not trust my love to be unconditional. Perhaps it is I who have failed, if I did not make my feelings known to you." Emily let her eyes wander to the ceiling. Genevieve sobbed harder, her sensitive heart beating painfully. "No difference of birth could erase all we have shared, dear Genevieve. But I understand now, why you were so eager to see Landhilton and so disappointed with the result."

Emily stood and reached for the tiny girl she had taught to walk and talk. Genevieve flung her chair over to squeeze her older sister. Lord Worthing clenched his jaw.

"We are sorry, Em. Perhaps we should have paid more attention when the Wingraves came to Tripton. It might have been our greatest failing to think you could protect yourselves without the knowledge required to do so. Such a miscalculation almost cost us two of our precious children, not to mention a year's worth of dreadful spirits. If anyone else has anything they'd like to inform the table of, do so at once," he said.

"Mary accepted my proposal," announced Peter.

"Finally, some good news," said Lady Worthing, beaming at him. Emily righted Genevieve's chair, and sat her upon it with an entreaty to finish her breakfast lest she never get as tall as her sisters.

"Up a wife and down a sister, is that a net profit?" Emily asked, glaring at him.

"I thought you were being unreasonable," said Peter, holding his hands out.

"I will thank you to let me think for myself. As it is, you have a choice to make. You are either my brother, or his." Lord and Lady Worthing choked on their food. They had thought the trouble past, yet a new explosive argument erupted before they could rest.

"I won't go back on our oath," growled Peter, going frown for frown with Emily.

"But you'll go back on your blood? With the exception

of thinking you dead, you have never hurt me as much as you did last night. You have continued to choose his wishes over mine, and I will not have it any longer." Emily, despite her feminine stature, was more frightening than her brother when angered. Bridget and Genevieve wisely did not intervene.

"My table has become a battleground! What did you do to cause such ire, Peter?" said Lord Worthing.

"He refused to leave Reddester though I implored him with all of our blood ties. I had to set off on foot by myself until Mr. Annesley kindly treated me as one should treat a sister," said Emily. Their voices rose above courtesy, but no one could say anything against Emily's reasons. For all she had done, as a sister and mother, Emily deserved Peter's respect.

"Why are you so angry? The Captain risked himself against Jude, so that we could all be done with this business," said Peter.

"How do you think the loved ones of martyrs feel? Do you think they rejoice in death because it brings good fortune for everyone else? The only reason you are all at peace this morning is because Jude Annesley has poor aim. I am not so overjoyed with that stupid man you call your Captain, and before it all turned out well, neither were you," said Emily. Peter slammed his hands on the table.

"I am not pleased that he could have sacrificed his life, but I do respect it. He did it for his sister. That is something I can only admire. Believe me, I would take a gamble like that for you." Peter stared her down until Emily sniffed at oncoming tears. "Please, I didn't mean to hurt you... I saw last night differently."

"You're both so stupid," mumbled Emily, taking her seat and shoving her palms at her eyes.

"I love you, too, dear sister. All of my sisters. I look forward to starting anew, now that all has been taken care of. Which reminds me, I promised the Captain that I would bring everyone to Reddester today. He wants to personally apologize, but is under strict orders not to travel," said Peter.

Emily shook her head violently, but Lord Worthing said, "It is only right. It will be the first time we've met with no addendums or hidden agendas."

"Pardon, but I am exempt from this happy meeting of friends. Since the Wingraves have come to Tripton, I've had my feelings dismissed and ignored by nearly everyone. Today, I refuse," said Emily, rising from the table.

"Emily..." said Peter. She waited for him to go on. He sighed. "See that you eat a good dinner. You're looking pale."

The rest of the Worthings were dressed and gone before noon.

"Em... be sure you do not ignore your feelings most of all," Bridget had said as she stepped out the door. Emily raised her brow, but said nothing.

Emily settled into a favorite library chair, and before opening the day's book, rested her head with her eyes closed. Then, she faced the truth, the real truth that she had wanted all along. Elijah Wingrave loved her enough to put the Worthing family above all else. He could have, at Fort Jennings, told her the rest, but he'd refused to expose her parents and Genevieve to ridicule. Capt. Wingrave had begged her to leave it be, and even when Emily insulted him he did not sacrifice others to save himself.

Emily hated that she loved him, her petulance still a voice though her hope began to blossom. What stood in their way now, but her own prideful resistance? The answer far from effortlessly admitted, Emily got up to search for her outing clothes.

"Excuse me, my Lord, but your carriage driver asked me to inform you he saw Miss Worthing headed for the garden," said the housekeeper, curtsying out of the room. As one, the room looked to Capt. Wingrave. He thought, smiled, then excused himself. It was a run of bad luck for Bridget and Lady Worthing for they could not rightly spy from the window without appearing rude.

"Miss Worthing?" She waited for him near the old rose bush at the back wall. Clear of overgrowth, some of the buds had already bloomed crimson.

"How is your shoulder, Captain?" asked Emily. She reasoned that it could not have been too horrible; no sling had been affixed to his person. Indeed, he looked unchanged except for a slight bump where bandages pushed his sleeve out.

"'Twas a light grazing. The doctor worries more about infection than the actual wound. Did you walk here?" Unburdened by any secrets or restraints, Elijah found he could not take another step. Nothing was left but to take her in his arms and yet he was afraid. Unreadable eyes and an expression lost in thought gave no hints as to Emily's feelings. He swallowed and tried to remember what she'd said the day before.

"I did. It gave me much needed retrospection." Emily watched his uncertainty mellow into humor.

"You told me yesterday that today you would have something to say to me," he said. Elijah moved closer, until they were ten feet apart.

"Yes, there is," she paused for effect, "You may call me Miss Emily in conversation. Miss Worthing is too stuffy for friends such as us."

"You are teasing me? How awful," he said.

"Am I not allowed any mischief? You have caused your fair share, and I thought it to be my turn." Emily strolled from side to side, taking pleasure in his doubt.

"What mischief do you accuse me of?" he wondered.

"You arrived in Tripton to see Genevieve and falsely

recommended yourself to me."

"I never encouraged your affection for anything other than my personal feelings." Offense knit his brow together until he saw her smirk of amusement.

"You left without warning, after securing my affection."

The Captain squinted, "For which I have apologized."

"Attached my brother to yourself, knowing it would frustrate me," said Emily. Her heart beat fast as he took a step forward.

"Peter is a good man, and very clever. I genuinely befriended him on his own merit. Frustrating you was a happy byproduct."

"Left me in Dunbarrow with doubt and bitterness."

"I never wavered. Any doubt was of your own making," said Capt. Wingrave. He followed her progress, from left to right, agitation growing by the moment that she would not hold still.

"Found a way back to Tripton so you could insert yourself in my company again, and argue with me?" Elijah smiled. Emily's pace reminded him of a prosecuting attorney in court.

"Yes. I missed that the most."

"Intentionally caused me pain yesterday eve?"

"One moment of pain for a lifetime of joy? I would do it again," he assured her. Emily froze in anger, and opened her mouth to protest, but Elijah closed the distance between them and kneeled.

"If I ever cease apologizing for how wrongly our romance has gone, I need only remember your face at this moment. I was unprepared to meet you last spring, but... you have caused an explosion of growth and admiration in my very center rivaling the creation of the earth. You are searching for the safety that should accompany the greatest of loves, the kind that binds souls together as ours have been. I can freely offer you that safety, and every piece of me, with no exceptions or sacrifices this day.

"I've waited so long to make love to you in any fashion that I wish, please end my banishment from your good opinion, and marry me."

"Elijah?" said Emily.

"Yes?" He held his breath.

"I love you." A tear escaped the corner of his eye, and he smiled.

"Are you still teasing me?" he whispered.

"If I was, would you break the engagement?"

"Never."

"Then, yes." Elijah gathered her up, and they kissed with all the need held back over months of despair and insecurity. It was a revelation to them both just how complete each of them felt with no objection or obstacle between them. Feeling propriety slipping away, Emily pulled back, but allowed him to hold her, head against his chest.

"Do I know enough of the world now to wisely choose a husband?" she asked.

"Maybe a little too much," he chuckled, "Even my Swordofficer told me I was a fool to allow you, who stirred up the entire fort, to escape me. Earning your hand has been the most difficult task I've ever undertaken."

Emily laughed, "A weaker man might not have survived."

"Aye. I've come close to finishing off a few myself." Emily gaped at his confession, to which Elijah only grinned.

It was a famous wedding, known throughout most of Endland, in which the three Worthing siblings married two Wingraves and an Annesley. Many attended, friends, family, and hidden, not to mention obvious, rivals. Rumors of Jude Annesley's exile had spread with enough tangential information that no one could ferret out the truth, though Mary had finally come to a peace with it being known. She had decided that acknowledging her mistake, should it become common knowledge, would make her stronger than acting in a way that assumed she was ashamed of a daughter like Genevieve, one of the sweetest souls she'd ever encountered.

Edward Annesley had made every possible amends to Bridget, and though she had understood from the beginning that his intention was not based on emotion for Emily, Bridget did not allow him to win her over easily. She cut off any possibility that he might think it easy to turn his back on her again. Jude's absence relieved him, allowing Edward to see how much of his life he had based on the illicit actions of his brother.

Mary Wingrave found true love in the arms of Peter, and over time, forgave herself for fourteen years of fear. Lord and Lady Wingrave admired such a son-in-law, and, heightened by the spirits of their children, welcomed people to Landhilton. They met with Genevieve again, and began to understand how her upbringing had turned out a fine young lady.

Elijah and Emily played duets clear of any lurking sadness. Emily's real beauty had been uncovered with love, and Elijah became all the more enamored of her as it grew daily.

Swtnt. Worthing became Swordofficer Worthing with his new assignment as the chief of operations at Endland's School for Officers. Capt. Wingrave played his role of strict Headmaster when necessary, but usually spent his time growing Reddester, and adoring his new family.

What is feeling if it is all for naught? Where is the line between logic and love? What is the value of a secret when its sacrifices may cost more than its revelation?

"Not a chance I would answer those questions for you,

my love," said Emily.

"But why?" inquired Genevieve.

"Firstly, you will do as you please, as do most. And secondly, how dull would life be, if you knew everything this instant? What would you do with yourself?" Genevieve thought this over.

"Yes, I suppose you're right. But, I'm afraid of being wrong," she said.

Elijah answered, "Act honestly by your own values, and no one else's. Many a misstep can be avoided with simple truth." Emily arched an eyebrow at him, and he smiled at his wife.

"You have learned the pitfalls of deceit," said Emily.

"And you, the purpose of mystery." Genevieve looked between them, viewing the tangible love they had, and was content with not knowing.

Gratitude and Author Information

Many thanks once again to Brice, my partner and extra pair of eyes. He tore the manuscript with his sharpest teeth.

Thanks to my other beta readers, Jocelyn, and of course, my mom. Loves!

And thank you to my children for putting up with the hills and valleys of a creative career.

Please visit my website for more information on books I've written and will write.

www.rachelfrancisbooks.com

<u>Paranormal Fantasy</u>
LIFE ON FIRE, Mages Book One

Map of Endland

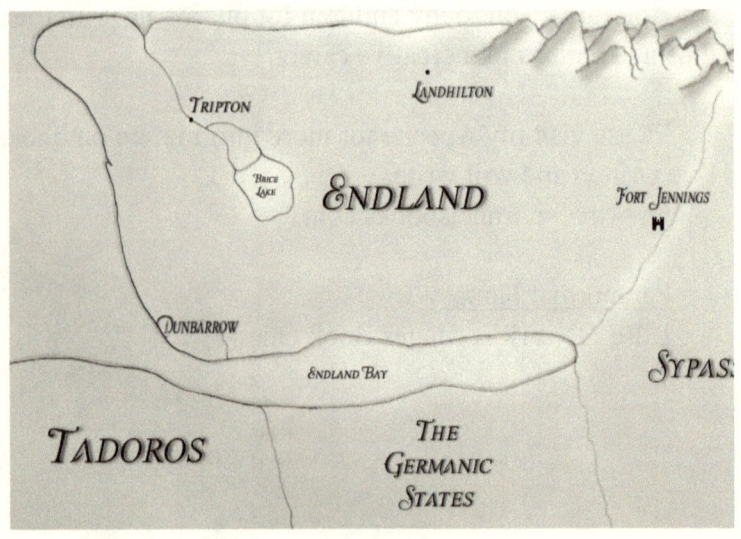

Introduction

There will always be more than I can say about any one world that I create. That being said, I felt it more than fair to the reader to explain a bit more about the parts of Endland that are not obvious or central to this particular story, on the off chance they found it interesting or confusing.

History & Religion

The religion of Endland is based on the legend surrounding the founding of the country. The legend of the Four Virtuous tells us that four people, two women and two men, came upon a land they loved at once. The two women were given Purity* and Honesty from the Divine Character, while the two men embodied Wisdom and Bravery. The four of them chose Wisdom as their King and so Endland began.

*Purity is actually a mistranslation from Old Ender. The correct word to use would be Clarity, and has caused great debate within the Church focused on the sexual nature of man. Purity teaches sexual repression (unattainable perfection) a.k.a. "We don't have sex out of wedlock because it is evil," whereas Clarity teaches sexual responsibility (attainable self-awareness) a.k.a. "We don't have sex out of wedlock because children are created that need the resources of both parents."

Nobility in Endland is present at birth, but titles come from land ownership and are as follows:

King- His country

Provent- Within the Kingdom there are 10 provinces

Count- Within each province are 4-8 counties

Countylord- Lord owning more than 1 tract

Lord- Owns 1 tract

Sir- A knighted Tradesman

Military & War

The border war with the Sypass has been going on for almost a century. The cause lies in the mountains that stretch from Endland into Sypass in the form of natural resources. Between coal and pockets of combustible gas, each country wants the energy deposits therein. Unfortunately, most of the larger deposits lie on the Endland side of the border, and at the beginning of the war, far before our story takes place, Sypass only desired to conquer the mountains. Over time, hatred has grown between the two countries, or at least their respective rulers, and the Sypass are intent on conquering all of Endland now that the rest of the country has proven to be fertile enough to support a century-old war while the Sypass suffer, having all their goods and people sucked into the conflict. Endland's success has come from valuing the Four Virtuous and upholding those principles combined with fairly open trade with other neighboring countries across the Bay. The Sypass trade with only select countries, and proudly refused any treaty Endland draws up that would require them to pay for any resources mined and collected by Endlanders.

I arranged the military ranks to fit the organization of the

Endland war machine.

Grander Roberts - He is the head of the military and one of the chief advisors to the King

Warmaster - Very few earn this rank and the responsibility of overseeing entire regions of combat along the border

Batteran - Physically stationed where they can carry out the Warmasters' orders

Fortcaptain - The last of the officers involved in directing strategy and troops to essential locations

Fieldmarshall - Carry out Fortcaptain's orders on the battlefield

Lineleader - Direct the front, middle, back, and reinforcement lines

Swordofficer - In charge of small squads of men

Swordtenant - Swordofficer in training

Countries

I developed more than this, but only mentioned Sypass and Tadoros in this book. Sypass I've already given you an idea of in the War section. Tadoros would be the equivalent of Spain in our Europe with a few differences here and there. Don't want to spoil the surprises that may wait for future novels, so I'll end this here.

* * *

Conclusion

Thanks so much for reading this far! I sincerely hope you've enjoyed my alternate Europe, and Emily's adventures.